Storm over Belfast

Mary O'Donnell

Storm over Belfast
First published 2008
by New Island
2 Brookside
Dundrum Road
Dublin 14

www.newisland.ie

ISBN 978-1-905494-95-8

British Library Cataloguing Data. A CIP catalogue record for this book is available from the British Library.

Book design by Inka Hagen.
Printed in the UK by Athenaeum Press Ltd., Gateshead, Tyne & Wear

New Island received financial assistance from
The Arts Council (An Chomhairle Ealaíon), Dublin, Ireland.

10 9 8 7 6 5 4 3 2 1

Mary O'Donnell, originally from Monaghan, lives near Straffan, Co. Kildare. She has published five poetry collections: *Reading the Sunflowers in September*, *Spiderwoman's Third Avenue Rapsody*, *Unlegendary Heroes* (Salmon Poetry); *September Elegies* (Lapwing Press) and *The Place of Miracles* (New Island 2006). Her first short fiction, *Strong Pagans*, appeared with Poolbeg Press in 1991. Her novels include *The Light-Makers*, *Virgin and the Boy*, and *The Elysium Testament* (Trident Press, UK, 1999).

Formerly the *Sunday Tribune*'s Drama Critic, she is a regular contributor to RTÉ Radio and has presented several series of programmes, including one on European poetry in translation, 'Crossing the Lines'. A poetry and fiction mentor on Carlow University Pittsburgh's MFA in Creative Writing, she is also a member of the Irish academy, Aosdána.

Contents

Acknowledgments vi
A Genuine Woman 1
Storm over Belfast 18
An Invitation 35
The Story of Maria's Son 46
Fadó, Fadó 64
Pimiento 72
The Lost Citadel 86
The Sacrament of Feet 92
Smiling Moon 99
Twentynine Palms 111
Come to Me, Maitresse 129
Strong Pagans 140
Canticles 155
Passover 163
Charlie, St Joseph, Big-Hands & God 179
Border Crossing 188
Jethro 197
Aphrodite Pauses, Mid-life 204
Yugoslavia of My Dreams 211
Little Africa 226

Acknowledgments

Some of these stories first appeared as follows: 'Fadó, Fadó' in *Cúirt*; 'Twentynine Palms' in *Brandon Irish Short Stories*; 'Smiling Moon' in *Cork Literary Review*; 'Come to Me, Maitresse' in *The Irish Times*; 'Canticles' in *Phoenix Irish Short Stories*; 'Passover' in *In Sunshine or in Shadow*; 'Charlie, St Joseph, Big-Hands & God' in *The Mail on Sunday*, also broadcast on RTÉ Radio; 'The Sacrament of Feet', broadcast on RTÉ Radio; 'The Lost Citadel' in *Best Prize-Winning Short Stories*; 'Jethro' in *Odyssey*; 'Border Crossing', broadcast on RTÉ Radio; 'Strong Pagans' in *Strong Pagans*; 'A Genuine Woman', prize-winner in the V.S. Pritchett Short Story Competition 2000, broadcast as a play by RTÉ Radio.

A Genuine Woman

None of us ever cheered Hitler on, because quite early in the war, Mike knew about the Jews. He had read something in *The Manchester Guardian*, something so awful we could hardly credit it. And although some of our neighbours could be quite gleeful as Adolf advanced across the Continent and showed the English who was boss, we were not. Austria, I always felt, was not much different from Germany, so I did not really think about the annexation there in 1938. Of course, I know different now. And when Poland fell in 1939, we were not so worried either, even though it followed quite naturally on the mean way he took Czechoslovakia, and after him saying he only wanted the Sudetenland! But the early summer of 1940 was another matter entirely. Denmark, Norway, Holland and France fell like dominoes. Somehow, the war became real, no longer a game which we could watch from our safe little independent island.

The evening before our lives were almost destroyed with shock, I went into the garden and leaned over the limestone wall. I must have been quite still for some minutes, my thoughts drifting, for suddenly, the fox appeared. From the corner of my eye, I glimpsed it. Then I turned and all I got was an aftermath of orange, rust, the streak of his foxiness left like an imprint on the eye.

It's strange the things you remember. Not the event itself that joined us to the war. That doesn't come first, although it should, God knows it should. Often, it's the fox I see when I think of that day, because I also glimpsed one at daybreak, only two days later, as I stood at the landing window with Sean's old copybook in my hand as I read and reread his records: *Bag for Season 1939–40*. It's the fox I still see when I try to keep hold of myself after what happened, to keep the thing in my heart. It's not as if Mike doesn't know. I believe he does, that he tolerates it, tolerates my struggle with my own heart.

On Sundays, Sean would sometimes take his gun out. He showed me his log book the day before he died, and for some reason which I cannot recall left it behind him in the kitchen, everything written up in his square handwriting, a month-by-month and season-by-season account, dated and totted up to show the total bag for any season. For example, I know that in the first week of February that year he shot seven rabbits, two pigeons, two ducks, five teal and four snipe. His total bag for that month came to thirty-three.

'Ah, Kate, sure it's me you should've married!' Sean would tease me.

'You must be joking, boy!' I'd scoff, smiling in spite of myself, knowing what would come next.

'I might not be much, I know that ...'

That bit always upset me. Maybe he was smart, running himself down like that, or maybe he was truly humble. I think he was humble, quite different from Mike, who, when I thought about it, had had everything at his beck and call.

Mike was always coddled. Adored by all, his mother and father and the aunt and uncle that reared him. Loaned at the age of two to the aunt for a few weeks, sent the few miles down the road to their farm, he had them charmed before long. Just like he charmed me later on. His parents, who had children of their own, left him there. An act of compassion, you might say. Whatever way they loved him, it filled him with ideas and plans and interests. Now he is the creamery manager at the Shelburne Co-operative Society, Campile, and I am his wife. The aunt frowned on me. Still does. Not good enough. A dairy maid that spent her days whacking butter after the churning, shaping and squaring the pound and half-pound with the butter clappers till it fit the waxy paper. The ridges of the clappers had to be scrubbed till they were sterile.

'Sterility is everything! Everything!' Mike would roar at us girls, terrified of bacteria.

But he was a gentleman, I'll say that for him. That continued after the wedding too. When first I began to notice his interest in me, I was struck by his nervousness. He was almost cold. Almost. He can look very strict when he's not sure of his ground. Fear extends his tallness. He holds himself more erect than ever, the shoulders stiffen and his face is like a mask, the long hollows below his cheekbones full of shadows and the darkness which hints at where he shaves.

But then he began to consult me about things that were unnecessary and obvious to anyone but an imbecile. He would point out different aspects of the new machinery in the dairy, running his hand over the tinned copper piping, or along the side of the great vats. Everything in our working lives was milky. The smell of it, the froth of it as it rose in the vats when the farmers delivered, then the other smell that came when it was heated, for separation, to one hundred and ten degrees Fahrenheit. When the cream came off, it in turn was pasteurised to one hundred and ninety degrees Fahrenheit. The slops, the skim went back to the farmers for whatever use they wished. The dairy had a biscuity, safe odour, almost of the breast, except nicer and sweeter and there was maybe a thousand gallons of the stuff.

I wore a new suit for our wedding, dark green wool with a black velvet collar and velvet trimming along the edges. The buttons were in a lighter green, some kind of glassy stuff. He insisted on going to Dublin to choose the best he could afford. The wedding was reported in the local newspaper, ending with the words: *The happy couple are spending their honeymoon touring the West of Ireland.* We stayed in the Old Ground Hotel, Ennis, then we visited the Burren. A strange place, compared to what we were used to. I could not feel safe on those great plains of stone, no matter what unusual flowers and weeds grew there. The Cliffs of Moher terrified me. Mike became impatient with me up there because I refused to stand up in the huge gales that blew that day. If the truth be told, I often felt lonely on my honeymoon. The only place I warmed to was a coral strand in Connemara one evening as the sun turned the restless waters of the Atlantic to floating fires and the mountains behind us seemed the colour of a fox.

Afterwards, Mike thought of everything. He never wanted me to be worn out having children year after year, like his own mother before him. Ours were never to be reared with an aunt or uncle, no matter how kindly. So children we had. Two sons. Then no more children. He saw to that on his one and only trip to London. On his return, they didn't check his luggage at customs. It is one of those things that still fills me with mirth, to think of those grim-faced customs officers watching out for dirty books and pictures and preventatives of any kind. The things he brought home to Campile proved useful enough, once we understood how to use them. The book, which was written by a woman called Mrs Marie Stopes, explained everything. These items I kept in the mahogany tallboy, in a special drawer with a lock on it, for my woman's things (where I also keep Sean's copybook now). Mike thought that the best thing, that I would have recourse to the preventatives when and as I thought necessary. He was not, in spite of the care that he took to provide the things that helped us in matters of love, a great initiator. That was left up to me. Still and all, Mr De Valera up in Dublin city was well and truly foxed, hell mend him!

When the boys were six and four, Sean Flynn began to bring our milk up the road to the house in a bucket, the froth still on the top and it still warm from the cow. I pasteurised it my own way, by boiling it first, then leaving it to cool. When it had cooled, the crinkled skin, which we all hated, could be scooped off.

I was nicely settled in my married life, no worries of a material kind. On Sundays, Mike's mother and aunt would sometimes visit us, bringing flowers for me and sweets for the children. I hated those afternoons, stifling they were, with lots of talk about who was sick and who had just died. Of course, the old people, being nearer to death than most of us, liked to dwell on it. It wasn't so bad when Mike's uncle came too. He had an eye for the women, it was said. Either way, he liked me, and he liked the tea I made, strong and black. He would hug me longer than necessary when he arrived and when he went. He meant no harm. I did not receive such a lot of hugs when I was a child, and took what affections he gave. Sometimes Mike and I and the boys would take a drive in the motorcar, in and around the Blackstairs Mountains, uphill and down dale, always with our camera at the ready.

During the week when Sean called, he and I would get to talking, and could we laugh! That's part of the trouble between men and women. As soon as you can laugh together, there's a chance you'll grow close. At that time, it was no more than laughter. He'd tell me funny stories about the ones down in the dairy, or how Mike wouldn't let Pat the Wheels, one of the Wheels Lynchs, on account of all the cartwheels lying around their farm, deliver milk until he learned how to scald his churns properly. Mike was a devil, he was like something possessed when he started on that. But Sean made it sound a hoot, and even though I was laughing at Mike – we both were – we didn't mean it unkindly.

'You can't imagine what class of craytures would be in that milk, Pat,' Sean would imitate Mike, pulling himself up to his full height. 'Craytures that could kill us all and have the creamery shut down by the men in Dublin,' he'd carry on, 'things that'd have you rolling in the floor with the pain in your gut. Then where'd we be at all, at all? Peritonitis, is it? Is that what we want?'

Sean was small, yet somehow he could do Mike to a T, and I'd be falling around the place with laughter, burying my face in my apron.

'And then,' says Sean, gripping my forearm to hold my attention even more, 'and then Pat, he says like, all stammery, "Ye mean ... ye mean ... enough to kill a man?" and your good husband he says nothin' at all, just stands there tellin' it with his eyes, by gob but you should see him, Kate!'

Sometimes I stopped the laughing game before it ran its full course. If the children were up the fields Sean could spend half the morning with me. I'd carry on as usual, doing everything I would normally do – bread in the oven, eggs gathered – the only difference being that I was aware of Sean. Sometimes he brought a couple of rabbits, shot earlier in the day, and we'd skin them together. Eventually, I let him do it himself. Skinning creatures has never appealed to me, even though, properly done, it peels off like a little grey jumper. Sometimes he helped me scrub the bed sheets, up and down with the brush on the washboard.

'That's enough now, Sean,' I'd say, doing my best to be sensible.

'Ah go on would you Kate, sure what harm? Can't I give you a hand now and then?'

'No harm. But still.'

'Still what?'

I could never answer that. I did not want to say the words. But then, one day I did.

'You're a single man.'

'More's the pity,' he said, smiling slowly at me then.

'You know how I'm fixed,' I said, expecting him to take notice.

'Not a one cares. Sure, they think I'm a feather-head. An aul' fella with one aul' gun and no thoughts of an'thin' beyond his station.'

I turned my back then. I did not want him to see me blush. I was suddenly happy, a bit afraid too, but mostly happy. Perhaps something happens to us in spring. That spring, I was like a mad thing, full of the happiness that came from talking to Sean. His eyes were bright blue, with a dark scar above one eyebrow where he fell on glass as a child. He had a headful of curly hair, very little grey for his age, all his own teeth too. I used to watch as he moved around the kitchen, talking away about this one and that one. The hair curled lightly on his forearms, down to the backs of his hands, which were very long and strong. A lifetime's labouring had shaped them.

When Mike and I went to the pictures one night in Waterford, I came out of the cinema with my head full of notions. I could not help it. As Mike tucked the rug around my knees and ankles before he cranked up the motorcar, my thoughts whirled inside my head. The film, which was called *Gone with the Wind*, was in Technicolor. Oh, the colour of the ladies' dresses and Scarlett O'Hara's in particular. I will never forget it, all the dancing and laughter, the big talk from very handsome men. It was the most beautiful film I had ever seen, all of us there trying not to cry, pretending that cigarette smoke had got in our eyes. You could hear a pin drop at two bits in particular. The first was when Melanie died, the other was when Rhett Butler forced himself over Scarlett's body and we all waited, dying to see whether she would enjoy that or reject him because of it. Then there were the bits when he just kissed her, or the way she would look up at him. I also enjoyed the part when she flaunted herself before him and all of society in a dress made out of old velvet curtains. Yet as Mike let the brake off the motorcar and we drove away, all he could say was, 'Well, that's that.' I was so full of something unspeakable that I did not dare answer in case I screamed. At times like that, Mike could fill my heart with disappointment, anger too. Even though he did not mean it, even though he was a good man, the best of men, something began to churn in me. I thought of the old butter churns still used in the country beyond the creamery, and even the big creamery churns, turning and turning until the liquid separated from the lumpy bits, and I saw the bits of my own life separating, some of them drifting and sticking in shapes beyond my control, while the thinner bits of me, or the bits that seemed thin and of no consequence, just slopped there in unwanted pools.

Two nights later, Sean went to the pictures by himself. The day after, he came up to me as usual, with the bucket of milk from the dairy. He looked bashful, quiet in himself. Full well I knew what was on his mind though we'd said nothing to one another. He opened a packet of cigarettes, lit one slowly, sucked in hard, keeping his eyes down as he did so. Only as he breathed out did he look at me.

'Which bit did you like the best?'

His eyes stayed on my face. I felt myself blush horrid hot, so much that I wanted to run from the kitchen. Quickly, I turned and dragged a bag of spuds from beneath the sink, fired them into a basin. I took a knife and began to peel like blazes. The sound of the peeling had its own quick rhythm, because although I did not mean it to, the blade of the knife kept hitting off the blue enamel edge of the basin. They were the cleanest spuds you ever did see by the time they reached the saucepan.

'Did you hear me, *a stóirín*? Which bit?'

I kept my head turned from him, and I answered.

'The bit where Ashley and Melanie run towards one another. When he comes back from war.'

It's true I enjoyed that part, but not as much as some other parts.

'Have you stars in your eyes today, then?' he enquired softly from where he stood, with his back to the range. I glanced over my shoulder at him, then turned away again.

His look was amused, gentle. He was well able to tease just then, knowing that, somehow, he had the upper hand. Everything was quiet at that moment, save for the soughing wind in the apple branches and a couple of starlings fighting over a scrap of bacon fat on the window ledge.

'Put some coal on that range for me, would you Sean?' I called back over my shoulder with a light laugh.

He futhered with the lid for a while before he got it opened, then lifted the copper scuttle. As the coal tumbled in with a loud grating, black smoke puffed out into the kitchen so that we were both coughing a bit. He replaced the lid quickly. But he didn't let up.

'You have stars in your eyes, haven't you?' he said again, more teasingly, as if he was insisting on something.

This time I just coughed by way of avoiding an answer. I marched out of the kitchen and down to the henhouse. I wasted little time picking my bird, tucking her under my arm and marching back up the garden towards the kitchen. Sean was watching from over the half door. There was uproar among the hens, as if they knew what was coming. The rooks were circling the yard as usual, cawing and screeching. Two magpies cackled on the plum trees, scattering the white blossom in little darts and spirals.

'I'll give you stars in the eyes, Sean Flynn!' I took the chicken and wrung its neck. I was good at that. Swift and clean. The birds hardly knew they were dead. This one didn't even squawk.

I did not see Sean until the following week. Something had changed between us. Perhaps we had declared ourselves. I was truly agitated by the prospect of his return. I knew he would come back, wanted him to. Delivering our daily milk was, after all, one of his jobs.

My eyes wandered restlessly as I worked, drawn always

to whatever was happening outside the window, whether I was in the kitchen or the parlour, or in the bedrooms, or indeed in the bathroom, where Mike spent so much time splashing and preening himself every morning. (Small wonder the boys still brought chamber pots to their bedrooms. He wouldn't let anybody near the bathroom in the morning until he was well and truly finished. He had leathers and razors galore, nose clippers and ear clippers, blades and cutting implements for dealing with every kind of hair under the sun, no matter where it was located. Me, I never bothered much with the solitary hair that sprang from a small mole above my lip. Sometimes I cut it, but it didn't worry me. For some reason, the few hairs I once had on my bosoms fell away after the boys were born. Everything else is as nature intended.)

But that spring I was full of nervous strength. Strength, that was it. I was so bursting with it I could have mown my way through a field of ripe corn or danced all night, had I the chance, or done things which I dare not commit to paper. Instead I kept the house clean. I was busier than ever. I made myself so. Some of the rooms in the house I have never liked, the ones that are too dark or which show the old-fashioned taste of the previous manager's wife. A drab soul, she must have been. But our bedroom, with the shining brass bed and a creamy white bolster with lace edging, the dressing table on which I keep brushes, one ivory comb, some face cream and a bottle of perfume, is a delicious place. I enjoy being a wife, in spite of all. The wifely things, the habits and touches that go with my station, bring ease and civility and peace. The view from that bedroom window always pleased me, falling down the hill from the back of the house towards the big stream, and beyond that again the field with the beech trees and the sweet beech nuts that I gorged myself on when I was expecting both children.

One day I made myself stop the mad cleaning and polishing. The youngest child was with me, the other boy at school. I treasured the last few months of my baby boy's true freedom. In September, he would be gone from me to the schoolroom, to rules and regulations, so that he could learn to read and write and count and become a proper little Irishman during Mr De Valera's Emergency. Makes my heart ache still, to think of it. But there we were, and I playing with him in the front garden. I had the box camera. I settled the child on top of one of the pillars by the gate, all ready to take a photograph. He still wore his little winter boots and the grey socks Mike's aunt liked to knit. Terrible things to look at, but warm.

'Now, *mo pheata*,' I coaxed, 'you give me that big smile of yours, the one your mammy loves so well.'

He knew how to charm, little man that he was. My heart filled with joy when he smiled and I looked down into the camera, transfixed by his broad grin and the small white teeth as he pulled his face wide just to please me.

'Ah, there's the good boy, the best boy ever!' I crooned for a moment afterwards, scooping him off the pillar and into my arms. But this is the strange thing. I knew full well that my joy was not entirely for my son. I knew that my heart soared like a lark for Sean Flynn, who had just turned in the gate as I lifted the child down. I've heard of dentists who give laughing gas to their patients. Well, I imagine that if I had had laughing gas it might have felt as good as what ran through me just then. It wasn't that I laughed out loud. This was something within me, a spring in some secret mossy place that nobody before had ever discovered. I wanted to shout about it, to tell everyone, to let the spring overflow and make its way to the unknown, wild, beautiful ocean where I could dream and drown with the joy of it all. And I wonder if there's a difference between dreaming and drowning?

Sean was taken by surprise, seeing me there. Immediately, he put the bucket down on the gravel path, beside the polleny shrubs that tumbled around, never pruned when they should be.

'May I take a picture of you? May I? I'd like to, if I may,' he said, suddenly more polite and correct in his English than I had ever heard him before.

I was wearing a big hat that day, and a new blue dress from Switzers of Dublin, and little cream leather shoes with fine double straps and the very latest heels.

'Yes,' was all I said.

'You look a picture anyway, did you know that?' he said then.

'Thank you,' I managed to reply.

'Good enough to ate, *a stóirín*.'

I could smell him. A clean sweat smell, I saw it moist on his neck as he craned sideways to see where he would take the photograph. Little did he know what torments his neck and throat were to me.

'Now.'

'Now what? I haven't got all day,' I began, then stopped myself. I can always sound more severe than I mean to.

'Ah, don't be like that,' he said.

'Like what?'

'Bossy. Mike's wife.'

'But that's what I am.'

'And my friend,' he answered, his gaze firm.

It took ages for him to decide where to put me. First he set me beside the sundial at the centre of the lawn, positioning me this way and that, with my head slightly raised. Then he changed his mind and set me standing beneath the lilac tree, looking away into the distance, as if I was thinking of something and not in the least aware that my picture was being taken.

'You're very fussy,' I ventured to comment, watching him as he took stock of the situation in a way I had never before seen.

'A very important piece of technology, this is,' he said seriously, 'and the photographin' of a lady like yourself should be done proper.'

In the end he made me go back to the sundial, leaning one elbow on the dial itself. Just as I settled myself, Pat the Wheels Lynch went by with his donkey and cart and two churns. He took a good gander in, his two eyes glued to the little scene in the garden. Even if the other business with the Germans had not happened, I was done for and I knew it. Next thing Pat would be down at the crossroads shop filling Mrs Sullivan and her nosy daughter Mary in on the sight he had beheld. But I did not care.

'Now, turn towards me. No, no, look – wouldja folly me hand! Look where me hand is pointin',' he ordered. I did what I was told to, calm in those few moments when he held the shape of me in a little square bit of the box. It wasn't that he was looking at me so much as into that place called the soul, which the priesteens around the county so like to talk about, but with little understanding.

Later, when the pictures came back from the chemist's in New Ross, Mike hardly looked at the ones of me, though he took great care examining the child's. It wasn't that he was indifferent, so much as remiss. That happens, even with the best of husbands. Because they trust their wives, they forget that trust is not always to be guaranteed.

Not long after that day, Sean kissed me. It was an awkward, short kiss, as if he was terrified, which he was, but I held onto him when the kiss had ended, because with that kiss, he entered a part of me that no one had ever before entered. I put my arms around him and hugged him very carefully, so that he would know I welcomed him. 'There now,' I whispered, 'it's all right, hush now ...'

There was a new sadness in his face that day as he left, as if he had been disturbed. Perhaps his feelings were in uproar like my own, raided with desire as if something from outside our lives had dropped on the pair of us.

I still cannot believe what happened next. No, that is not true. But it confounds me. That summer was like any other until August, the days long, the fields and hedges and trees ripe. Meadowsweet, purple vetch, nettles, yarrow, the barley waving like a pale yellow sea. Sean and I whiled away many an hour together.

According to his records, which I slip from the drawer every so often, Sean bagged three rabbits in August, four duck and three teal. The previous August, he had bagged thirty rabbits, three pigeon, two duck and three teal. He shot no duck the December before, but six snipe, three woodcocks and twelve rabbits.

I will never know what notion took him that he stayed so long at the creamery restaurant that day. Probably to chat to the girls. What I remember is the whine, unlike anything I have ever heard before, getting louder and louder, so that we all knew it was not a fire siren, but something else, something deadly. The ferocious sound fell to its awful conclusion, thunder to cap all thunders, an earthquake sound because it seemed as if the whole world had been split asunder, a devilish, evil, roaring thing that shook us in our bones and souls. I was in the henhouse just then. The children screamed with fright from further up the garden, then raced down to me and clung to my legs. I could feel their bodies atremble, even though my own legs went weak as water. People everywhere stopped what they were doing. I crossed my chest without thinking.

That evening, when the worst was known, I could hardly stand for the weeping, so that Mike had to put the two boys to bed. I did not care. The *Irish Independent* carried a full account the following morning, although I did not read it for a week or more.

> *Three girls – two of them sisters – and one man were killed and others were injured when the creamery in which they were working at Campile, Co. Wexford, was wrecked yesterday afternoon when a German aircraft dropped bombs in Campile, Ballynitty, Bannow and Duncormick. The dead girls are: Mary Kate Hoare, aged 35, and her sister, Catherine Hoare (25), of Bannow, and Kathleen Kenny (25), of Tacumshin. Mr Sean Flynn (44), of Campile, also died in the incident. They were at work in the restaurant portion of the Shelburne Co-operative Agricultural Society, Ltd, when it was struck by a bomb and reduced to ruins. The bodies were buried beneath the debris and were dead when extricated ...*

Rumours spread, of course. People said that Shelburne Creamery butter wrappers had been found in Dunkirk and that the Germans must have thought it was a big source of butter to Britain. Others said the German pilot had lost his way or that he was getting rid of his load before returning to base.

It is no secret that I loved Sean Flynn. Mike knows it too, and has not been hard on me on account of it. Half the neighbourhood had been gabbing about us for a long time anyway. I imagine, however, that none of them today lie awake at night thinking about me and my little problems. They have enough of their own.

When I think back to before that time, I see my life running along smoothly, even though things often perplexed me. But I was happier than I knew. Everything was normal and ordinary, just as it is again. The ordinariness is not so good now. Nowadays, I live true to everything and everyone. I am what some might call genuine. I do not give a hoot for being genuine, not since Sean died. Through him I understood that surface sincerity is not everything, that sincerity has an underbelly that it is not always possible to be true to. Most people avoid that tender spot. It is the difference between a lake and the ocean. Both are water, but I would choose the ocean any day, for its greatness, its solid will. Nothing contains the ocean, only gravity.

It still cuts me to the quick to think of Sean ending his days like that, in a way none of us could ever have imagined, his life destroyed in an instant of pain and fire ... sometimes I can hardly bear it. I try not to think of Sean, who never did anyone any harm, least of all me.

We never did more than kiss.

Storm over Belfast

Roon had promised to go back and see Lettie, so there he was, grinding along at 120 kph, steering wheel steady in his hands, BBC Radio 4 voices explaining the world as his thoughts drifted.

For a mile or so after the Dundalk bypass, the road held good. Then he noticed the blip on the geographical radar, the subtle difference as he entered what remained of bandit country. He passed around the mountains, observed the first signs of a roughing-up. The furze-clotted vitiations would look better in the far south, in Kerry or Tipperary, he thought. He whizzed past the one big filling station between Dublin and Belfast, and the gigantic sign, TOILET, which drew most travellers to ease their bladders as they nosed north. But his bladder was quiet, his thoughts restive as he remembered the house where he had lived with Lettie.

He tugged at his chin. He hadn't bothered to shave. That was the way she liked it. He castigated himself then. Why should it matter what she liked? It was too late for them, after all, too late for him to return to the image she had loved. Roon, her unshaven, dark-chinned man of the earth. Ha.

After about ten miles the land calmed itself. It was serene and self-confident. He was now in a foreign country, the imagined loyal province of Saxon and Briton. She had never understood how comical he found it and why it made him smile. That was in her saner moments, when conversation was possible, before the one-way diatribe that passed for communication overtook her.

He passed by Hillsborough with its commemorative pillar, glanced at the gardens and earthen-bricked mansions of the wealthy and middle-aged. They had tried to create an England and, in a way, had succeeded. But all Roon had to do was look at the planted peasant faces of old Scotland or the sat-upon faces of old Ireland, genetically intact despite the English country gardens. It showed him something else, the plastering over of the Celtic genetic pool with the truculent cements of the conqueror. Oh, God loved a tryer, that was the truth. And they had tried ... and tried ... the kith of conquerors.

Get a grip, man, he urged himself. It was the kind of observation she detested. *You and your cocky Southern shite!* she'd sometimes rail when they'd had a few scoops. *It's not so long since your lot were digging spuds and had no indoor toilets. Christ's sake!* she'd laugh, her dark eyes glittering over her pint.

It was as well they never got hitched. He wasn't the marrying kind. Still, she drew him back, she was magnetic. This time, though, it was different. And this time, his secondment to the communities of Belfast was an added excuse, letting them in on the runes and secrets of the Irish language, the *cupla focal*, so that they could give the two fingers to *an teanga Bearla* and embed themselves more deeply in an imagined memory of the Gaelic dream.

They'd tried the whole cohabitation act. Back then, she was working regularly, in and out to the studios in Belfast, bending over backwards to accommodate the tastes of the mother country, what she called 'the mainland'. Her programmes were edgy, like herself, recording the smoke-deepened voices of those who lived on the edge. Falls Road. Coronation Gardens. Divis. Shankill. There she'd be, ferreting her way into the terrain, getting through somehow to the man in charge. There was always a Man in Charge, a head honcho along the barricaded gardens, the no-go lands, the Serengetis of either allegiance.

She was good at what she did. That was when they could still talk, and argue, though she always did more of that than Roon did. She was a fierce talker.

The roads were up as he approached Belfast. He missed his turn and headed for the city centre, then cut away over the Queen Elizabeth Bridge and out the A2. Trust him to take the long way around. Traffic was light despite being Saturday afternoon. The shopping malls were probably thronged with shoppers and kids, Roon thought, the holy afternoon both north and south, unmissable for idolators of the god of purchasing.

He hated driving. He preferred to concentrate on landscape, and as the town hoved into view he hated it even more, the long descent from the city drawing to an end, the sea shouldering in against the outline of the town. Everything was bypassed. To his left and right, the houses of the good burghers of the suburbs clustered neatly, gardens present and correct, flowering with military precision. Pebbles, cobbles, red-brick edging, pebbles, cobbles, red-brick edging …

He attempted to keep within the suburban speed limits, but his hands were clenching the steering wheel. Her phone call had unnerved him. He thought, but couldn't be certain, that she had sounded a bit disjointed. Elevated, he would say. But she did like to talk. Finally, down the hill and into the town, then out along the seafront, where the three-storey houses were tidy and occasionally colourful. No Vacancies, someone's window announced, even though it was low season.

He pulled up outside the house. Oh, *fuck*. He took in the sloping garden and the steep steps to the front door. He looked and counted, the eyes popping out of his head, his breathing quickening. Garden gnomes. He counted forty and hadn't reached a final tally. And glass shoes in different colours, pairs of them, like clogs, lining both sides of the steps. The clogs on one side pointed up towards the house while those on the other side pointed seaward. They were – Roon had to admit – beautiful clogs and he wondered where she got them.

Before he could do more than look, the big cerise-coloured front door burst back and the dog hurtled down the steps. The one time he'd taken Rodney, the animal entered an instant state of gloom in Roon's Dublin ground-floor apartment. He could only conclude that no matter how kind he was – he walked him, fed him, allowed him sofa rights – he couldn't adjust to the silence. By the time he left Rodney back to Lettie, he'd lost weight and she accused Roon of neglect. But no, the dog pined for her voice, despite all, for the river of throaty sounds defining his life.

Out she came, all dressed up. A lady in red. Her hair was a volcano of spewing red fuzzy curls – it reminded him of that ugly fashion designer from the Sixties who featured in the magazines, the Westwood one. She'd let it bush out in its natural curl. A sign she was letting what she called her 'real' self emerge. The true woman, unimpressed by the contemporary urge for the razor-straight, the robotic, wearing a billowing red dress with leg-of-mutton sleeves and silky tassels at the hem.

As he slowly stepped from the car, gathering himself, he knew they would embrace. But what kind of embrace would it be? How did he want it to be? His mind raced. Friendly? Erotic? Passionate? Everyone embraced, even people who despised one another. Down in Dublin, the artsy set liked to kiss on both cheeks now, Parisian style.

In the end, it was awkward. A rapid peck on the cheek, hands holding shoulders, then the quick push away as they both turned to go up the steps. Her skin smelled stale. He told himself she wouldn't affect him this time, that he was here out of kindness, to check up on her. He wouldn't like to see her come to harm.

'I thought you'd never come! I've been waiting half the day! Look you, come in, you'll never guess what I've been up to, look, I took to baking bread and cakes and I've got this pile of stuff just has to be eaten …'

She dragged him along by the hand, her face pink with excitement. It was true, the house was filled with the odour of recent cookery. The warmth of it gushed out the door and filled Roon's nostrils, making his stomach rumble. But she was still speaking, pouring forth like an undammed river. His eyes roved around despite his willing them to remain still and look at her, listen to her. The place was a shambles. The cobwebs astonished him. The hall, the living room, the kitchen were draped in the manner of Christmas decorations, opaque with swathes of ghostly grey spider-silk. Then the dirt. He was not a fussy man. It was one of the things she would harp on about in the old days. He wasn't keen on clearing up, changing beds, on sweeping and wiping. *There you are, like a ruddy great spider in that chair! Get up off your arse, you're not the only one holding down a job!* she would accuse him.

She was no philistine. She came from something. Her people were good, East Belfast folk. Not like his lot down south, everybody whizzing around in big cars, living in wide-winged homes with gravelled driveways and gold-painted eagles on the privacy-protecting walls. Fancy a whole nation of lower-middle-class philistines suddenly rising high, without an aristocracy of anything – whether blood, intellect or muscular labourers – to save them? That was how it was down south.

There was a leak beneath the sink. A pool of water had trickled out across the floor. She'd been walking in and out of it, trailing muddy footsteps all around the place. In some places, flour from her baking had fallen into the liquid. It lay thick and filthy, sticking to the tiles.

'I'd better clean that up,' he mumbled, still in shock at the state of the place.

'Aye, the mop's over there,' she pointed, mid-sentence, and took off at a gallop again about the colour of the sea and how it was really exciting and did he know she'd enrolled for art classes and the teacher said she showed promise?

In order to rinse the mop he had to remove a mountain of crockery from the sink. She hadn't cleaned up for weeks. There were mould and mouse droppings.

Oh girl of the great fuzzy hair, woman of the frontiers of intellect, his programme-maker par excellence! He saw her now, enrolled with the night-class artists: expert amateurs doomed to reject all criticism, determined to splodge their unsubtle therapeutic colours onto whatever canvas would accept them, to repeat the habit winter after winter, working towards some pathetic exhibition in the spring.

He squeezed the mop out again and again, then laid sheets of newspaper on the floor. The newspapers were everywhere, piled up, mostly unread. Some of the weekend magazines were flung around. She'd been cutting out. A scissors lay on the sofa. A number of capital letters had been cut out and left there. She intended to do a collage, she told him, using those letters but then painting over them. The words would tell something, she whispered rapidly – he could see sweat beneath her eyes, catching slivers of light in the pockets of her flesh – but that would be for the viewer to figure out, because she intended to paint over the words and use them as texture, overlayered thirty or forty times.

'Is that so?' he remarked.

'Yes, Roon, don't you think it would work? I mean, isn't there something about pushing back the boundaries of an idea?'

He shrugged. Most people pushed at boundaries, one way or another. 'Well?' she demanded, two hands on her waist as she stood watching him.

'I think it's a good idea. No, a *great* idea,' he eventually said carefully.

'Hmm,' she said, doubting his conviction. 'Don't patronise me, Roon. Anyway, it's something to be going on with until I get my life back together again. I'm going to be back at work within two months. That's a guarantee!'

'Is that so? For certain?'

'Aye. I've been on the phone to the office. Well, what I mean is …'

Off she went again, obfuscating, justifying.

'You've stopped taking your meds?' he enquired softly, putting the mop down, replacing it in the corner of the kitchenette.

She regarded him balefully across the worktop. It was marked with stale tea and coffee rings. Mugs were discarded, empty biscuit packets, cigarette cartons, milk cartons. The smell of her baking was beginning to recede, to be overtaken by the house's natural odours: of filth, rot and decay.

'Of course I've stopped! What does it bloody look like? See, I'm back to normal, I really can cope, love, despite what the doctors say. Oh, I know all about it, I know they're saying I'm in denial about my fucking *condition*, as they like to call it! Huh.' She turned her mouth down and raised an eyebrow as if daring him to contradict her.

A bark from out the front interrupted them. She whirled quickly out to the hall and opened the door. The dog ambled in, sniffing, his tail wagging, pleased to see his mistress again. She always said that if it weren't for Rodney, she'd die, that the dog especially was always glad to see her, no matter what.

'There's the great boy, eh?' She rubbed his black head gently. 'Who's the great fellah, eh? Who's Lettie's best boy?' She continued to gush for a few minutes, the dog lapping up all the attention like the eejit he was. He looked oddly guilty as he accepted her attention.

For something to do, Roon turned on the tap and filled the sink with hot water, scraped stale food into the overflowing bin, then let the pile of delph sink deep into the bubbles. That lot could soak there for half an hour. Then he turned to her and folded his arms, adopting what he hoped was a casual pose against the draining board.

'Do you think it was wise to come off your meds?'

'Wise?', she responded with an incredulous smile. 'Now there's a strange word. Of course it was bloody wise! Do you think I could stay on that crap for the rest of my days? Do you want me to grow fat and slow and uncreative? I can't live like that, you know I can't!'

Her voice rose, her face reddened. He turned his back in an attempt to defuse the situation, pushed the sponge idly through the pile of soaking crockery. Already, some of the residues were loosening.

'I didn't mean—'

'Oh, you never mean anything, do you? Do you?' she stamped her foot. She looked as if she would strike him, but some thread of restraint held her for the moment.

He did not reply. But that too was an offence. She started to scream. How come it was her that was taking pills? Wasn't it always odd that it was the woman in any relationship who ended up on tablets? She hated the labels. *Bipolar. Depressive. Psychotic.* Terms that were inapplicable, she jabbed the air.

He knew where it was leading. He felt panicky, three years with her flooding back with their mixture of erotic fevers and distressing, disturbing anxieties. She would say it was him who needed the anti-depressants, not her, that he was projecting his problems onto her, that as a typical male he was not taking responsibility for himself and was instead burdening her. There was always a victim, she used to say, when someone in the household doesn't take emotional responsibility.

She would say such things when she was really down, and then he pitied her. So, to satisfy her, he took the pills. Just once, for a month. And yes, he knew what it was like to be untroubled by anything, to be instantly sociable, how to tolerate all kinds of fools and treat them as equals. He also discovered he was now impotent, but even then they laughed in bed together as he compared making love to climbing Mt Everest in a blizzard. He never got beyond Base Camp. So he stopped taking the pills.

He could half-handle the depression. The elation was something else. She turned into an over-energetic sex maniac, a shopping-mall addict, binge drinker and incessant, repetitious spinner of tall, illogical tales.

He noticed that the dog was shivering nervously. He was leaning his big black body against the radiator, sitting in his basket, observing the exchange between them. His eyes darted anxiously from Lettie to Roon and back again.

'I think you're scaring Rodney,' he murmured, then swivelled his eyes towards the animal.

'He's my dog and I know how to handle him,' she straightened up, the voice rising again. 'I know what he wants! Don't I Rodney, eh, there's a great boy!'

She lunged towards the dog, who cowered.

'Leave him alone, Lettie. He's afraid.' For fear of repercussions, he did not add *of you*. Once, she'd punched Roon in the cheek, cutting the flesh with the wallop she gave. She was wearing the big sparkler she'd bought with her credit card, a two-carat solitaire knuckleduster. The shock of it had made him weep.

She squeezed the dog's ear gently. He submitted, then she sighed and attempted to control herself for him again. She was trying – he knew it – like a child desperate to behave well before an adult.

'Let's have a cup of tea,' she whispered, eyes flashing. 'There's all them cakes laid out for you, eh?'

She strode across the kitchenette and pulled at the kettle, filling it from the tap. Almost immediately, it began to sing as the water heated. The sound was a relief. He needed something else to fill the space of the house where all was anger sloshing on the air, breathed out by her, emanating from her pores.

Ten plates of breads and cakes awaited him on the worktop. There was brown bread and white bread, then white bread studded with raisins. There were fairy cakes, the old-fashioned kind with the tops cut off and replaced like butterflies' wings. There were coconut cakes and even a Battenberg cake. The colours of the Battenberg cake had run into one another. They should have been diametric pink and yellow in four squares, but instead she'd been heavy-handed with the colour and the cake was a violent swirl of red, intercut with chrome yellow. He controlled his tightening stomach, reached out and took a coconut bun.

'I'm going over to my group later today,' he said as casually as possible.

'Oh. Still peddling your wares with the activists, the *Gaelgóirs*, then?' She pronounced it *Gale Gores*. When the few Irish words he taught her found their way to utterance, it was like language carpentry. She could not accept that the consonants of Irish merged into certain vowelish sounds, so she had cobbled together a mixture of phonetics and her own instinctive disdain.

She was smiling. Charitably, he thought.

'They can manage quite a bit of conversation now.'

'All women, isn't it?'

He nodded.

'Typical of you.'

'How so?'

'No chance there'd be any men in your group.'

He rose to it. 'No more than there's any chance of

women in your radio interviews.'

'Touché,' she replied grudgingly, then laughed.

He felt relieved as he chewed the coconut bun. That was a remarkably sane and ordinary man–woman exchange, he thought.

She made a pot of tea, took two mugs from the sink, rinsed them, dried them, laid them on the worktop. Her hands were shaking. She reached up to the shelf and drew down a bottle of whiskey.

'Just a wee dram, eh?' she whispered, looking up under her eyebrows mischievously.

'Not for me, thanks.'

'For Christ's sake! Have a drop, it'll do you good!'

'No.'

She poured less than half a mugful of whiskey for herself, as if to spite him, then added the tea.

'You'll kill off all the alcohol anyway. The tea's too hot,' Roon could not resist saying.

'What would you bloody know?' she snapped. 'You're all buttoned up, aren't you? A bloody buttoned-up *man*!'

'I didn't come here to be abused.'

'Fuck off.'

'That dog's terrified of you. And you an animal lover!' he remarked deliberately.

She whirled around. 'Don't you ever – EVER! – say a thing about THAT DOG!' she roared.

Again, Rodney shivered in his basket. Roon apologised. Why would he want to goad her? Desperation? Remorse? Bitterness over lost love? Nothing so high-minded. He wanted to goad her because he could and because he felt sorry for the damn dog. It spurted from him suddenly, the realisation that he had the power to drive her up the walls. It wouldn't be him who would have to deal with her in the coming weeks. There was probably a list of mugs like him to whom she made pleading phone calls. Even so, he apologised a second time, urged himself to recognise her frailty despite that booming, hysterical voice.

'The women in the group have named themselves,' he remarked by way of steering the subject into temperate waters.

She shrugged as if to say so what.

'They – they're calling themselves *Sliocht*.'

She repeated the word, crammed her mouth with it, *sshl* and *ocht* and *th*, testing the syllables as if for size.

'What's it mean?'

'Descendants.'

'Oh, that's bloody great, that is. *Descendants*? Of what, pray? Descendants of what, may I ask?'

'Lettie, that's the point, love.' He softened before her bafflement. 'They want to find a way back to something.'

'Even if that something was never there in the first place?'

'Even if it was obliterated,' he amended. 'Even if they have to imagine the something.'

She gulped at her tea and whiskey. 'Well,' she conceded, 'I suppose it's important to imagine something. For all of us.'

For the first time, there was peace.

'I see you're into garden gnomes,' he said then.

'Like them, do you? I think they're great.' She was beaming. 'I bought the lot up at the garden centre. The man said I'd left none for anybody else, but I told him to go away off and reorder, that I was a customer like anybody else and could buy what I wanted.'

'I like the glass shoes.'

'They're new,' she said, looking uneasy.

'Where'd you get them?'

She shifted on her stool, as if uncomfortable. 'It's a long story. Well, to be honest, I knicked them.'

'From where?'

'You know that co-operative near Glengormley? The glassworks I did the programme on? I went out with the intention of buying. They were all away at lunch or something. So I helped myself. You won't tell, will you? Promise!'

He nodded. The dog was asleep in his basket.

For a few minutes, neither of them spoke. He rested his eyes by looking past her head, past the cobwebs in the window, past the dried-out shells of dead flies and wasps, out into the bay. The little boats were out there as usual, tilted against the wind, tearing along with the tide. Down on the seafront, a man upended a bag of crusts. The gulls descended, dived, shrieked and tore, mad for food.

All the ordinary things defeated them, Lettie and him. They might, had things been different, have seen those gulls together. Might have absorbed a sane view of the landscape. But Lettie, being out of kilter, would never, ever look at those gulls and feel happy at the unfolding scene. She would always want to rearrange something, would always be dissatisfied and contentious, making arguments in favour of the abolition of gulls or the rearrangement of clouds on her part of the seafront.

The whiskey softened her. She reached across from her stool and placed her hand over his.

'So why did you come?' A smile brightened her eyes.

'To see you,' he answered.

'Well, you've seen me.'

'I have.'

There was an awkward pause. 'Come to bed awhile,' she

said.

It was not what he had intended. Back in Dublin, it crossed his mind as a possibility, but so remote that he dismissed it. His intimate life with her was in the past. What remained were bonds of a different kind.

'Come on, ah do,' she coaxed softly.

How many times had it ended with the two of them rolling around in bed, assuaging their differences for an hour or so, departing on good terms, only for her to unearth something new from her trove of discontents and renew her assault? Oh, she was good at sex, probably still was. Off her meds and high as a kite, she was a cracker. Briefly, despite himself, he remembered her collarbones, her breasts, one of them with a small mole below the nipple. The silk of her thighs. The taste of her. Her response.

For the first time, he knew what not to do.

He shook his head. 'It wouldn't be right. Not any more.'

He drained his mug and began to pat his pockets as if searching for car keys. It was a signal to her. He was about to leave.

'What wouldn't be right about it?' she persisted. 'Surely we're old pals, Roon. Old lovers. You're my …' she screwed up her face as she tried to recall something, 'my *anam cara*, isn't that right?'

Stop, stop now, he screamed inside. *Don't debase yourself any more.* He remained mute. She sighed heavily, pressed her knuckles to her temples, and he sensed the terrible confusion in her.

'Okay, so. If that's how you want it. Get out now.'

'What?'

'I said GET OUT NOW!'

The dog had begun to tremble again. He crawled

stealthily from his basket to stand at the back door, his bony back in a hump. For a large dog, something about him suddenly seemed very small. Roon made a mental note to contact animal welfare.

'I didn't mean to offend you,' he told her.

She began to scream, a tirade of self-hate ballooning from her lips and throat. Who did he think he was coming up to snoop and watch, oh she was on to him all the time – she knew – she knew that he had set up a virus both in the computer and in her soul, she knew she was being watched. He was behind it. Because of him she was infected and deadly. Did she imagine that those glass shoes were outside for decoration?

'They're for my protection! That's how bad it's got! I have to put the fucking glass shoes in a certain way so as to ensure my own safety!'

She blasted on and on about it being his responsibility, firstly for dragging her to the doctor three years ago, secondly for not sorting out his own problems, thirdly for being a total bastard in every way.

'Get out, you useless waste of space! GET OUT!'

She was weeping horribly now, her face folding in on itself, her lips wet with saliva. It was all too much for the dog, who trickled a puddle of urine at the back door, then rushed, embarrassed and fearful, back to his basket.

'Oh for Christ's sake, Rodney!' she roared, moving as if to strike the animal.

Only then did he touch her. He caught her by the wrist. Despite himself, he twisted slightly, just enough to halt her in her tracks. He felt small bones, sinews, her terrible tension.

'Don't touch that dog,' he warned. 'Please don't touch that dog.'

'He knows not to do that!' she bellowed, still struggling.

'No, he doesn't. He's afraid. And so am I,' he whispered urgently, bringing his face close to her left ear, where the heat of his lips and breath made her go still.

Her body relaxed in his grip, or perhaps from the proximity of another body, something humanly intimate.

'I'm sorry. You're right. Poor Rodney.'

'I have to go now, Lettie. Promise me something.'

'What?' she said in a dull voice, her left foot toeing the ground.

But he could not get the words out. He wanted her to promise not to harm the dog. He wanted her to go to the doctor, or to ask him to take her. But it was no use.

He went into the hall and she followed.

'You're really leaving me?' she asked quietly.

'I'm not leaving *you*,' he said, 'I'm just *leaving*.'

But it was a lie.

He did not look back after the door closed. She did not follow him. He left her to her misery, and to Rodney. As he drove in towards the city, to the little community hall in West Belfast where the group awaited him, he was filled with dread. He would make the necessary phone calls. There was, perhaps, nobody else to do it.

It had begun to rain. Over the mountain, an electrical storm was breaking. He watched the clean zigzag of lightning, but that too brought him back to her, to hospitals, to electrodes. Despite the encroaching rain, the city centre was lively.

An Invitation

It was Dorian's ninetieth birthday. Someone had decided it was high time to honour the author whose work had flowered modestly throughout the second half of the last century, until recently, when a mild stroke had made him forget his words.

Kevin was undecided about attending. It wasn't that he had no regard for Dorian's work. On the contrary, he was an admirer of the lyricism, the slight bawdiness, the secret sense of a different kind of knowledge conveyed in tone and narrative. Critics referred to him as 'the last of the Big House writers', referring to his portrayal of love and loss in one such collapsing Ascendancy home.

'I won't be late,' Kevin told his wife, who was bent over a bed of hostas.

Tess nodded, glancing at him, then turned to touch one of the emerging dark leaves that unfolded in the May evening.

'See? No snails this year,' she said with satisfaction.

Spurred by curiosity as much as obligation, he turned the car through the iron-gated entrance of Charleville

House. The avenue led towards the pseudo-Gothic mansion now owned by an Italian antiques dealer who had thrown wide the doors for the sake of this link with the past. He cast his eye along white-painted windows Dorian had looked through as a child, then up at the crenellated roof, before finally surveying the restored grounds and the antique hermitage far down the garden.

Within the arched doorway, people stood around, greeting, recognising. There were committee women too with welcoming smiles, willing everything to go smoothly.

The organiser stood to speak. Kevin looked around carefully and found the old man himself, hunched in a grey cardigan and denim jeans on one of the sofas in the reception room, where dampness and mould had been long since banished during the restoration of his former home. Leaf-shadows quivered on yellow walls. Two dachshunds trotted busily around before settling in front of the log fire. The cream-suited Italian sat on an ottoman, stroking his dogs, murmuring as they pressed close to his slim ankles and satin-slippered feet.

And there *she* was – Gwen – Dorian's companion, whom Kevin had never met, but had occasionally thought about in the three years since her vitriol appeared in an English daily newspaper. She bent attentively towards Dorian, patting his hand, whispering in his ear.

This wasn't the occasion to stoop so low as to snub her. It had occurred to him once or twice that if more reviewers were actively confronted, if they actually heard the angry, unembarrassed words 'You destroyed the sales of my book!', it might caution them. His wife considered him naïve. The woman who, Kevin reminded her, had not published a book in three *decades* clearly couldn't give a toss about the fact that her review portrayed him practically as a pornographer. She had lampooned his dialogue, then went on to find his descriptions of lovemaking to be *masturbatory*.

It had been quite a lot to take in, one September Friday afternoon when he had innocently perused the literary pages and found the piece grinning malevolently out at him. But no, he had not been innocent, for no writer lived in such a state of grace.

The organiser finished speaking and everybody applauded. Someone else stood and spoke about Dorian's childhood and the relationship between his family and the local village, now exploding with housing developments edging closer each year to the fields around Charleville House.

'Hey! Kev! Over here!'

He turned. It was Jago Kinnane.

'Good to see you, man!' Kevin's face broke into a smile. He reached out, relieved to have met a crony with whom he had shared many a glass in the privacy of one of the city snugs or even in the Shelbourne lounge, where fires blazed and there was room to spread oneself and gossip.

Jago had driven over from the West with Dorian and Gwen.

'We're neighbours, you know,' he remarked contentedly.

Kevin nodded. Despite his friendship with Jago, he'd never had any doubts about his allegiances, all three former alcos now imbibing sparkling water or freshly squeezed juices. But he guessed there was other history too. The three shared a cache of divorces, affairs, troubled adult children, bisexual dalliances, the full braggadocio of drink and disarray trailing between them like a mark of honour. Kevin knew he belonged to their number by default, when it suited Jago.

Unlike them, he had chosen stability. He loved his wife. None other would suit. Yet there were times when he was aware of feeling excluded, as if he could not know what they knew, or write with the full complement of experience at his disposal.

When the speeches closed, Kevin offered Jago a lift.

'Where are you staying?' he enquired.

'At the Linden,' Jago replied airily.

'Ah, the castle hotel. Nothing but the best,' Kevin winked.

Briefly, Jago turned away from him. 'Hang on a sec, you must meet our honourable guest,' he said quietly, moving towards a tall, wide-shouldered woman. Kevin drew himself up as Jago murmured something and ushered her around from the other side of the drinks table.

Carole M., novelist, lived in complete isolation in the middle of Montana. She wrote about men of character and men of weakness who struggled with land and cattle, who shaped land and respected land. The recent movie of one of her novels had divided the viewing public into polarities of liberal and edgy caution.

When Jago introduced her, Kevin noticed how she looked at him. She met his eye and did not allow her gaze to glide away as so often occurred with people who were well-known. She took him on trust, he felt.

'Forgive me, I'm jet-lagged,' she said, wrinkling her brow at him.

'Nothing worse, nothing worse,' Kevin commiserated.

'I want to crawl into bed, but I suppose I'd better eat something first.'

'You'll feel better tomorrow,' Kevin said.

'You're right. I'll need energy for my reading tomorrow.'

He offered her a lift, to which she readily agreed.

The conversation during the few miles to the hotel was general. Jago sat silently in the back as Kevin explained the area and its relationship to the city. The city, he told Carole, wasn't so far away despite trees and rolling fields and the great green plains that stretched to the foothills of the mountains.

'We've got a little bit of green at home right now,' she remarked. 'But I guess that's as good as it gets.' She stared at the green corn as the car pulled up a hill. 'By the time I get home, it'll be burnin' up in the sun,' she laughed.

At the hotel, Kevin nosed the car into a space near the stables.

'You'll join us for dinner, eh Kev?' Jago leaned forward and tapped him on the shoulder.

Kevin hesitated. 'Let's see now …' he breathed in through his teeth. 'I told Tess I wouldn't be late this evening.'

Carole got out and yawned. 'Good Lord,' she chuckled, 'a man who listens to his wife? Are all Irishmen like that?'

'Probably not,' Kevin replied, feeling his face go hot.

'Oh, come on!' Jago grunted as he hauled himself out of the car. 'Call her and tell her you've fallen in love with the siren Carole. Tell her anything!'

Tess wouldn't mind, he knew. She probably wouldn't even read his text message, down on her knees in the scarcely controlled wilderness of the garden.

He wished she was with him. She was as familiar with the great woman's works as he. But it would be impolite to drag her over now, when the visitor herself was clearly exhausted. If Carole met Tess, it would have to be when she was fully awake and in possession of herself.

*

Over the weekend, he dipped in and out of lectures and seminars, chatted with or avoided various people he knew. By Sunday, it was clear that things had gone well. Dorian's first novel was reissued and launched with a great deal of champagne and well-chilled wine. The organiser prowled around as speakers interacted and mild controversy developed between a novelist and one of the city journalists. Throughout it all, committee women adjusted microphones, got the coffee ready, straightened rows of seating during breaks in lectures.

That afternoon, he found himself again sitting with Jago, following the debate between Dorian and a visiting academic. Carole, also on the panel, intervened with the occasional moderating comment, clarifying, cutting through faulty digressions. Although she was smiling, Kevin formed the impression that the visiting writer held herself at a remove from self-indulgence.

'I wouldn't like to get on the wrong side of Carole, eh?' Jago muttered, nudging Kevin.

He recalled how Jago had offered to endorse his own first novel some twenty years before. They had agreed to meet in a Dublin pub, but he arrived to find Jago so completely drunk that he could barely sit straight.

'What do you want me to say?' he had slurred.

Kevin had foreseen a typed sheet on which Jago's praise for his maiden voyage into fiction would appear. Instead, he was invidiously forced to compose the entire blurb himself as the pub filled with office workers out for the night. Jago agreed with everything, dozed off, woke up again and continued to agree as Kevin hastily scribbled. Finally, Kevin shouted the paragraph at Jago, who leaned over and scrawled his own name in jagged black ink.

Not for a moment had he considered leaving the rank

bar without an endorsement, not for a moment did he hesitate to stoop to the hodge-podge of self-written lauds and the indifferent signature of a drunk. When he escaped to the night, leaving Jago slumped over the stained table, he felt nothing but relief. He hurried along the canal bank path, avoiding prostitutes, head down, a sheet of paper rolled in his fist.

He told himself that Jago was a canny literary bird who felt safe enough in his company to reveal his private carps about the literary tensions that crossed the country like ley lines, unseen by the majority, electrifying to the few.

Now, halfway through the afternoon, he suggested that Jago and some of the other guests return to his house that evening. He was enjoying himself, so why not have them over, friends old and new?

'Ah sure, I'm in the mood for a party!' he announced, having already mentioned the possibility to Tess, who had wondered about the wisdom of inviting Dorian and Gwen. But Kevin had replied that it was time to rise above past slights. In any event, he had hardly exchanged two words with the woman all weekend.

Jago was interested. 'Good man! I'll tell the others, eh?'

'I'll organise something simple. Pasta, smoked salmon, drinks,' Kevin said. 'All very welcome, *chez nous*,' he added warmly.

'We'll liven things up for you! A night to remember! The last bohemians!' Jago growled mischievously.

His mind raced. What did it matter if Gwen had disliked his novel? It seemed too long ago to care about. His thoughts moved to what interested him most. To think that Carole M. would in all likelihood drop by! He texted his wife, instructing her to kill the fatted calf, the gang would probably arrive sometime around eight o'clock.

When had he ever had the opportunity to entertain so many from his own world, in his own home? To cap it all, never in a million years could he have foreseen that Carole M. would descend among them, trailing dry-ice brilliance, uncomplicated intelligence.

Again, he found himself driving Jago and Carole back to the hotel.

'I might see you later,' he nodded at Carole.

'Thank you so much for the invitation,' she said politely, stepping from the car, 'and thanks again for the ride.'

He slipped her a brown envelope.

'You might like to read that,' he said shyly.

'That's so generous! I'll read it on the plane tomorrow.' She leaned in, smiled as she took the package, then made her way to the hotel entrance.

It wasn't quite the response he had expected. On the bloody *plane*? Where oxygen-deprived passengers turned to all kinds of drivel to pass the time?

'I'll work out the details,' Jago called as he hurried to catch up with Carole. 'Dorian might like a little lie-down. Call you at seven.'

'And if it doesn't suit, I'll drop over and join you for a nightcap,' Kevin shouted.

He drove home and felt as if he was flying. He pressed a button and all four car windows opened. He turned on the radio, only to hear his favourite organ piece spilling forth. Widor's *Toccata* caught the rush of devotion and ecstasy he was now experiencing. He drove faster, ripping the car through the bends, enjoying the blasts of air that tossed around his head and neck. He'd phone his two painter friends in the next county, admirers of Carole M., and other friends twenty miles away, a pair of women poets equally avid about this great writer. They would have an unforgettable night, a spring revel in which reservations would evaporate and they would be joyous together.

He pushed in the front door. Tess had cut long stems, then thrust them in vigorous twists into pots and jugs. He smelled cooking. Parmesan cheese. Garlic. He smelled uncorked bottles of wine, noted her home-made rosehip lemonade on the worktop too. She was busy separating slices of smoked salmon.

'Great stuff, my love!' He bounced through the long kitchen, taking a little run at her and gently squeezing her buttocks. She turned and smiled.

'They're coming?'

'Jago'll ring in a few minutes.'

Tess looked puzzled.

'To confirm numbers, that's all.'

As he was about to call his friends the painters, the phone rang. He glanced at the caller display, recognised the hotel number.

'Ah, Jago – very punctual!' he boomed. He knew he was letting his guard down, eager and, for once, not afraid to show it. Tess threw her eyes up and shook her head.

'So – what's the story?'

There was a pause. He could hear Jago's heavy breathing, and what sounded like the shuffling of papers.

'Well, we've had a discussion about your idea … together … and, um … it's been decided that we're all tired, and going to have a light meal here in the hotel. Then perhaps early to bed …'

'I see. So you're not coming over?'

He waited for Jago to suggest that he return to the hotel to join them.

'I'm afraid not. As I say, we're rather tired.'

'Mmm. I suppose these weekend festivals can be … intense.'

As the words left his lips, he was annoyed at himself for being so rational. He waited, held the silence that fell. Jago would invite him to the hotel. Surely he would do that at least. But no. The breezy bastard carried on.

'It's been great to catch up. Marvellous of you to come to the event.'

'It was nothing,' Kevin said, unable again to muster the words he needed.

'I'll probably retire early. Do a little light reading.'

He heard a thin clink, as if a glass or a piece of cutlery were being laid down.

'If you're ever in the West … you do come West sometimes?'

'Never. Do you come to Dublin?'

'Off and on. I'll give you a call.'

Silence.

'Goodbye,' Kevin said.

'Cheerio for now. See you anon.'

Tess's brow knotted in that way she reserved for whenever one of his kind failed him. She was, he knew, his greatest audience.

'At least I hadn't put on the pasta,' she said in a low voice.

His eye fell on the shapely jug of flowers on the table. He took in their home and solid life, which failed nobody. She had put on the kettle for him. He pottered around, took two mugs from the press, teabags from a tin with painted scenes of the India of the Raj. Jago's voice resounded in his ears, the blatant, velvety lie. They had had a better offer, he guessed, dinner at Charleville House, a convivial post-mortem on the weekend with the organiser and the Italian and his petted little shits of dogs.

Later that night, he lay on his back as Tess snored. She had shed tears and berated him for being too trusting. Then she had fallen asleep, mouth open. She looked surprised, her hair in an untidy fizz on the pillow. Despite the snoring, he would not disturb her.

The long dusk slipped through a sliver in the bedroom curtains. The spring birds were not yet silent. He listened, then turned on his side. In the continuum of stories that bound them all, he felt his own life's unfolding epic.

Tomorrow, Carole M. would return to Montana. He imagined her frank, uncompromised eyes. He tried to sleep.

The Story of Maria's Son

This is the story of Maria's son, but it is a story with two endings.

Maria lived in a small neglected suburb on the edge of the city and at the foot of the mountains. She had one son, and he was her world. His life was her life, and her thoughts were directed only to him. Eighteen years before, she met his father on the one holiday she had ever had, in Spain. Herself and the girls in the biscuit factory had clubbed together and booked two weeks in Benidorm. Her first glimpse of the turquoise sea as the plane droned down into the Spanish dawn made her eyes prickle with astonishment and joy at such postcard beauty. The world was full of marvels, she thought then, and life was beginning.

Most of the girls met men on that holiday. Some had a quick fling, or even several one-night stands. But on the second night, Maria met Jorge. As far as she was concerned, that was it. He was the man of her dreams, with golden brown eyes, dark skin that felt like satin when he touched her arm and a sweet bucket of a mouth that she wanted to suck all the kisses out of forever and ever. Jorge was a printer. He wooed her and stuck to her like a clam throughout the holiday. He brought gifts of specially printed notelets and cards with her name on them, and clever drawings of two hearts entwined. He told her he loved her and she believed him, because she loved him. It did not seem possible that the love she felt could not equally be returned. It was also the first time she had fallen in love, and as it was her nature to be giving, she gave herself to him, heart, soul and body.

Things had moved swiftly. In retrospect, she believed she became pregnant on the third night of the holiday, which was the second night with Jorge. She saw no reason to withhold herself from this man, who was good, charming and whipped her senses to a delirium. At the end of the holiday, she had a vague sensation of unwellness. She noticed, as she lay roasting on the beach one afternoon, waiting until Jorge would come from the printers to join her for the last hour or so by the water's edge, that she felt not quite herself. It was not exactly a sickness, but an odd sensation of having been slightly pushed out of her own body.

Around her, voices of other holiday-makers rose on the air. People played in the water like children. They dipped their overheated bodies into the Mediterranean and swam around for a few minutes, whooping with pleasure, occasionally splashing someone else as they went.

On the final evening, Jorge arrived with a generous heft of pink, scented writing paper on which her address in Ireland was printed in delicate slanting writing, fresh from the printing press. *So that you do not forget to write to me*, he murmured close to her ear in his delicious accent, making her forget her earlier feelings of physical displacement. She felt weak with love for him, and that night they fell again insatiably into one another's arms.

Back in Ireland, she did not forget to write. But after three letters, and once she relayed the news of her situation to him, Jorge's correspondence suddenly ceased. At first, she did not want to believe that such a thing could have happened to her. Her mother, who in her way was sympathetic, told her not to be a fuckin' eejit and did she think she was the first girl to get knocked up and then dropped like a hot potato?

'But Ma,' Maria wailed, 'he told me he loved me!'

Maria's mother threw her eyes to the ceiling and folded her arms. 'Daughter dear, you weren't the first he said that to. Now the best thing you can do is forget the louser. You'll manage. Trust me, you will!'

Over the years, Maria placed her trust in her mother's advice. She managed very well indeed, all things considered, with a small, adored son whom she christened George. Eventually, she moved away from her mother's house and into the suburbs. She mostly forgot about Jorge and concentrated instead on George, determined to raise him to be a good man, a reliable man, although he had no father to show him how to be a man.

For George's sake she took two jobs, one of them with a domestic cleaning firm, the other as a waitress on Saturdays and Sundays, when she cycled to a restaurant perched on a thickly wooded hill halfway up the mountains. She scrimped and she saved so that George would have the right clothes for school, the right trainers, the right pencil case and ruler, a proper boy's lunch box and, after school, some decent computer games. Because she did not trust banks, she saved money in two ways: at the credit union and in a narrow tin box kept beneath the crimson layered skirt of an ornamental Spanish doll, bought at the airport by Jorge as the lovers said their tearful goodbyes. The doll stood in a Perspex case on the landing window. She congratulated herself on her cleverness in secreting money in such a way. As time went on and George grew older, she knew that she had almost equal amounts of money stashed in both locations. It was a comfort on the rare occasions when she awoke at night to know that there were literally some thousands right there in her home, to be put towards George's education.

He was showing signs of being exceptionally good at maths and her heart ached with pride in him. Although she would never admit it to her neighbours, like many mothers she dreamed of him joining the professional classes. Someday, she thought, he might become a doctor. He would heal people. She hoped he would never go for law, however. In her opinion, solicitors had big mouths and necks as thick as a jockey's bollocks, and it was universally acknowledged that they overcharged. Medicine, please, she prayed, not law.

So it was for George's sake that she knuckled down, literally, on the floors of some of the grand homes in which she worked, poking her fingers into unsavoury corners of domestic filth, sticking brushes down many toilets, spraying and swirling clean scents into places where clean scents would not otherwise be found. It was for his sake too that she worked overtime some evenings, to have that little bit extra, so that George could go on the school tour to Paris or Barcelona or wherever the teachers decreed was the place to go that year. Sometimes, she would meet the very same people whose houses she cleaned in the restaurant at weekends. At first she used to feel awkward about it, but after a while she couldn't be bothered dealing with such feelings. Occasionally, they blinked in comfortable Sunday surprise, recognising her as she awaited their menu choice.

No starter for me, some cashmere-wrapped woman might murmur modestly, or, *I think I'll treat myself and go for the goat's cheese*, as if that was a really daring thing to do. Once she heard a woman remark softly to her silent husband about how great Maria was *to hold down two jobs to make a go of things*.

At home and school, George was diligent. The school was ten miles from the estate, far from the local one, which Maria regarded as too rough. He had local friends, of course, but, miraculously for the times they lived in, appeared to hold himself at a slight remove from trouble. This pleased her. She did not worry that when George was busy tweaking at his mobile phone there could be anything other than boyish conversation going on between him and his mates. She would eye him fondly, her heart swelling as she observed him, his vital, straight shoulders, slim hips and the golden brown eyes which reminded her of his father. Like his father, George would be of interest to the girls, she surmised. Unlike his father, she hoped she had knocked a bit of character into him, mainly by not spoiling him and by teaching him the value of a euro.

'The world owes none of us a living, son!' she once said.

'I know that, Ma. You've told me that before!' George had replied, impatient by now at the familiarity of this mantra.

'So long as you know,' she said softly, dropping the subject.

One day in late May, when the air was heavy with the scent that rose up from crushed grass, the one scarred horse chestnut tree and the few wanly flowering shrubs at the edge of the estate, Maria waited at her gate for George. The domestic help suppliers were on strike because of a dispute regarding van rosters, and to her dismay she was off work all that week. There had been the usual May rain and despite the pleasant, early summer scents, she felt irritable and wandered impatiently up and down her own path.

It was a week before George's Leaving Cert and, encouraged by his maths teacher, he had applied for a place in both Oxford and Cambridge University, in England. *He really should go for Oxford*, the teacher had advised Maria at the spring parent–teacher meeting. *Nothing to lose and everything to gain. I think he can do it, I really do …*

Oh, she had replied, astonished at George's brilliance, which even she had not fully realised.

We should hear something, maybe a provisional offer of a place by the end of May.

A neighbour passed.

'Waiting for George?' said the neighbour pleasantly. He stood for a minute to adjust the belt of his jeans and wipe the sweat of the damp day from his face. He was an old widower who passed much of the time voluntarily collecting litter from around the pavements of the estate. Everywhere he went, he carried a long fork-like gripper and a light plastic bin.

'Clammy weather despite the rain, isn't it?' he said, idly opening and shutting the litter gripper. 'It'll be a hard bus ride across the city for George this afternoon. The traffic's gone crazy. I wouldn't like to have to face a long bus ride on a day like this!'

'Ah, George doesn't mind. He studies on his way home!' said Maria with the pride of one who'd never studied much.

Minutes passed. She kept looking up at the sky.

'I suppose a few clouds never did us any harm!' she said at last.

'Clouds, if you get enough of them, can be disastrous,' said the neighbour absent-mindedly as he pulled a discarded milkshake carton from the gulley below the pavement. 'Think of the rain in '87! Savage! The whole of Ringsend and Ballsbridge destroyed when the river burst its banks! Oh, you could lose your life with too much cloud.'

'Still,' said Maria peaceably, not wanting to offend the neighbour, 'at least we're in a big city and not out in the sticks. The floods can be really bad out there. Global warming has changed things,' she said knowledgeably.

'That's true, I suppose,' said the neighbour. He looked at his fingernails. 'Well, it's the biggest city in Ireland now,' he said earnestly. 'It's a cosmopolitan city now. It's big, oh, very big and full of foreigners. Not so big it can be seen from the moon, I'd say. Not like the Great Wall of China. But it's a big, big place.'

Maria was beginning to wish her neighbour would move on. She wanted to concentrate on George's arrival down the long road. The man must have sensed her inattention, because he said goodbye and headed off in search of litter.

When half an hour had passed, it became apparent to Maria that George must be delayed. She texted him.

Are u stuck in traffic?

A minute later the reply came. *Yea, c u l8r, round 6. Gud news Ma!*

She reread the message, afraid to believe what she thought the good news might be. Oh, God, she panicked joyfully. That must mean …

She raced back into the house, opened the tin box beneath the doll's voluminous skirt, and pulled on a light jacket. The supermarket was a ten-minute walk, but if she was quick she could get there and back in half an hour.

There was obviously something to celebrate. As she raced along the road, she had no time to do more than greet her neighbours in the most cursory fashion, a nod here, a quick hello there.

Once in the supermarket, she delayed, fascinated by the sheer choice of foods, most of which she would not ordinarily buy unless they struck her as good value. Although she had not intended to, she took a large trolley instead of the small basket she would normally have chosen. She took her time along the supermarket aisles, examining sauces and pastas, rich, sweating cheeses and the warm, yeasty aroma of breads that lay piled provocatively within wicker baskets. She bought Italian breads and French breads, then added some Polish bread for good measure, on the grounds that it was good to experiment. Then she added two thickly cut steak fillets, a head of lettuce, garlic, vine tomatoes and small new potatoes from Cyprus. For dessert they could have that rich ice cream George so liked. Strawberry cheesecake flavour, she remembered, reaching into the ice cream cabinet and withdrawing two tubs.

She walked home as briskly as she could, but weighed down with groceries, the journey took twice as long as it normally would and she arrived at her gate breathless and with tired arms.

The moment she looked up the path at the house, she knew something was amiss.

The front door was half open. She noticed too that the upstairs blinds were closed. Had she forgotten to open them that morning? No, it was not possible. Forgetfulness was not her style. Once inside the gate, she dropped the groceries and ran. She pushed the door back fully and raced down the narrow hallway, glancing wild-eyed into the small sitting room at the front as she went. The cushions of the sofa were all over the place, the sofa itself had been ripped and the television stolen. Worse, to her mind, was the sight of George's school rucksack on the floor beside the open kitchen door.

It was only afterwards, when the harm was done, that Maria began to think that it might perhaps have been the presence of that doll in the landing window that gave some peering Peter, some crack cocaine addict, the idea that she had nice, worthwhile *things* in the house, that it might be a worthwhile place to turn over.

'George! George!' she screamed, flailing around for some sight of him. But the kitchen, which had also been overturned, with broken crockery everywhere, and the fridge door wide open, was empty.

Some instinct made her pause before she went upstairs. She thought of the Spanish doll, perched in her display case. Some dread seized her. She began to take the stairs in twos, screaming as she went, calling out her son's name over and over in the silent house.

He lay there on the landing floor, collapsed and crumpled in on himself the way a dog that had just been killed might be.

'Oh, God, oh, God, let him just be unconscious, let him be alive!' she screamed. By then, the neighbour she had spoken to earlier was on his way down the road again, noticed that something was different about the house, and arrived at the top of the stairs, along with two women, just as Maria knelt down by her son. He lay near the window, where the doll was not smashed, but overturned, her porcelain legs sticking up ridiculously within her rumpled skirts.

'He's only passed out!' Maria screamed and she urged the three that had gathered around her to do something for him. 'For God's sake, get the doctor!' she cried, pushing one of the women towards the head of the stairs. 'Get a move on! Doctor! Ambulance! Phone 999!'

But the other woman and the man were crossing themselves already and fell to their knees beside her, for it was clear that George was dead. His blood had spread in a bright, uneven pool and there was a deep cut on his head.

'Can you feel a pulse?' Maria implored the man, whose hand was on her shoulder, who was hushing her in an attempt at consolation.

'Let's carry him to the bedroom,' the man suggested gently, looking into her eyes.

'What was he at, trying to stand up to those knackers? Why didn't he let them take the money? What's money? Is it worth poor George's life?'

But after a time she stopped raving and looked from one face to the other.

'Why didn't he just slip out of the house again before they saw him?' she sobbed. 'Why did he try to hang onto a tinful of money? Didn't he know he was worth more to his mother than an old tin that would be opened to pay his fees one of these days? Why did he do it? Why? Why?' she wept. 'Now I can hardly pay for the funeral,' she murmured to herself.

The neighbours had begun to weep.

'There now!' they said. 'There now!' That was all they could think of saying and they repeated it often, even after the guards arrived, and the doctor.

'There now! There now!'

In the years that followed, whenever Maria spoke of her son George to the good neighbours who dropped in to keep her company for an hour or two in the evenings, she always had the same question to ask; tireless, gnawing, unanswerable.

And they always gave the same answer.

'There now!' they said. 'Time will help! Let time do its work! We're here for you, always!' they impressed on her. And they sat as silently as Maria herself, gazing towards the flat-screen television on which the events of the world were reported in an unceasing tide of colour, blood and anger. Whenever Maria saw blood on the faces of children in the Middle East wars, she would weep, because it always reminded her of George and the waste of young lives everywhere.

But surely, some of those neighbours must have been stirred to wonder what would have happened had George not decided to go bald-headed in defence of his mother's store of banknotes? And surely some of them must have stared into their own flat-screen television sets as the activities of the world unfolded before their eyes, as great towers crumbled in New York, as famines and despair ravaged the people of Darfur? Surely they pictured the scene of the tragedy again, altering a detail here and there as they did so, and giving the story a different twist. For her neighbours knew Maria and her intensities and follies, just as they knew George, and when you know people well it is sometimes easier to anticipate what they might say and do under certain conditions than it is to remember what the facts actually were. In fact, sometimes invention is far more satisfying than accurate retelling, because without invention, the real history of our presence on this planet, which is storytelling and gossip, would wither and die.

So, let me tell you what I myself think might have happened had George not been so courageous. It is no more of a fiction than what I have just recounted.

To be honest, in some respects the new story is the same as the old.

It begins the same way, too. There is Maria working hard to make ends meet, holding down two jobs, fussing and caring for George so that he might have a better life and be able to hold his own with the sons of the professionals she half admires. There, too, is the neighbour, stopping to chat to her. When he opens his mouth it is to utter the same remark as before.

'Waiting for George?' said the neighbour pleasantly. He stood for a minute to adjust the belt of his jeans and wipe the sweat of the damp day from his face. It will be remembered that he was an old man.

'Clammy weather despite the rain, isn't it?' he said, idly opening and shutting the litter gripper. 'It'll be a hard bus ride across the city for George this afternoon. The traffic's gone crazy. I wouldn't like to have to face a long bus ride on a day like this!'

'Ah, George doesn't mind. He reads books all the way home!' Maria crowed with the pride of one who'd never studied much.

Minutes passed. She kept looking up at the sky.

'I suppose a few clouds never did us any harm!' she said at last.

'Clouds, if you get enough of them, can be disastrous,' said the neighbour absent-mindedly as he pulled a discarded milkshake carton from the gulley below the pavement. 'Think of the rain in '87! The whole of Ringsend and Ballsbridge half destroyed when the river burst its banks!'

'Still, at least we're in a large city and not right out in the country. The floods can be really bad in low-lying parts,' Maria said reasonably.

'That's true, I suppose,' said the neighbour. He examined his fingernails. 'Well, it's the biggest city in Ireland now,' he said earnestly. 'It's cosmopolitan. Full of migrants.'

Maria was beginning to wish her neighbour would move on. She wanted to concentrate on George's arrival down the long road. The man must have sensed this.

'Well, I'd best go on. No doubt you want to spoil your lambkin son!' he teased gently.

Maria turned on him. 'Are you talking about George?' she asked. 'George was no lambkin, not from the day he was born!'

'Oh now, oh now,' the man said in a knowing voice before moving on.

When half an hour had passed, it became apparent to Maria that George must be delayed. She texted him and he replied that he was on his way, that he had good news for her.

So here she is now in the supermarket, shopping carefully for the anticipated happy meal. She has bought the breads, fillet steak, a bottle of red wine I forgot to mention in the first story, and of course the ice cream: strawberry cheesecake flavour, George's favourite.

When Maria arrived back at the house, pushing her way tiredly up the concrete path towards the front door, she noticed that it was slightly ajar. George was home, she thought happily, dragging her groceries into the hall and laying them down carefully on the floor.

But all was not what it seemed. George came thundering down the stairs, his face red and furious, eyes blazing. At a glance she also noticed that the downstairs was wrecked, the television gone.

'What is it?' she shrieked.

'Oh Ma, Ma, the money's gone!' he shouted in agitation.

Maria screamed and threw her arms up in the air and

ran outside in a panic. Just then, the elderly neighbour was making his way past her gate again and, spotting a drama in the making, decided to come in. At the same time, two women from across the way came running.

'I couldn't help it, Ma. I couldn't help it. They must have been followin' me. I didn't notice till one of them was holdin' a blade to me throat!'

Maria ran upstairs and lifted the overturned doll. She stood for a moment, examining it all over, holding it by the head and letting the long, wide skirt dangle in the air. She ran down again into the hall, where George, the elderly man and the two women clustered anxiously. Then, catching the doll by the feet, she raised it above her head and brought it down on George's back, in blow after blow, delivered with venom, and the doll smashed on his head, which got another cut so that blood flowed over George's face and hands, over his white school shirt and even dripping down onto the hall floor. It was as if her whole life was unravelling like a huge sweater in which there had been one tiny tear. She saw it clearly, the yarn of her life, her sweating daily effort which was all poured into her dreams of George's future, unravelling and falling to a heap of nothingness.

'You stupid, stupid blockhead!' she screamed between blows. 'How could you not have seen them? How often have I told you to keep the front door locked as soon as you come home? How many times, eh? You must've known they were on your heels. It wouldn't be the first time some of the lads from round here turned on you!'

She turned to the old man. 'Shouldn't he have been more careful than to let those yobbos run him down and into the place?'

'Well, I suppose you can't be careful enough these days,'

said the old man uncertainly, his eye on the broken doll in Maria's hand.

'There you are!' Maria said. She flung the doll on the floor. 'You saw the doll on the landing window, knowing what lay beneath,' she raged at George, 'but you made no attempt to divert their attention! Never crossed your mind to phone the guards! Right? *Right?*' she screeched, twisting the lobe of his bloodied ear.

'Ma! No, no Ma! Sure, what could I do? They knocked me around the place and began waving knives and hammers in me face!' George's lip trembled.

'You could've texted someone!'

'Ma, are you mad or what? They'd have killed me if I'd taken out the mobile. Christ's sake, Ma, they'd have killed me!'

'I mean, did you do it on purpose, like? Did you want to avoid going to college? Is that what it's all about? Sudden laziness just when success is yours? You've got an offer in one of those big-smoke English universities, right? The kind of offer nobody around here gets in a million years?'

George nodded, his face reddening. 'Yeah, I got a place. Two places, in fact,' he said in a dull voice.

'Oh.' Maria dropped the doll, the truth of his words taking the wind from her sails. So he'd done it! He'd done it. He could – if he wanted – now take a scholarship place at Cambridge or Oxford. Instantly, she wanted to calm the whole situation, to be rid of the gaping neighbours who should not be present for such good news. But they were staring at her. The words of the old man still prickled in her mind. The thing about George being a *lambkin*. Lambkin, how are you! She imagined them now, sniggering behind her back after the display of unfettered rage and after the crazy logic of her thinking which, in the heat and panic of the moment, had let her down. She, who had always and for so long held their lives together, had slipped. Well, she wouldn't satisfy them!

She turned to George. 'So, you've got two scholarship places, eh?'

'Yes, Ma,' he replied, looking at her, his eyes suddenly mistrustful.

'Scholarships!' she said sarcastically, at the same time trying to lighten things a bit. 'I suppose you'll be too good for the rest of us from now on. I suppose you think you can do what you like, when it's not so long ago I was wiping your arse and mopping up after you!'

The neighbours laughed at that and the tension was broken. But the moment the words were out, her heart burned at the sight of his embarrassed face.

'Get into the kitchen!' she commanded with a forced laugh, giving him a shove in the back. 'Let me see to those cuts while we're waiting for the cops, scholarship or not!'

Again, the neighbours tittered. She wanted to get him away from them. She hated them suddenly. If they had not been present, things might have been different. At least she had the groceries, the special meal she had bought so carefully, spending far more than she would usually for an evening meal. She wanted to get the potatoes sliced and parboiled, and the cheese grated, and the garlic sliced, so that she could make cheesy potato pie for George. It would comfort him.

But George only poked at the food when she served it up. And even after he had washed himself clear of blood, there was a new sullenness to him. The guards came and made notes. They spoke kindly to Maria. Immediately after the squad car left, George said he was going out. She passed the evening uneasily, her eyes half-witnessing the events of the world as they were relayed on the news station, no longer caring about them, because her world had shrunk and she was poor in a manner she would not have thought possible.

She went to bed around midnight. She thought she heard George let himself in sometime during the night, turned over, and then slept deeply because the drama had tired her out.

The following morning, she went in to wake him for school, because it was revision week, the last precious week before the Leaving, but his room was empty. His bed had not been slept in, and when she examined the wardrobe, she saw that his best clothes were gone. She rang around the neighbours' homes, but he wasn't in any of them. She thought she could sense the little judgments as she hung up after each one and phoned another. He wasn't at school either.

The guards did their best, but there was no news. Nor would there be for three weeks. A long text arrived saying that he was well and that she was not to worry. He was working in the midlands with a team of block-layers. There was plenty of work and no need to go abroad. He would not be returning home, he said. In time, he added, he'd replace the money that had been stolen, but she would have to wait. The text was simply signed, 'George'.

When she read that, she screamed to herself and jumped up and down, clenching her fists, holding bare knuckles against her teeth in an attempt to silence the screams, but still they emerged from her throat, high and pitiful.

… And so people may have let their thoughts wander as they sat before the television with Maria, listening to her voice repeating the same thing, over and over.

'Why did he try to hang onto a tinful of money – no matter how much was in it? Didn't he know his life was worth more to his Ma than an old tin that would be opened to pay some stupid university fees? My boy, oh my lovely boy!' she wailed.

Occasionally she thought of Jorge, George's father, and of the seed he had planted on her third night in Spain.

Perhaps every action has a double life, the potential for alternatives. In the end, it is only by paying absolute attention to the heart within our hearts – the invisible one which beats beyond the physical, vital with instinct – that we follow the path destined for us. Because no matter how tragic *that* path may be, it is better than the needless tragedy we bring upon ourselves. We witness daily, on our television screens, tragedy and needless tragedy alike. Even so, we learn nothing.

This story was written in response to Mary Lavin's 'The Story of the Widow's Son'. I have deliberately followed the form and tone of Lavin's masterpiece, although the context is contemporary. My purpose was to explore the possibilities of a morality tale with two very different outcomes in an urban setting.

Fadó, Fadó

He waited in the car park three floors beneath the shopping centre. His daughter Katy had promised to meet him there at three thirty, leaving enough time for the usual crawl across the M50 to their home, just beyond the suburbs. It was now four o'clock and no sign of Her Nibs and the over-sexed fourteen-year-old Sorcha, who was her current Best Friend.

He'd read the newspaper and had absorbed the columnists' views on everything from the Middle East to current national prosperity and immigration. He flipped his phone open and laboriously texted with big fingers: *Where r u? Fone me NOW. Dad.* He now quite enjoyed the abbreviations of the mobile phone, even using them when staying in touch with Joyce, his wife. Today, she was at the hairdressers for her biannual mortgage-sized haircut. It was left to him to bring the two girls, on the last Saturday of the summer holidays, across the city to the southside shopping haven that drew them like bees to honey.

After a few minutes, he decided to phone Katy. He waited, then tutted as her voice cut in with the usual cutesy stuff about not being there right now, *but leave a message and if you're lucky I might, just might, get back to you!*

As so often of late, he could feel his heart pumping with anger. It was always an anger that had to be suppressed. Any word from him and Joyce would modify it, making less of his admonitions and advice, sometimes even in front of Katy, urging him to encourage rather than inhibit. He understood where she was coming from. Both of them had long memories of feeling small, a well-absorbed sense of inconsequentiality learned in childhood when parents and teachers sang in perfect harmony to the wisdom of the Irish version of an education. There'd been a lot of humility, not being seen to be big-headed, and certainly no showing off.

He got out of the car and slammed the door shut. The escalator went up five or six levels before he arrived at what was supposed to be a ground floor. The place was humming with its eager constituency of women and yet more women, groups of young fellows in blue and white striped rugger shirts, gaggles of tanned young girls in high-street couture T-shirts and pearls. *Pearls*, for heaven's sake! When he was young, only his girlfriends' mothers would be seen in pearls. Now pearls were the far edge of cool. Katy wore them too.

He scanned the vast mall. Where was she? Should he find an information desk, get her paged? Could he do that? And would she hear her name over the babble of discriminating, magpie-eyed shoppers? He observed the crowd, focusing occasionally on a bag-laden woman in casual wear. Clichéd as it was, they'd all come a long way, and he wasn't so sure he liked the distance.

Katy could do with a spell down in Limerick with his Uncle Seanie. A few nights at the farm in Clonfadó would open her eyes. It sure as hell had opened his, thirty-five years ago at the age of fifteen, when his parents took a trip to London and thought it a good idea to renew family relations by sending him down to Seanie's place. That was how he discovered East was East and West was West, and as far as he was concerned the twain would never meet. He had reeled through the seven days in a state of quiet shock at his parents' misjudgement, appalled by the savagery of his uncle, who had inherited Clonfadó House. It took a year before he could even begin to forgive his father, not only for sending him there, but for having a brother like Seanie, whose wife lived in fear of things he could only guess at and whose children – his cousins – were a pitiable crew, dragged up by Uncle Seanie's begrudging, swearing ebullience. It was like something from a jagged satire by Myles na gCopaleen, except that it was real, so real he quaked.

They had no indoor toilet. In the centre of every room hung a single, unshaded light bulb. The strong tea tasted strange, acrid. He didn't discover the reason for this until his sixth day in Clonfadó, when he noticed Aunt Eylie pouring the water in which Uncle Seanie's two eggs had been boiled into the teapot. When he timidly enquired about this procedure, Aunt Eylie whispered that it saved on electricity. No need to boil water twice, she said, her cheeks flushed.

He found it difficult to get to know his cousins. One of the two girls was impudent, a year older than he, well able to stand up to her father, who favoured her. She would throw him long, unsettling, glitter-eyed looks that made him feel oddly naked. Bafflingly, she also shared that particular gaze with her father. The other girl, like her mother, was mostly silent, embarrassed and perspiring. The boy, the same age as he, had a severe cast in one eye.

'Ah, sure, the fairies got to that fella!' Uncle Seanie would roar at mealtimes. 'An' he should've bin *dhrowned* at birth!' Then he would laugh, his voice cruel and triumphant as his only son scowled.

When he got back to Kildare, he wept with relief and rage and challenged his father about it.

'Why did you send me there? Why? Why?' he blubbered, the urgency of the question rising over his tears.

His father looked helpless and shrugged. 'I didn't know it would be like that. Honest, son. Seanie rang me a month ago, first time in five years, so I thought ... and he offered to take you ... I thought it would be a holiday. I meant no harm.'

He meant no harm. Even so, harm was done. He would never inflict the equivalent on Katy, even if she needed a root up the arse from time to time and thanks to her mother never got it.

He sighed. Where would he find her? He texted her again. By now, he was walking quickly past various shops, Tommy-this and Ralph-that, Harvey-something, House of something else. He was afraid to take the plunge inside for fear of what he'd find there, yet they were just shops. Places where people bought things. But all he felt was anxiety. He needed to be in a land, a safe haven that lay somewhere between the chosen impoverishment, the spirit-wreckage of his uncle in Clonfadó and this new, bewildering zone which people embraced frenziedly. Where did he fit in, he and Joyce, who remembered the old days when everybody was smacked down? Now, reward was automatic for the stupid, the passive and the evil, and everybody dressed like characters from a southern California soap series.

For a moment, he heard his own inner rant and saw himself in Grumble Mode, all his own once-young-man's laughter long gone from him.

He glanced to the left, into a lingerie shop. Just as he was about to force his eyes to glide away from the sight of so much feminine apparel, he saw them, Katy and Sorcha at the checkout, handing over their purchases. Joyce had told Katy to get herself some new underwear, he remembered as he entered the shop, approaching them. Their girl was growing. Soon she would be a young woman. He imagined her in the future, a slightly intimidating Amazon to the faint-hearted, but otherwise grace and ease on two legs.

Already, he could hear the giggles. He had long ago conceded that most young females spent a lot of time amused at very little, as if they carried a built-in radar primed to receive the comic and the absurd so that they could break their guts laughing at it.

Sorcha spotted him first and hissed something in Katy's ear. There was a sudden rush of activity between them as the purchased items were hastily deposited into bags. The girls approached him.

'Hi,' Katy smiled up at him. 'I know, my phone was switched off. I didn't mean … I forgot, Dad.'

'That's okay, love. I found you, that's the main thing.' He smiled at her, then glanced amiably at Sorcha. 'Have a good time?' he enquired.

The girl stared frankly up into his eyes.

'Oh John, we had a really *cool* time of it. *Savage!*'

He took a deep breath. What had happened to *Mr*? Before he could say anything, he noticed how she held his stare. Who had taught her to look at a middle-aged man in such a way? His mouth tightened and he said nothing. He looked straight ahead as they walked down the long mall towards the lift, pacing himself, trying not to react so much.

The girls whispered and laughed, responding to everything they saw. As they went, he noticed how the eyes of men of all ages rested briefly, assessing both girls. Katy suddenly darted into one shop, a gleaming bazaar-like haven where accessories were sold. The residues of childhood were in her still, the need to rush towards the beautiful, the magical, trusting in all she saw.

Eventually, they reached the car.

'You have to see what Katy bought!' Sorcha announced as they flopped into the back seat.

Katy shot Sorcha a venomous look. So some things were private.

'Go on, show him!' Sorcha urged, trying to grab one of the shopping bags.

'Piss off, Sorcha!' he heard his daughter warn, but then she laughed despite herself, maintaining a firm grip on the bag.

The journey home was subdued. The girls shared an earpiece each from Katy's MP3 player. Every so often one of them would say something. No matter what was said, laughter followed. Despite himself, he found it charming.

That night, he called in to say goodnight to Katy. She was stretched out on the bed, supporting herself on one elbow, book in hand. At least she still reads, he thought approvingly. Then his gaze fell on something. His daughter noticed and frowned, eyes darting desperately down to the bottom of the bed. But it was too late to conceal the tumble of airy fabrics that had caught his attention.

Thongs. Thongs worthy of a pole-dancing professional, whether in Bangkok or Allenwood, scraps of meticulous adornments, with rudimentary triangular and transparent front pieces, silky ribbons that could have been woven by fairies and the finest of satin strings holding it all together.

He left the room before steam hissed from his ears. He would speak to Joyce, who was so busy trying to paddle a middle way between their daughter's childhood and womanhood that she was in danger of pushing Katy out into an un-signposted savannah. Then he changed his mind and turned back, roughly slamming the bedroom door wide.

'Never, ever wear those things with a miniskirt!' he thundered, gasping at the thoughts of what the child was being allowed to do to herself. A projectile of spittle whizzed out of his mouth as he spoke. Katy spotted it, but it didn't amuse her. Instead she shrank back, suddenly timid. At the same time, he moved towards her. He took in the full sight of her – luscious and alive – yes, he could see that for himself, as could any eejit who might pass her on the street or as she hung around the school gates, texting and tittering with her pals. Despite himself, he reached forward. Again, she shrank back, not understanding.

'It's all right!' he pleaded. 'I only want to—'

As if to prove that she was safe despite his anger, he touched her cheek with the back of his hand. Her skin, smooth as a plum, was warm. She was still uncertain. Now he could imagine her if the wrong type caught her. The pupils of her eyes were dilated and she gazed up at him. She was trembling and tight in herself.

'Maybe I overreacted a bit,' he mumbled, taking his hand back from her face. 'Did I?'

She pulled a sulky face now and turned from him. He left the room then, ignoring her alarmed cry as she attempted to follow him.

'Dad! Dad! I didn't mean anything. They were so pretty ... and *cheap*, too!' she pleaded.

'Just be careful!' he called back over his shoulder, lest she see his eyes, ablaze with the twin passions of love and anger. He thought of all the young girls, oh, the young girls with their fabulous bodies, the little fripperies out there with which to adorn them, and of all the men, of any age, of whom he was one, struggling to be men.

Pimiento

Out towards the sea, over the tops of the one-storey cottages on the street opposite, Bunmore Head lay jewel-clear, green as a gem. It was a sign, Ella thought, that the funeral demanded colour. A man was being buried and all the Mackeys would assemble to mourn him. She imagined his sisters with hurt and noble faces, burying their brother, their boy turned man turned older man, whose heart finally failed.

She had deliberated over whether or not to attend. Her brother advised against it.

You shouldn't bother, you know.

Why not? she texted back.

Makes no difference now.

She flung back the wardrobe doors, then sniffed with pleasure. It still smelled new, modern. She turned her back momentarily on carefully hung silks, suedes and wools and let her eye glide over the bedroom. The king-sized bed – rarely shared, and since the split with Aidan only three or four times with Tom – was positioned towards the back but facing the front so as to avail of the view beyond the roofs opposite. With help from her brother, she had ripped up the ancient carpets after their parents died, then sanded the floorboards before painting them silver grey. A modern, hand-made rug shimmered in the centre, drawing the eye, a thing of its time and for future times, with suggestive primitive notes. A bleached canoe, perhaps; a harpoon; fleet human figures. Colours were cerulean, black and pimiento.

She associated black with the eight years she had been Aidan's lover, although in the full flush of it she would have imagined red, green or yellow. When she thought of her childhood, she saw it as a sky-tinted stream, incredibly peaceful in comparison to the scarified inner life she now knew. After school, she and her brother would spend hours around The Stores, the family hardware co-op. It was a time of tractors and trailers, of the search for spare parts for farming machines that were intended to serve not one, but maybe two generations. They played within the vault of the reinforced shed, mounting hills of bagged grain, pellets or even peanuts. When a German family moved into the area, peanuts became a big thing and birds were fed. Other Germans arrived and soon the demand was established. She occasionally thought that their village must have had the best-fed birds in Ireland, with the fanciest feeding trays and balls of suet, all supplied from The Stores.

Tom had urged her to attend the funeral, but that was typical of him, she reflected, peering into her wardrobe. Reasonable to the last, making himself generous and wise, perhaps because he wanted her more than she wanted him.

'He meant something to you, after all.'

'Yes, once,' Ella had replied, burying she knew not what in those two words.

In a way, Tom had taken up where Aidan Mackey left off. But should she feel guilty if he wanted to be with her, when surely he sensed that she was not exactly driven to bed down with him? She hoped she had been clear about that. She didn't feel ready, she had said, open to neither love nor lust. She was *fond* of Tom, who wanted to please. But now that was a problem, especially today. She didn't need to be pleased by anyone.

Eight years had taken their toll. When Aidan's wife left him, even then he prevaricated, so Ella finally began her reluctant withdrawal. The tearing apart got underway. Weeks of it being on, then off, then on again with promises of never ever parting, love to the grave and beyond. *Para siempre*, as he used to say in Spanish, believing it still charmed her. But then old hesitations would creep in.

'Sometimes I think you're ashamed to be seen with me,' she speculated accusingly, keeping her tone teasing, not nagging, obeying a centuries-old code absorbed by her gender. She would think of their special haunts, the car lodged safely beneath the trees at a secluded lakeshore far from everybody they knew. But even then, the idyll had been disturbed. Once, just when she had abandoned herself to the pleasure of his hand between her thighs, a text arrived. Aidan stopped what he was doing. He actually stopped, as if it was an emergency call on his clinic bleeper, which it certainly wasn't. When she'd first gone to him as a doctor, she'd had his complete attention.

Grand day for sight-seeing, Aidan!

'Lie down! Keep your head down!' he'd urged, frantic as he scanned the lakeshore. A metallic gold van with bull-bars was parked some three hundred yards away, facing them head on.

'Shit. A cousin of mine,' he sighed wearily. 'No one you know,' he added, giving her bare thigh a consoling stroke.

But it *was* someone she knew, a regular at The Stores. From then on, he winked every time he had to stock up on materials, teasing her about special discounts for special customers. There were no secrets, she realised, sensing knowing sniggers behind her back as she went about her business in Bunmore. A single, middle-aged woman. Always good for a salacious comment or two, especially when rumour had advanced to confirmation.

Once, she bumped into his wife, Joyce, behind the church at the Saturday morning farmers' market, the pair of them standing side by side at the mince pie stall, both pointing at the same batch of pies.

'Oh, I'm sorry!' the other woman said as their hands accidentally touched.

'Oh. Hello.' Ella felt her face blaze with embarrassment, aware that the goon on the other side of the stall was observing all with open curiosity.

'Just getting a few things for myself,' Joyce said calmly, turning to Ella. 'Hard to know what to buy when there's just one of you, eh?' She stopped suddenly. 'Not that I meant—'

'No, no, not at all,' Ella took up, desperate to cover their joint mortification.

His wife was smart, she concluded rapidly. She had looked straight into Ella's eyes in a manner that left her in no doubt but that she knew. And she was damn civil into the bargain. It had made her feel ashamed, to be slinking and sliding around the periphery of their small community like that, with this woman's willing and imminently ex-husband. But it didn't stop her, not even the sudden inkling that perhaps his wife felt happier without a lovesick husband on her hands. Because Aidan was her drug and she was addicted.

In an effort to smother such uncomfortable reflections, she made a suggestion on one of their trips, in the wilderness of Wicklow. They had just made love and again she was full of him, flooded by him. He lay warmly in her arms. Outside, the wind whistled in the high firs so that the whole world seemed hushed.

'Let's go out tonight when we get back. A restaurant. How about Botticelli? Or Le Grenouille?'

'Darling, you know I can't.'

The usual, hopeless excuses. He didn't want to run into his wife's friends, not until everything was formalised and the divorce underway. He didn't blame his wife for leaving. He'd been a complete pig, he said, almost making a virtue of it.

She agreed with that, and it was an insult to the pig, she added. The fact was, he was ashamed of her occupation, of dungarees and forklifts, the piles of green wellington boots, the sacks of seed, grain, oats and fertilizers that occupied her working days now that she and her brother managed The Stores.

He sighed wearily. 'I never knew you had such a chip on your shoulder.'

'But what else am I to think when you won't step out with me in broad daylight?'

He shook his head. 'This is hopeless, Ella.' He tilted his dark head back and regarded her down the length of a fine, straight nose. 'The fact is, I – love – *you*. If you can get that into your skull …'

But she couldn't. Something about it always rang false, even if he believed it himself. For a time, texting was frequent enough, ending with the telltale X or even four Xs if either party was sufficiently heated up again. But gradually, even the final solitary X was omitted. After that, silence.

She had been free of him for the past year and a half. She corrected herself as she gazed into the wardrobe again. Until the day before yesterday, the day of his death, she had been mostly free of him – his kisses, his ardour, his off-the-wall, funny compulsions whenever he dropped his guard. Black times kept at bay thanks to anti-depressants prescribed by a different doctor in a different village, she grew accustomed to seeing his metallic blue Alfa around the area as he moved between two gleaming private medical clinics. Gradually, the sight of the car caused her no pain. He had bought an apartment, she heard, overlooking the river, close to a supermarket.

She moved on. Work was satisfying. The atmosphere of the bustling, extended yard behind The Stores was lofty, dusty and full of house martins, pigeons and thrushes. Men drove in and out, lifting, hoisting, directing. Invoices were waved and separated, customer dockets brought to the collection point where goods were delivered. She oversaw all, known for her stamina and acumen. Her brother ran the office, but she was out and about, observing, transacting, doing the chatting and bartering. Her head was full of holding effects – brass taps and fittings, screws, rawl plugs, drill bits and outdoor wear, German spades versus English or Irish spades, hammers and masonry nails, wire nails and yard brushes, cattle feeders, calf nuts and mineral licks, crowbars, axes and nailbars. Her mobile phone contained a log of jokes from men she was on good terms with. Funny jokes, stupid jokes, putrid jokes, sent in a spirit of mateyness.

Aidan scrolled through her joke log one night when they lay in bed and remarked that it was a peculiar use of her Cork university degree, which she had scraped through twenty-five years ago with a lazy pass in History, Maths and French. But history was always happening, she had told him. *We're in it. We're making it*, she had murmured drowsily. And in the village Aidan had suddenly left, it was happening excitingly, they were living on the unpolished edge of a happening world. All she had to do was glance around the yard at the extra staff – Lithuanians, Poles, Russians, several Nigerians – to see who was doing the work now. All she had to do was watch the Irish-owned BMWs, Audis, Mercs and four-wheel-drive Range Rovers backed up outside The Stores, or near Tom's health shop. Every evening, similar vehicles nestled together around the village's two brasseries. This was how she knew that history had buzzed on the doorbell of the native culture, announcing change.

Yet one winter evening when the days had shrunk and she felt dulled and alone, she had phoned one of his sisters, the one Aidan confided in. Desperate for consolation, for some signal that things would work in her favour, she introduced herself.

'I love Aidan,' Ella risked. 'I think that he … that he might … do you think he …?'

There was a long pause at the other end. A spool of failure rolled into a universe of its own, deep within her.

'I'm sorry,' came the reply, 'but to be honest, I'm in the middle of stirring something on the cooker – I don't think I can comment.'

'Oh.'

'It's none of my business anyway. I really don't want to get involved.'

'I understand,' Ella had replied, stung.

Apologising for bothering her, she hung up. She didn't understand how anyone could *not want to get involved*, as the sister had put it, evasive as a local politician. For fuck's sake, she simmered. It was amazing how everybody in his family closed ranks and pretended the relationship hadn't occurred. She bumped into them often enough, on the road, in the supermarket. She would find herself on the receiving end of a vague, slightly hurried smile, the kind that village matrons specialised in as a means of keeping at bay the hoi polloi or those who had in some way broken rank.

There was absolutely no requirement that she should go to his funeral, none whatsoever, she reflected, staring into the wardrobe again. On the other hand, she was damned if she was going to hide away.

Cutting across her funeral deliberations was the question of Tom, today more sharply prodding than ever. Aidan's death had brought something to a head, she mused, fingering through skirts and trousers, suits, blouses and coats.

She heard a knock at the front door and swore. A peep out the window, and she spied Tom's brown thatch as he shuffled from one foot to the other. *Shit.* Quickly, she grabbed a red silk skirt and top and flung them on the bed. 'My pimiento rig-out,' she muttered. 'I'll wear it for the funeral. One final blast!'

She raced downstairs and pulled the glass-panelled door open.

'What were you doing? All out of breath!' Tom growled gently, giving her a light cuff on the cheek as he entered the hallway.

'Deciding my funeral attire,' she said with a roll of her eyes.

'Something respectable, I hope, as fits the day?'

His solidity drove her to distraction. He spoke so sanely

about Aidan, as if he had never felt insecure. Forget about ownership and possessiveness, he impressed on Ella again and again, hushing it like a magic spell into her ear on the few occasions they'd gone to bed. Oh, knowing him was easy. The problem was, she realised, Tom was in love with her.

She had never intended this lazy choice, born from the need for distraction and companionship, for relief from loneliness too. The thorn – no, the wedge – that was Aidan had still not been levered from where it had lodged.

'Don't worry,' Tom breathed over her shoulder as she led the way upstairs again, 'you don't have to face this alone.'

'It's all right, hon.' She immediately regretted the careless endearment as it slid off her tongue. 'I'll manage.'

'I won't hear of it!' He patted the bed invitingly. 'Sit down here, beside me.'

She froze. The red outfit was laid out behind him. She wanted to get dressed, slowly and alone.

'I've got to keep moving.' She sounded vague, approaching the outfit from the opposite side of the bed. Just as she lifted the skirt, Tom half turned, placed his hand on hers.

'It's all right, you know,' he assured her, looking into her eyes.

Oh, *man*. Again, she stiffened. 'What is?' she asked lightly.

'Your feelings today. They're bound to be mixed …'

All of a sudden, her patience snapped. 'Will you please stop analysing me!'

'I'm not analysing you. I only meant—'

'Whatever you meant, please stop it.'

He stood up, brushing his brown fringe back from his

forehead. 'What's got into you?'

Bracing herself, she pulled a face and bit her lip, feeling every inch the defiler of innocence.

'Look, if it makes it easier, I can accompany you,' he suggested before she could speak. 'I'll go with you! How about that?'

She didn't believe what she was hearing. Jesus Christ, as if she needed him on her elbow in the church like a tasteless announcement to the world that they were an item. Which they bloody weren't.

'And look.' He rummaged in his trouser pocket and withdrew a small bottle. 'I thought a few drops of vervain. Might pick you up. And some St John's Wort.'

'Oh for God's sake, would you stuff your remedies up your—' She stopped and swallowed. 'This isn't the right day, Tom. No day would be right, but—'

'What are you on about?'

'Us.'

'Well?' He began to move from one foot to the other.

She blurted a few key words. *Can't carry on.* And, as an afterthought, *Not fair on you.*

He looked at her, blanching.

She took another stab at it. 'It's not right for me to be seeing you ... the way I have been.'

No matter what she said, it was going to sound like dismissal from on high.

Tears sprang up in his eyes. 'How can you say that?' He paused to control himself. 'It's a pity you won't wake up and allow yourself to have feelings for someone else apart from that *shit*!'

'Stop right there,' she said, the palms of her hands wet as she gripped the silky red outfit and held it close to her chest. 'It's not a case of won't. More like can't.'

He watched her.

'I'm just not ready, Tom.'

'I know, I know.' He looked at the floor as if reading it.

'You know? Well why the hell have you allowed this charade?'

His body sank heavily onto the bed. 'Charade?' he asked in puzzlement.

It wasn't the word she had intended, but now she pushed her advantage home. She reminded him of who had pursued whom, of how he had placed himself as central consoler of Ella-the-broken-hearted, how he had taken her on.

'*Charade?*' he repeated.

'I don't want to do to you what Aidan did to me.'

'How bloody *considerate*!'

'It's time to tell the truth.'

'Which is?' He shot her a look. For a moment, she hesitated. She didn't utter the actual words.

He jumped to his feet, and for a moment she feared he would hit her. 'I'm sorry,' she mumbled.

'You're *sorry*!' Tom repeated. 'Well, I'm sorry I spent these months practically coaching you!'

'I didn't need you to,' she reared up, suddenly ready to fight.

'I'm not talking about the *body*. I'm not talking about skin and hair and *touching*. You know nothing of the heart, *nothing*!'

'And you can't stop passing judgement!' Standing near the wide open window, she screamed at the unfairness of it, aware that the little drama would fall, as usual, on interested ears below in the street.

In four strides he crossed the room and lunged at the red skirt.

'*No!*' She held tight to the garment.

'Give it to me! Give me the shaggin' thing!'

There was a tear, the hint of seams about to split, thread about to give way. She cried out, released her right hand and walloped him with the flat of her palm. He stepped back, holding his jaw, a scrap of a red frill in his free hand. 'You lousy bitch!'

She trembled, clutching the skirt. Finally, she spoke. 'Let me go.'

He stared at her in silence, regarding her as if for the first time. 'You know what, Ella? I don't know how to make you respond. I think you might be *frigid*.'

After he stormed downstairs and slammed the front door so hard a pane of glass broke, she released her hold on the red skirt and top. It was crumpled from her grip during the struggle. Still trembling, she shook it out and examined it while the word *frigid* circled her mind. So that was it? Tom, understanding counsellor and all-round alternative good guy, resorting to schoolboy jibes? How revealing. And what a strange, old-fashioned flavour the word had, she thought, half-amused, like something from a women's problem page forty years ago.

There had been violence in the air, a sense of bullying. Only violence could finish it, violent words, hard to hear. Now it was over. She felt like throwing up in the bathroom, but told herself that she was free again, something she valued above all else. She held the vivid skirt to the light. Miraculously, apart from the piece of lace trimming that came away in the tussle, the garment was intact. Aidan had spotted it as they strolled through the evening streets of Jerez. *You must have it. Try it on!* he had urged.

It still fitted. Her fingers fumbled as she pulled up the

skirt. She closed the zip, imagined wave after wave of hot, pimiento red embracing her belly, comforting her. Who would comfort her now, she thought, running her fingers along her belly and down towards her groin. She pulled on the little top with the fluttery cap sleeves and clinging bodice. She felt sick and weak.

At the funeral, nurses from the local clinics formed a guard of honour. Family pride was riding high and Ella made herself sympathise with his relatives. Sprays, bouquets and wreaths were stacked around the coffin. His sisters, as anticipated, were noble but impregnable and she felt a pang of envy as they clustered around Joyce, the woman he had married and then abandoned. After Mass, the sister Ella had once phoned spoke with dignity. They were to join the family at the hotel, she added calmly, all were welcome, whether from near or far.

In the cemetery, she watched as each sister turned a small shovelful of soil into the open grave. This couldn't be real. Desperate now, she recalled how they had once made love with her wearing the red outfit, how he had lifted the skirt and buried his head in her, saying she tasted of hot, sweet pimiento. She wanted to tell his sisters that in the end, she had had the best of him. Except that she could not be certain.

She felt a gentle touch at her elbow. Surprised, she turned to find Joyce gazing into her face.

'Hello again,' she said, taking Ella's hand to shake it, her voice mellow. 'You knew him too, of course,' she added with a discernable tightening of the lips, yet reminding Ella of her open manner that morning at the mince pie stall.

'I did,' she replied without thinking. She felt faint. It was as if she had just been touched by goodness.

'It must have been hard for you to come here today,' the other woman went on softly.

'It – yes, it was.' The words slipped from Ella's throat, as if freed from their moorings, instinctively truthful.

'And in Bunmore – well, Bunmore is …' Joyce sighed, still holding her hand.

'Too small,' Ella whispered angrily.

Joyce gave a faint smile. 'And our lives are so messy.'

Ella glanced down the hill. A sea mist was rolling in from Bunmore Head. Her cheeks were wet. It was harder than she could ever have imagined, and now someone – Joyce – had reached into her and at a touch released the wedge that had tormented her for so long. The other mourners drifted and hovered, seeing all, seeing nothing.

She wished she had worn anything other than red.

The Lost Citadel

Until today, the only guarantee of escape was to swim. Thea says it's an obsession. Perhaps it is. Either way, every evening at six I drive to the shore and strip to my underpants. If the tide is high, I wade out to the Gull Rock, until the waves buoy me in such a way that I am deposited quite gently on the shelf. My backside has grown accustomed to the abrasions of mussel shell and limpet.

Then I clamber across to the southernmost tip and prepare to dive. In that moment the sea drowns out everything, receives my pale flesh with its own visceral embrace. Imagine the weight of thoughts that float out of every swimmer into the ocean! How easily we are absorbed by our first element, how becalmed the mind as the body dives!

What I can never fully explain to Thea is almost inadmissible, even to myself. The sea has always helped. Until today, that is.

I know that by the time I have swum ashore to pat myself dry and unpeel my sodden pants, she will have collected the child from the crèche after work, that as I walk in the door she will in all probability be making him eat his tea or making him wash his hands. *Making* being the operative word.

So today, it all rushed back, as it does occasionally, a feeling that sparkles like ice or diamonds impaled in me with chill precision. Even though the whole thing happened a year ago. The memory always coincides with conflict of some kind. And besides, we had a bad row only yesterday. She said I exaggerated, that I overreacted.

'I do not overreact!' I answered in a staccato voice.

I would rather spoil him, as she would call it, than do the opposite. Much as she wishes it, I will not collude in the strategies of adult tyranny.

'It's not tyranny!' she practically scoffed. 'Someone has to discipline the child, for God's sake, even if you can't!'

'There *are* other ways.'

'Like what?' she challenged. 'You tell me how we stop him screaming night after bloody night when he knows we're in the house, when there's absolutely *nothing* wrong with him!'

I was helpless to respond. His screams return again and again, circling my skull, jabbing at my stomach.

Today the tide was quiet, viridescent, then as I struck out, the sun spattered the bay between Giant's Crag and the Cove. I might not have ventured in had I sensed what would occur. The air seemed warmer than on land. Not for the first time, only minutes into my swim, I detected that rank odour. It is distinctive. Smoke. The kind of smoke that wafts from food being cooked in the open, smoke and charred animal flesh.

Thea and I can talk about such things, the unusual, the singular or the inexplicable. Naturally, she long ago concluded that it was a folk memory, though how a folk memory can strike the olfactory senses is beyond me, even if the old Norman citadel was located right there above the cliffs, even if it was big and bustling and a place for trading.

For a woman of such intuition, she can be harsh where the child is concerned. Dim, dare I say it.

I always looked forward to the prospect of bringing him out with me, of gradually teaching him about water and about his own strength and weakness. Of course, he's only six. And when I pick up the acrid tang of smoke and flesh on the sea air, I wonder if he will ever smell what I smell. And will his eyes come to rest on the cliff face as mine do, probing the crinkled erosions? Will he casually search the tawny encrustations for traces of lost settlements, places where men and boys were joyous and sure of themselves, now buried between the sand martins' nests and the kittiwake ledges?

Backwards and forwards we go, Thea and I, like contestants in some kind of batting game. Except that one of us doesn't always want to bat ball and the other is all too eager. Every so often she talks about women always being the ones left to do the disciplining and then getting blamed for it.

'You're lily-livered where he's concerned. What're you afraid of?' she goads, the veins in her forehead bulging with anger.

When she comes out with that, I grit my teeth. How many domestic crimes are averted through the most rigid self-control, a seizing up of the facial muscles as the weak or inadequate or irresponsible spouse stands accused by an all-too-triumphant partner?

Not for the first time, I thought again today of the lies spoken in the name of childhood. That childhood is a time of inviolate growth, that there is peace and discovery and fun. Lies, lies.

This evening, I came into the house wearily. My hands were still cold, unusually so, the fingers tingling with numbness. There he was, struggling with his shoes, which she claims he should be able to manage himself by now. He looked too innocent, too innocent by far, grunting and whining as he forced the left shoe onto his right foot. She could see him too. She sat quite still, feet curled beneath her on the sofa, her nose, as usual, in a book.

I bent to help him. She looked up and sighed.

'Can't you let him be?' she said, not unkindly. 'He has to learn for himself.'

'But we have to show him, Thea.'

'If I've shown him once, I've shown him forty times. Can't you see? It's all for *attention*!'

Once more, beaten into a cul-de-sac. He stopped pulling at the shoe, tugged it off again and ran towards me.

What torments me most is the quality of his forgiveness, which seems absolute and unmarred by fear. And yet I wonder at his notes, the scrawled messages delivered to both our pillows in new, shaky writing.

'To Daddy and Mammy, you are good to me.'

Or 'Thank you Daddy and Mammy I love you I will be good.'

I quake at the thoughts of him. I still hear him scream, I still see the little legs kicking out in an attempt at childish defiance which he could not possibly sustain.

And again, again, I ask myself why I did it, why I listened to her.

For a short while today, the sea soothed me. This time I stripped completely standing by the jeep, firing my clothes into the torn passenger seat. Pieces of his Lego set lay on the floor. Complete nakedness felt good. There was nobody around except for a mooning couple some few hundred yards up towards the sand bar, too absorbed in one another to notice a pale, greying man.

I was cleansed again, swam eight hundred yards breaststroke, turned and swam eight hundred more front crawl, turned again and backstroked, my eyes open and my head singing with the sounds of ocean and gull and the smell of the Norman fires which I now took for granted rushing to my nostrils, and then – at first I wasn't certain – voices. Mens' voices, powerful laughter, which crushed over my body and faded too suddenly, as if washed through with something more sinister.

Then I heard it, as clearly as if Thea and I were in the bedroom, or arguing in front of the child, or at our own hearth with the logs hissing and the coal crackling. Well out of my depth, I stopped swimming and floated, my ears throbbing.

Not even the sea could save me. The current beneath became a shaft of ice, fixing me in a state of solid fear. But it was more than the current, and I continued to float in an attempt to recover my equilibrium, told myself that it would be all right, that things would sort themselves out in time, that timc was a healer. Yet when the ancient voices faded, all I could hear was one child's voice, the screams and the fear of one child as I tried to please her, doing my best to see things her way. It was the middle of the night. He'd been calling for hours, whinging and sobbing. Finally, it was my turn, and I bore her rage like a ball of steel, grabbing him from beneath the bedclothes. He roared as I shook him. Then I struck and could not stop. I flailed at his legs and arms with my man's strength, as if to finally quieten him or show him that this was the way and once and for all, he would behave for her.

'No Daddy! No Daddy! Oh please, no Daddy, I'll be good, I will, Daddy, oh Daddy!' he wailed and gulped, slipping once from my grasp and running to the bathroom, where I missed him again and he jumped into the bath, screaming, the tears bursting from him, crouching finally, hands over his head as my blows rained down and his forehead struck the faucet.

Thea stopped me, her face white and wet.

'Not that much, not that much!' she called, catching my arm.

I think I almost drowned this afternoon. Perhaps I wanted to. Or else it was my own weeping, inaudible amidst all that water and salt, a great weight crushing my lungs as I lost my breath and slipped under for those few moments.

I love the smell of him. His skin. His soft hair. His breath, which is always sweet.

There is nothing he cannot – could not – do, given the right chance. There is nothing we could not accomplish, a father and a son. I would die for him.

The Sacrament of Feet

Nancy's view, when she stared up from the basement flat on days off or sat in the sunny patch outside her doorway, was of people's feet and the upper branches of a weeping ash in the park opposite.

The language of feet was a gradual discovery in which she learned how to read people, how to decipher the fallen arch, cut ankle or hen-toed gait, as well as the elegantly turned instep. It was like breaking through new frontiers, each set of feet characterised by separateness, carrying a varied insignia of chewing gum, dust, leaf particles or glossy leather.

Occasionally, when bathing a patient at the hospital, she would recognise a pair of feet, but of course couldn't say so. Why bring further dismay to people already rendered vulnerable within the modern institute of healing?

Her gentleman friend, as she chose to call him, laughed at the idea, clapped his hands together, whooping with delight.

'Oh, *meine liebe* Nancy! Dear, dear Nancy!' he chortled. 'You are a child of truth, a purveyor of ironies!'

'Rubbish,' she scoffed, 'I'm a middle-aged woman gone to seed.'

Stefan shook his head. He was twenty years her senior, his large hands graceful, with amber and onyx rings on each forefinger; on his feet embroidered slippers and green silken socks.

She could have seen more of him, but chose not to. His days were filled with music, art and butterfly collections and the Wicklow sheep farm which he managed vaguely, especially in winter, when two local men sorted out the lambing problems.

At the hospital, her skin absorbed smells of disinfectant, formaline and antiseptic during her shifts, with night duty one week in four. At such times, the colour and sense of white was all she knew; white uniforms, sheets, towels, bandages, the battle against filth and infection pitched in an ambience of piped music which made some of the patients cry. Away from work, there was real music, nights out with women friends or afternoons in old furniture shops, slow dalliances with dusty clocks and antique screens, the search for what Stefan would call ein *Kunststück*.

The flat was spacious enough for dancing with Stefan to the sound of Maria Callas's *Carmen*. She had the whole basement to herself, a large sitting room with brocade chairs, a cinnabar-coloured chaise longue and a tiled fireplace. An old ormolu clock with four coloured enamel spheres spun with unhurried elegance, and as a result Nancy thought of time as a series of slowly expanding circles rather than a straight line on which lives were notched up between God's idea of points A and X.

The flat had a guest room, and her own wide bed was fresh and scented. Stefan would sometimes join her for a drink, and they would listen to Callas while the ormolu clock spun and spun. She would compare him to other men she'd known. He was different, held few fixed ideas about nurses. She was used to old fellows in hospitals running their hands across her rump in moments of real or contrived delirium, but Stefan was a man of discrimination.

She could keep an eye on him too, monitor his condition. If anything, he was only a borderline case. Life was difficult enough without imposing brutal recovery regimes on others. She'd heard so many lectures from po-faced social workers out to convert the world – the anti-drug brigade. They reminded her of members of fundamentalist churches she'd met years ago in the States, the Latter Day Jehovah Plonketty-Plonks or suchlike. What harm if she helped Stefan every so often? She would not see him suffer or hector him into giving up the habit *for his own good* – the phrase made her shudder – he who had opened her mind and heart with such generous imagination.

At work, during her rounds with the medicines trolley, she saw herself as from a great distance. To some patients she was an efficient dispensing machine – busy, plump, hurrying to administer painkillers, antibiotics or laxatives. To others, though, hers was the hand that brought relief. In the maternity unit, she had felt herself trapped on a carousel that wouldn't stop, the air stifling with pollen from too many carnations, the smell of talc and babies and amidst the greenhouse temperatures, the uncertain humour of post-partum mothers.

But the elderly had something to say for themselves. Their bodies were as fragile as one of Stefan's priceless decorated eggshells, as ornate with sheer living as any of his antique Russian bowls. Sometimes their voices were mere whispers, their joints swollen, veins a dark purple breaking the surface of tissue-like skin as the body relinquished its taut epidermis.

Above all, she enjoyed their feet, the horny skin built up from hundreds of thousands of miles' walking; or the way women's feet were often unnaturally narrow, the toes colliding with one another after years of being shod according to fashion, rising in a mound, reminding her of Stefan's comments about the bodies of the Jews when the doors of the gas chambers were finally unlocked.

Toenails could be thick and dense as bone, a testimony to time, to things half done, well done or not done at all. The feet of travellers were firm and free of deformity because such people wore supple, roomy footwear when backpacking in the Himalayas or exploring the Tierra del Fuego. The tendons and muscles attached to the tibia and fibula of an experienced walker remained bulky right to the end. Only recently, on night duty, she had attended to the body of a renowned mountaineer who suddenly decided to die. A frantic wheeze alerted her. Eyes glazed, lips dry, he struggled for breath. Nancy took his hand, then bent close to catch a final triumphant whisper: 'The Jura – was – the *best*!'

She slept poorly that day, perturbed by his death, yet gratified that at such a moment he could invoke enthusiasm, that it should be for a place and not a person. Later, she drove out to see Stefan.

As they embraced, she paused to explore his eyes. The sun cut across the top of his head, turned the hair to a fuzzy halo of light. Inside, the place smelled of incense.

'Sandalwood?' she sniffed.

'Lotus Blossom,' he corrected in an intimate voice. 'Like it?'

'Mmm.'

Tea from the silver samovar, poured into small blue Japanese cups. They sat before an open fire on the chaise longue, an exact replica of Nancy's.

'Are you tired, my dear?' he asked.

'Not tired. A little tense, perhaps,' she ventured before describing the mountaineer's sudden demise, his final words.

'Vas he happy?' Stefan wondered.

Nancy leaned back against a tapestried cushion that depicted mediaeval peasants piling grapes into a vat. 'I'd say so. But he needed to tell someone how well he'd lived.'

They sat and sipped. Outside, bats pipped and wheeled in the dusk.

'Vitality is everything,' Stefan remarked, refilling her cup. 'Taking pleasure in the moment. That's the only message death can offer.'

'But Stefan, do you really believe that? What about the genocides, what about the people who have no choice?'

He sat back and took her hand. 'Makes no difference. If ve go, ve go, not a damn bit of difference ven. Ve must live vell, let others live vell too. Even if ve don't like the vay they live.' He shrugged, then moved closer. 'I know vot you need.'

Nancy shivered, then settled back again and stretched her legs, her head resting on his shoulder. She heard the slow throb of his heart. Steady, strong. A sign of good health. Her eyes drifted around the room, examined the butterflies mounted on blue velvet, their spotted wings, startling antennae or bands of white and orange. Long Japanese panels formed a triptych, classical scenes of feudal love and adventure; delicate women, samurais with fierce expressions. All, she noted, had small, neat feet.

'Shall ve begin?' Stefan suggested. Nancy reached up

and caressed his face. The skin was freshly shaven. He rose, switched on Maria Callas, then lowered himself to the floor and removed her shoes. His expression was intent, Callas's voice flooded the room, his hands brushed the soles of Nancy's feet.

'Oh!' she gasped. It was always surprising. She opened her handbag, rooted around, then placed a small package on the table beside his blue saucer.

'For you. A gift. Call it a standby.'

She always managed to filch what she needed. Just enough. They couldn't prove a thing.

'May I?' Stefan asked, almost as if he had not heard. His hands slid beneath her skirt, undid suspenders, rolled each stocking in turn until her legs were exposed. Nancy pressed her spine deeper into the plump cushion. His hands glided down, paused for a split second on the right calf before finally descending. Deftly, he drew each stocking in turn over her heel. He paused, holding the wisps of dark nylon across his palms, testing them with his thumbs, stretching each until it was taut. Then he relaxed his grip and draped them across the back of the chaise longue, a smile making his lips turn upwards at the corners.

He worked expertly on her toes, bent gently, massaged each in turn, then moved to the pads of flesh beneath until she was in a frenzy of quiet pleasure. Darkness fell, cinders crackled in the grate.

Je veux vivre dans ce reve, I want to live in this dream, Callas's Juliet sang in the transcendence of first love. By the time Stefan's fingers had pressed into the arch of her right foot, Nancy's eyes had closed. Every so often she would lean forward and stroke his head. She felt the delicate skull, the scented warmth of fine hair as his hands worked exquisitely. She thought of the old mountaineer who preferred the Juras, his smooth, well-walked feet which she'd washed only two days ago. As Callas hit the final top G she heard the incessant tread of feet – busy Russian feet, Chinese feet, French, Greek and Irish feet – moving and doing as they carried people towards enthusiasms, eager for pain, passion and a future.

Smiling Moon

She hadn't expected mosquitoes the size of jets launching an attack beneath the fold of her right buttock while she showered, nor the constant proximity of saucer-sized spiders, especially at night.

Another day switches itself on with the sound of whistling birds, screeching parakeets and cockatoos and in the trees up the hill from the bay, a laughing cookaburra. The bird's hit the right hilarious note, she thinks, perched in bed in a roomy holiday apartment which should be full of flip-flops, sailboards and Rip Curl beachwear. Instead, all her writer's things are strewn around the bedroom. A new laptop bought with a loan, pens, a notebook, several novels. She is reading three at once, divides the day so that there is time to absorb three very different styles and plots. Unthinkable at home.

A door opens and closes, followed by the sound of a lock turning. Her Chinese companion has taken over the bathroom. By now, a week and a half into their joint residency, she is familiar with his routines. Water gushes for a long time, the toilet flushes at least twice. Afterwards, he retreats to his room and begins to slap himself hard. That is what it sounds like, until he explains that he is practising *qi-gong* and that one hundred and five slaps to the kidneys are a necessary part of daily meditation.

It has taken days to adjust to the quietness of this man, to gear down notch by notch from the episodic quality of her time at home – driving the children to school, writing until lunchtime, avoiding phone calls, avoiding encounters with people she detests, remembering not to become the perpetually smiling middle-aged mom, coping and capable, doing it all. A little bit of this, that and the other. A typical writer's life. Check. A typical married female writer's life, she amends, eyebrow raised laconically. She is grudgingly accustomed to the enquiries of people who cannot understand her book titles. Basic words, but string two or three of them together and they are a riddle to the trash addict.

It's a joy to be away for five weeks, remote from contemporaries, remote too from the slight condescension that envelops most writers when they meet the local movers and shakers, who spout quick words like hot tea and never read anything properly unless it suits an agenda. Why do some of them feel the need to say something nice and meaningless at launches? Why do they imagine they must always say something? She considers their pleasantries, utterly empty, a comment here and there about some story of hers that they read perhaps twenty years ago.

With Wong Tian, everything is orderly, respectful. He carefully examines her latest novel, which will surely take him two years to read, she guesses. He asks questions about the impressive-sounding endorsements on the back cover. Already, she has observed his monkish devotion to his work, which is comprised of reading as much as writing.

The language barrier is a problem. She was not expecting to be cohabiting with someone whose grasp of English – although vast in comparison to her non-existent Mandarin – is mostly literary. She has to explain many things.

By the time she rises every morning, he has used the bathroom and gone to have breakfast. Today, as usual, he is sitting at the wooden table out on the terrace, a mug of cold green tea and a well-thumbed copy of *Soul Mountain*, banned in China, before him. He smiles as she approaches, bustling towards him to conceal a slightly guarded manner, fully dressed, as always. His face widens to a welcoming white crescent of a greeting.

The routine of breakfast requires some work on her part. He is happy to be there, in Australia, fussed over by the Chinese community, to give interviews and readings. This is his profession and like herself he is pleased to be doing what a writer should when the writing is complete.

'Merry, Merry …' he begins. In his mouth, her name sounds like the first words of a Christmas carol. He turns to her as she takes a spoonful of muesli to her lips.

'What is … what means this word?' He points to an opened page, his smooth brown fingertip resting beneath *style*.

'Style?' she asks.

'You say – *sty-il*?'

'No, no. Not *sty-il*. That's just my accent,' she smiles and chews. 'It's more like' – she marshals the correct pronunciation – '*styyyll*.'

He repeats the word until she nods in satisfaction. Mostly, she does not object to this word-work. When was the last time anybody outside of a writing class bothered to ask anything about 'style', unless it had to do with clothes? Who among her friends – even the writers – mulled over definitions of anything outside of relationships and relating, that complacent monster-word of the West?

'What *styyyll* mean?' he presses, sitting back expectantly, arms folded as he awaits her opinion.

'Ah, that's a tricky one. It depends on context,' she replies, still munching.

'Con-text?'

She sits back and fans herself. Nine o'clock and already it's humid. The deep green fronds of subtropical foliage at the edge of the terrace keep them in shade as she warms to the topic.

'It depends on what you mean,' she explains.

They set off on a journey through style – as appearance, as a way of doing something, a way of writing, a distinctive pattern or description. Finally, he understands. Breakfast proceeds in silence. He reads, she listens to the birds, considering the long day ahead. There are pleasant cafés and bookstores, shady places where she can perch in peace for an hour or two. She likes to watch backpackers rove up and down the streets in colourful bandanas and swirling skirts, guitars and flutes attached to their luggage.

An hour later, as she heads briskly to the beach, the problem of the whole trip rises in her mind again. It's all a bit much, she has begun to think. The organiser had no right to lumber her with the Chinese man for so long. Everything about the place is beautiful. Location, minimal residency work, time, accommodation. And yet this domesticated holiday setting is not quite what she had envisaged. For one thing, there's no writing table, not even in the bedrooms, which are dark and shaded during the day, and not conducive to the vital rush that pushes words up out of her. For another, her companion rarely ventures out alone, does not prowl the town the way she does, examining shops, cafés, wandering restlessly, exploring the deep overhang of forest up from the beach. Up there, she encounters wild turkeys, parrots, one drowsy koala.

One evening, when they both return from the supermarket, he with his string bag full of fresh greens and noodles, she with a frozen pizza and a plastic bag of pre-washed lettuce, the manager of the complex leans out through an office window.

'G'day, how's it going'?' he grins.

'Fine, fine,' she replies.

'No problems in the apartment?'

She shakes her head. Wong Tian has already moved on down the passageway towards their door.

'Tricky, is it, stuck with your man?' he leers, a smirk on his face, tossing his head in the direction of the apartment.

She can tell that he expects an outpouring of confidences, senses a smug white-skin-blue-eyes conspiracy at work in the exchange.

'Everything is fine,' she says. 'We're very comfortable,' she adds lightly.

But she feels hemmed in, whether by the apartment or her Chinese companion, she cannot tell. She writes very little during the day, heads out some mornings for the seafront, spreads her towel and lies reading for hours. On several occasions she has ventured into the waves, but is not up to the ferocity of the Pacific shore. She studies the way most people have learned the knack of diving beneath them to emerge safely on the other side, beyond the point of the actual impact, but is unable to master it herself. Content in the shallows, she hovers up to her thighs in the shifting mass of water. It pulls and drags at her. She is fragmentary, teasing what she should not. Even then, she has to turn sideways to avoid being swept off her feet as each wave rushes in, crashes, then pulls heavily backwards so that her feet sink and the world undulates. Once, knocked off her feet, she gives way to the force, trusting it to land her in the grainy sand. As she holds her breath, her brain flashes a memory of Keem Bay, Achill. She was fourteen and thought she would drown when that wave snatched her, pulled her out and flung her back, finally, onto the beach. Back then she could not swim, only struggle. Now, a swimmer of sorts, she knows how not to fight, how to turn her body into an arrow of stretched limbs and tucked-in chin so that the current will work in her favour.

Nobody bothers her on these solitary beach forays. She brings a camera, photographs brazen seagulls that land right at her feet, sharp eyes inspecting her red-painted toenails, observing her sandwich bag, waiting for scraps. They hop around on tangerine, webbed feet, fighting with one another, jealously guarding the prospect of grub.

One night, a Chinese thing occurs. It is like a story from ancient times, could be painted on a plate. Willowpattern and Moon, she calls it.

They are halfway through the visit. The man remarks on the full, bright moon one evening after they have eaten.

'We two … go watch moon on water,' he suggests.

They make their way along dimmed streets towards the beach. The tide is roaring. People have retreated for the night. Beneath the rocks towards the back of the beach, snakes are coiled. She knows this, is not uneasy about it. Snakes, she assumes erroneously, are not nocturnal creatures.

At the beach, he removes white trainers and pads to the water's edge. She has already perched herself against a boulder a little further back. After a while, he returns in her direction to stand nearby. They do not speak. They look. The moon, the lantern which everybody from the north of China to the south of Tasmania can see that night if they wish, hangs there. It is a smiling moon, and the smile is split into a kaleidoscope of other moons upon the heaving water.

'Moon laugh,' he says, pointing.

'My children would like this moon,' she remarks, suddenly missing them.

He reaches out, brushes her arm with his fingertips. 'They see moon in twelve hour,' he consoles.

They say little more. He is lost in thought. She tries to second guess him. Does he think of his dead wife, whom he nursed through the final stages of Parkinson's disease? Does he wonder about his grown daughter, now living with her boyfriend? But he has a woman friend as well, she knows that, spotted him once peering into the window of a jeweller's on the main street of the town before disappearing inside. Later, when she took a look into the window, she noted that it was full of opals, the cheaper kind, and of necklaces, some with small rolled-gold hearts.

Suddenly he turns to her and laughs. 'Merry, Merry, it is good we two writers see moon together!' he exclaims happily.

On the way back to the apartment, they weave past the local hell-raisers spilling out of the bars. Wino Aborigines are playing tom-toms and pan-pipes before an open brazier. One of them sits drunkenly, a didgeridoo resting between his legs.

As they return to their rooms, she imagines how the scene would look on a porcelain plate. Two people, probably lovers, staring out to the Pacific, the moon above broken into shimmering minor moons on the water, making poetry in their souls, stirring loneliness, awakening thoughts of absence and longing. On the plate, though, the man and woman would stand closer together.

But a few days later, she makes arrangements for new accommodation at the other end of the beach town. She has packed her things and is waiting for a taxi. She cannot write in the apartment, she explains. It takes a while for him to understand that she is leaving. He looks bewildered, then withdraws. He is searching for words not available to him.

'You will come? Here tomorrow?' he asks.

'No. Not tomorrow. The next day. On Thursday,' she promises.

The phone rings and she answers it. The taxi has arrived.

'I will see you soon,' she impresses on him, shaking his hand. He nods, but his eyes show confusion and dismay.

I am not responsible for him, she repeats to herself as he lifts her luggage and drags it along the passageway, out to the front of the complex. It is loaded up and the taxi draws away from the pavement. Already, he has retreated back into the depths of the building.

Halfway up the hill on the way outside the town, she asks the driver to stop. At first he does not hear her and the vehicle pulls slowly along the winding suburban road of timbered, split-level homes, tree houses and the occasional tent.

'Stop! Please stop!' she cries urgently.

Ten minutes later, she is back knocking at the apartment door. Inside, all is silent. She buzzes and then knocks again. She hears the sound of rustling, then soft footsteps.

'Who?' comes a suspicious voice.

'Wong Tian! It's me, Mary. Let me in!'

The door opens slowly. He looks at her in surprise.

'You back! What happen?'

She mutters something about it not being such a good idea after all and drags her stuff inside again. She cannot leave. Not like that. Although he can manage without her, it would not be easy for him. He would be quite miserable, she senses, and rather lost. Up here in the resort, the tiny Chinese community has not exactly been tearing the door down to hear him read.

Something changes between them. They go grocery shopping every second day, trawling the supermarket together, pricing things. She explains to him what is expensive and what is not. On the way home, he carries her shopping bag as well as his own. Sometimes, they stop and he telephones someone in China. He needs her to explain how the prepaid phone card works. She observes him on the telephone, how different the strength of his voice, how animated his face, the urgency of saying a lot in very little time impressed on his features as he speaks in runs of swallowed consonants, creates little balloons of vowels and *ussshhh* sounds in his mouth.

One day, he makes another decision. He has observed her going in and out each day, changing her clothes to take a long walk on the beach or heading down to sunbathe.

'Go together to beach?'

'Good idea,' she says cheerily, her curiosity mounting.

He prepares for this as for everything else – assiduously. Packs a picnic, makes sandwiches, squeezes fresh oranges and makes juice for them both. On the beach, she feels a little awkward. As on the night when they observed the moon, they place themselves at some distance from one another. Their towels are spread with the width of at least three bodies between them. She is sure that he is surreptitiously examining her, as curious as she. He is tall, the skin on his smooth muscles remarkably pale in comparison to his face and hands. His nipples are cherry-red, small and tight. Like buds. She has never seen anything like them. Before they eat, they each take a brief swim, allow themselves to be tossed around in the bulk of seething water. He tells her about his exile and re-education during the Cultural Revolution. He talks about the first time he visited Shanghai, how he had never seen such beautiful girls before, how glamorous it seemed. He does not use the word 'glamour', but that is what is meant. Later, they sit in silence, looking out to sea.

She is aware of his eyes watching her now, differently from before. At night, she can hear him pacing up and down the living room area, long after she has gone to bed, read her book and put out the light. Her unease grows. There is no lock on the bedroom door, she notes.

One night, as she tries to sleep, she listens again. This time, she hears soft moans as he paces the apartment. She lies flat on the bed, her hearing sharpening. Finally, what she dreads – a knock. For a moment she dithers. To feign sleep or to answer? In the end, she opens her mouth.

'Yes?' she calls, feigning the voice of one disturbed from the depths of sleep.

The door swings open cautiously. She clicks on the bedside light.

Dressed in his immaculate check pyjamas, he crosses the room timidly. She half sits up, but as he approaches finds herself shrinking back, drawing the cover up around her chest. She is wearing a long T-shirt.

'I can't sleep,' he whispers, his hand reaching for her.

There is no doubt now, only panic. 'Go back to bed,'

she instructs firmly. 'Go back to bed, and you will sleep.'

He hesitates, hand in mid-air. Then, even more timidly, he reaches for her head and pats it gently.

'You very good,' he says before turning to leave.

She listens for a long time for sound in the apartment, but he is in his own bed now. She senses his obedience, pictures him sleeping, not restive.

They leave the resort together, heading back down to Sydney from where he is to depart immediately for Melbourne. Prior to the flight, they separate at the airport. She wants to shop. She will meet him at their gate, she tells him, not certain if he understands but trusting that he will go ahead anyway. She takes her time examining the perfumes and cosmetics, buys a stuffed kangaroo for her daughter, a couple of printed T-shirts for her son. By the time she reaches the gate, most of the other passengers have boarded the plane. Pleased with her haul, she puffs her way up the steps, passes the stewardess and makes her way down the aisle. Then she sees him, waving, pointing to her seat.

'Sorry about that,' she explains happily, 'I was engrossed.'

He is distraught, his face a shifting network of emotion. 'I thought – I thought I lost you!'

'You did not lose me,' she says, looking at his eyes, which are in commotion.

They travel mostly in silence. He seems absorbed by the clouds and the landscape below. But as they approach Sydney Airport, his mood changes again. Suddenly, he grips her hand and holds it tightly. They look at one another. He smiles at her. It is a moment of quiet uproar. He nods his head and smiles at her, then squeezes again.

Inside, before he moves off, she hugs him. She imagines the porcelain plate now, and how the figures have really moved very close together, how the imagining artist is leaning in with the finest brush so that the couple share the same view of the moon on the water.

Twentynine Palms

After his big fists smashed the face of a pretty boy outside a gay bar, Bob was sent to the brig. Connie wasn't surprised. Somehow, the remorse that accompanied every hangover didn't ring true. She knew Bob had lied about attending AA meetings. She recognised the effortless innocence, the way he looked her in the eye because he was forcing himself to, because he had trained himself to act honest. Once or twice he made her feel as if she was the one with the problem. In the end, she despised his innocence. No way was she going up the mountains with a lush like him. The fight resolved her dilemma. From what she heard afterwards, the gays weren't having any of it, though by the time the cops arrived it was too late for the guy he'd picked on.

Early in the mornings as she rushed to get to work, thoughts of Bob arose, like shards breaking the surface of something barely calmed. He might, had he wished, have possessed her; not by force, but when they weren't tripping, by sheer contemporary charm, with endless discussions about their 'relationship' and the direction it was heading. In the end, though, always getting his own way.

'What the point of a guy like that, eh?' Maria would say, throwing her hands in the air. 'He have nothing, he know nothing. His folks crazy on God. What the point?'

Maria knew all about folks who were crazy on God, about statues and candles, pieces of charred wood, beheaded chickens, their necks drooling sticky blood, crucifixes and ecstatic dances. San Diego verged on being her home. She didn't plan on heading back South, yet she loved Oldtown, with its souvenirs of the South, the painted crosses, the glamorous skeletons for the Day of the Dead.

The God-groupies didn't freak Connie. She'd never known fundamentalism, even in Ireland. Now, she accepted it as a natural part of the exoticism of exile, part of the self-conscious thrill that came each time she experienced otherness, in whatever form.

'You watch him. He get like his mom and dad. You wait,' Maria had warned. But Connie picked and mixed her cultures, her religions, her music and her food. Even on her baby-minding money, she loved the place. The heat had made her thin; the dry, relentless breath of desert air had shorn the saddlebags on her hips and the generous heft of her breasts. What remained now was a slight, youthful frame.

There was little time for anything but work. Her habit, confined to weekends, mostly amounted to a few snorts on Sundays, often with Bob. She liked to treat herself, kept some Irish pound notes rolled and ready, just in case.

For ten dollars an hour six days a week, every second weekend free, she expended herself on the infant child of a couple who also worked long and irregular hours. Jeff was a square-skulled army husband. Shirley, sweet and cutesy, was in charge of human resources at a microchip factory. Every Thursday night, she stayed up to bake gingerbread cookies, cornbread and apple pie with cinnamon. On Fridays, Connie sometimes had to do the weekly shopping, but between the coupons and special deals which Shirley and Jeff always knew about, it often involved a trip in multiple directions, from Coronado right across to Lemon Grove and on to the Parkway Plaza at El Cajon. Mostly, Shirley organised the shopping trips. With those big Bambi brown eyes, it was hard to imagine her dealing with staff at the factory, never mind sacking anybody.

Once they left the condo, Jeff in his brown and silver saloon, Shirley in an older sports model, Connie's day began. She smoked in the garden and played with the baby, jigging him on her knee to songs from her own childhood, faster and faster until he giggled and clucked with delight. Maria's employers forbade smoking, even in the garden.

'Where a girl supposed to smoke?' Maria would fling her arms in the air. 'Under the sheet in the dark? Huh? In the shower? That suit them of course, these American dopeheads.'

'Maria, Maria,' Connie would say patiently, 'dopeheads these people are not. Come *on*, Maria. You've got to improve your English if you want them to take you seriously.'

'I guess,' Maria would sigh.

'So listen to words, Maria. Listen to me.'

'You not perfect. You Irish.'

'But I speak good English and these people – *not* dopeheads – like the sound of what I say.'

*

The baby usually woke sometime around mid-morning. Connie would feed and bathe him. She enjoyed his solid, confident weight, the way he would suck her cheeks and chin, ravishing her in his sweet slobber. How bizarre, yet how normal, she thought, to be so clean inside your body that even your saliva was sweet.

Jeff and Shirley liked the way she spoke.

'Sure is a million times better than that last Irish girl we had. She was from *Cork* – right, honey?' she called to Jeff.

'Kerry, sweetie, Kerry,' Jeff intoned from the bedroom.

'No, hon, that was the one before her. Cork, darned sure it was Cork.'

'Ker-ry,' Jeff sing-sang in his patient, bossy voice.

Shirley gave a tight smile in Connie's direction. 'Anyway, wherever she was from, we never could tell just what she was sayin'. Her voice went up an' down, all over the place. A real Colleen.' Shirley's smile was affectionate when she looked again at Connie. 'Hell, you're fine.'

Connie started that same day because Shirley thought she should familiarise herself with the baby's health and allergy profile. She listened and nodded continually, wishing Shirley would just shut up. The next morning, she cast her eye along a three-page list of instructions, written in careful, elegant cursive.

Life swung full circle. Things that had once made Connie uncomfortable now guaranteed all-round approval. As a teenager, her accent seemed all wrong. There were times and places when the whole family sounded out of place, in restaurants, in certain Dublin shops, even on holidays. Once, when she was thirteen, they spent two weeks in a castle in Wexford where most of the guests were English. The only time she'd felt comfortable was at Ballyhealy beach, when she and her brother Gavin would wait till high tide before diving off a solitary mass of rock.

At dinner every evening, English voices announced an unfamiliar, yet approved of, standard. In comparison, their softer Irish tones seemed obliquely related to the language they shared. On that holiday they became islanders, hobbling after their betters.

One day, as the four of them picnicked at Ballyhealy, two of the guests, a blonde and a dark-haired woman, stopped to chat.

'Splendid day, isn't it?' the blonde one beamed. She was wearing the smallest psychedelic-green bikini Connie had ever seen. Connie wanted to cringe as both her parents, normally competent, able people, pulled themselves together hastily on the sand-covered bedspread they used as a beach blanket. They'd never got around to acquiring a satin-edged tartan Foxford rug, or any of the million and one aids to beach life in a windy climate which the English acquired – the stools, chairs, collapsible tables and windbreaks. The bedspread was torn in places and soiled with paw-marks. A layer of dog hair was evident from the times when they would throw it along the back seat of the car so as to save the car from the dog's muck.

'Oh, fine day indeed,' her father replied too eagerly.

'We're trying to organise a volleyball team for this afternoon,' her friend continued, tossing straight black hair over her shoulder, then snapping her finger beneath the bottom of her orange and black polka-dot swimsuit so as to snap it down over a tanned left buttock.

The blonde took up as if on cue. 'Should be a spot of fun. Care to join in?'

'Ah, no. No. Thanks all the same. We're …' her mother stammered, lost for words.

'We're not great ones for sport,' her father took over again.

'Oh, it's nothing serious. Come on, you two, buck up,' she teased. 'High time you took your noses out of those books!'

The women haw-hawed at her patents' upturned novels, already smeared with Nivea and sand.

'*Do* think about it,' the dark-haired woman urged.

'Well. Sure, we'll see,' her mother relented.

'*We'll see*? Splendid!' she said in a high, victorious voice. 'I know that's Gaelic for yes!'

The women waved at them and headed on down the beach at a brisk pace. Gavin and Connie looked at one another as their parents murmured and mumbled, her father briefly imitating the dark-haired woman's voice, her mother falling around the place laughing at his feminised 'Splendid!'

Connie couldn't remember now how the volleyball episode resolved itself, recalling instead the feeling of exclusion that dogged her throughout that holiday. They weren't excluded, of course, but for the first time, she discovered that the things she took for granted – turns of phrase, her accent – were *alien*. She, her parents, Gavin and all belonging to them, and all the people to whom they weren't related, the citizens of the island of Ireland, were *different* by virtue of the way they used language. To outsiders, they might even seem comical, speaking in a *brogue*.

She thought of her parents that day, at peace with their books, her father dug into *Strumpet City*, a fictionalised account of the last poverty-stricken years of English rule in Dublin. Her mother, she recalled, had confiscated *Last Exit to Brooklyn* from Gavin, but in the meantime was herself absorbed by its dense, forbidding print, her face dismal, uttering the odd gasp, the occasional 'Oh my *God.*'

Years later, the feeling of bewilderment returned when a musician she knew, a native Irish speaker from Kerry, said how he hadn't known before the age of ten that people spoke anything other than Irish, that what he had been reared with was of no importance in the context of world languages. He had wept, he said. No other discovery, neither the challenge of sex, nor the knowledge that Santa Claus did not exist, had the same effect on him.

Connie hadn't wept on that holiday. She'd enjoyed the two weeks, despite being outraged when the owner of the hotel described a local man brought into the castle one evening to entertain the guests with his stories as a 'native'.

By the time they returned home, she had decided that nobody would ever think less of her on account of the way she spoke. If people didn't progress beyond judging according to accents and words, she reasoned, then nothing ever changed. Some people were so stupid that they would always need the reassurance of having their own accents echoed back. Those people didn't matter, but if they had power over you? She began to work at her own accent, learned to inflect her voice, saying 'little' when formerly she would have said 'wee', and 'scold' where once she would have said 'give out'. She stopped saying 'but' at the end of her sentences, a local peculiarity in her county.

Maria, intent on making money in California, possibly even marrying an American, wasn't bothered about her clumsy Spanish patois. Her mouth, throat and tongue seemed to burst with unshapeable words. Although her vocabulary grew, with every syllable, her accent remained defiant.

*

The baby kicked and cooed in his basket. Connie unplugged her iPod. '110 and rising,' the weatherwoman had said. The weather was never like that back then. No drama. Nothing to be watched, monitored or slotted, as it was now, into the mythology kit of the urban pioneer. In Ireland, moisture and the weather were inextricably entwined. Something else from the day at Ballyhealy beach surfaced – her father, heating water for their picnic on 'the Volcano'. It was a metal contraption, a cylinder within an outer hollow ring. Just as he'd packed the central cylinder with tight balls of newspaper and had set it alight, Gavin had muttered under his breath and nudged Connie.

'It's them.'

Connie tutted. The newspaper began to curl and flame, eventually reddening. Just as the water in the outer ring began to simmer, the Englishwomen stopped again on the way back from their walk along the beach.

'Oh, how *won*derful!' the dark one exclaimed, a piece of bleached wood clamped under one arm.

'Soopah, absolutely soopah!' The blonde clapped her hands in delight as the water sang and hissed malevolently in its outer ring, within which the newspaper roared and writhed.

'What a clever idea! Where did you find it? Do tell, it's just the sort of thingummy we could use on our moors hikes.'

Connie's mother and father stared at one another, as if puzzled.

'Where *did* we get it?' her mother said. 'You see, it's always been with us, just one of those things.'

'Second-hand shop?' her father queried.

'After we tied the knot?'

They both nodded.

'There was never anything like it in our family anyhow,' her father said firmly.

'Nor mine. I think we must have picked it up in Flaherty's auction rooms, that's it,' her mother added.

'Isn't it sweet?' the blonde gushed.

They watched in silence, momentarily lost for words as the water suddenly bubbled, boiled, then surged in its container. In the end, Connie's mother gingerly poured the boiling liquid into a teapot, swearing quietly as a drop of water slopped onto her bare foot, her face red beneath the admiring gaze of the two women.

'When you see that Bob again?' Maria enquired late one Friday night as they finished a bottle of red.

'Who knows?' Connie said, emptying her glass.

Maria smiled grimly. 'You meet someone else. For sure.' She settled her hands into her lap, as if awaiting confidences.

'I don't hate him, you know,' she said.

'He too bad for that?'

'I'm indifferent. I've grown indifferent.'

'Those were good times, though,' said Maria, crossing her ankles and stretching back in the leatherette armchair.

She felt too old now for good times like that. What it had amounted to was one long brawl, an endless, laughter-filled crawl from bar to bar in Hillcrest, then back to the condo, his or hers, his if he was out of his head (he could damage his own place but she wouldn't let him cross her threshold if he was going to behave like a bear on speed).

'You throw out all that junk last night?'

'You know I did,' Connie replied. Souvenirs from the Bob months: stolen plates, glasses, spoons, even a chipped yellow crutch swiped from a smackhead outside a strip joint. Somehow, it had ended up at the apartment and Bob had forgotten to reclaim the spoils of war.

There had been only one good night, a twilight when they'd strolled together along the beachfront outside the Hotel del Coronado. He'd talked seriously about getting a job, about how good he could be. Around them, sandpipers thrust their long beaks into the wet shallows and the sky was hard as a sapphire. But it had been all talk. Bob couldn't hold down a job for more than a week without finding something wrong with it. Apart from that, he couldn't stay sober.

She couldn't go back to Ireland, not just yet, not without a visa for re-entry. Sometimes she wanted to visit her parents. They still asked about Bob, but Connie had heard her mother's sigh of relief when she'd had to explain what the brig was. The night she met Blue Hawk, he was with a boy of no more than eighteen or nineteen. Blue Hawk was clean but the boy was stoned. They had a couple of shots together, bourbon for him, Frizby Dix for Connie, then listened to a crooning Mexican-Indian singer. The woman swayed behind the mike, her broad hips shifting slowly beneath a close-fitting black satin dress that came to her knees. Her stockings glistened beneath the pink and blue lighting as she swivelled from foot to foot in pink suede shoes.

'So what kind of place is Twentynine Palms?' Connie asked Blue Hawk.

'High desert. Ain't nothing much up there.'

'What do people do?'

'Do?' He clapped his hands on his knees and thought hard. 'They live there.'

'But what do they do?'

'That depends,' he said doubtfully.

People clapped lazily as the woman finished her act. A young Korean stepped up in her place, smiling as the spotlight zoomed on his face, eyes bright with undistilled fear. He positioned his instrument, a four-stringed oblong, and began to compete with the absorbed hum of voices.

'Ain't much craftwork up there. That what you mean?'

He knocked back the remainder of his bourbon, then looked at her. 'I suppose you have a dream catcher.' He smiled. 'All white women seem to have dream catchers.'

Connie smiled, feeling silly. 'As a matter of fact, I have.'

It hung on the wall over her bed, a circular piece of wood criss-crossed with pieces of gut surrounding a central hole. The idea was that bad dreams became entangled in the mesh of gut, beyond which they could have no ill effect on the dreamer, but that good ones slipped osmotically through the hole.

'Well. No harm in that, I suppose,' Blue Hawk replied, smiling.

The following weekend they drove to Bombay Beach in his pick-up. They walked and talked. Around them was desert, pure grey-white wilderness. Whatever parts of herself needed losing, she thought, whatever she was in flight from could be left in the slackening waste. The desert held her, much in the way the beaches in Ireland had once held her. It was a recognition, the purest moment of perception.

'Strange name for an Irish girl,' Blue Hawk remarked on Saturday evening as they sat by the lake. The sun dipped low, a thin disc spreading like a shimmering layer of crimson foil on the surface of the water.

'Short for Constance. After a famous revolutionary, a very progressive woman. Constance Markiewicz.'

'Never heard of her. But maybe I'll call you Constance. If that's okay.'

'Can I call you Blue?'

Three months later, Blue met her off the bus when she arrived at Twentynine Palms. He grasped both her hands, his look measured as he held her at arm's length, then guided her towards the cream and brown convertible. His hair, she noted, had grown longer. He wore blue jeans, a red shirt and a turquoise-beaded suede belt. The journey had been long and tiring. She had barely registered place names. Morongo Valley, Yucca Valley, Joshua Tree. Finally, Twentynine Palms and, beyond it, the Indian reservation.

'How do you feel about *that*?' Connie asked when they got to the hut.

'About what?'

'*Indian* reservation. I mean,' she was hesitant, 'isn't that the wrong word? What about …'

'Oh yeah, the PC stuff. *Native American*? Somehow, Native American reservation has never sounded right to white folks. They ain't never got around to puttin' it on road signs.'

The weekend slipped by. She owned nothing, she knew, absolutely nothing. She was as great or as inconsequential as the sands. The people of the earth owned nothing but owed everything to the Great Mother that gave them life. On Sunday they set out early in the cold dawn air, food and drink for the day strapped to their backs. When the sun rose, the chill gradually melted and heat filled her. Slowly she brimmed with light and sunshine, until eventually she was scorched and wet. She was glad of the broad hat she wore and the long-sleeved white dress which covered her body.

'Tell me more.'

'What d'ya want to know?'

'About your people. About the way you live.'

They sat, partly sheltered from the midday glare by the stiff spread of a giant cactus on a bluff that overlooked the plain. In the near distance, mountains, white and grey, places from which some people never returned, too dehydrated, too lost or just freaked by a cocktail of acid, poppers and the sun. They saw things, that was for sure. Connie removed her sandals and rubbed sand across her feet, like a child awaiting a fairy story. Blue opened a bottle of bourbon and gulped slowly. He breathed out, then held the bottle towards her.

'No. Not during the day,' she replied.

'There y'go now. Damn Injuns just can't keep away from liquor,' he laughed quietly.

'It's not like that. That's not what I meant.'

'What did you mean then, Constance?'

'Ah, it's got more to do with the months when I knew Bob. I told you about him.'

'In the brig. Right.'

'Here.' She took the bottle from him. 'Just to prove myself.' She didn't even like the stuff. Here she was showing her bona fides to Blue on a heap of dust in the back of beyond. She swallowed and grimaced, then squinted up at the sun, wondering if she was worthy of her name. It was a bit of a farce, the obsession with naming, one people imposing themselves on another people, another land, parents inspirationally imposing their ideas of honour on newborn babies. The recipient never lived up to the original dream. The native country, the native child, heroes, heroines and politics, crumbling to nothing in the end.

'Don't do that. You'll damage your sight,' Blue said gently as she squinted at the sun. She was thinking about Bob. It had been all play, no work, or as little as possible. She'd handled her hangovers during the week, after the skites from bar to bar in the company of two Latinos, a Swedish woman and a giant of a man, an art professor from Decorah, Iowa. They put their lives on hold, letting deeper reactions build beneath the surface as they drank and snorted. It was a pressure barely perceptible to Connie. They raised hell at weekends. Shirley had remarked on Connie's pallor one Monday when she arrived for work, her eyes glazed, her body like a live, sparking wire. Sometimes they'd buy enough stuff for a couple of weeks' modest snorting but blew the lot in one weekend at the Swedish woman's apartment on Orange Avenue. They'd hang out of her fourth floor window and howl like monkeys at passers-by, yelling and jibbering to catch the attention of drivers, waving until they were waved to. Sometimes they heated tinned soup or Connie would microwave a couple of Linda McCartney organic dinners. But the idea of food was mostly a joke: between the arguments about sharing the stuff, whether everybody had enough, between Bob and Connie's rushes, then the long hours of sex, give or take a Black Bomber or two, time flowed away. Sometimes, Bob and the others would shoot up. When they awoke from comatose sleep, they needed an instant upper. Connie wouldn't touch heroin.

In the end, the pressure got too much for Bob. She was glad she hadn't witnessed that crazy, belligerent attack on the gay place. Just as the cops arrived, the Swedish woman told her later, Bob puked all over the place, spattering the police wagon, the police and himself with a mixture of red wine and tortillas.

'Fool,' she whispered.

'Let him go,' Blue whispered back, taking a quiet gulp of bourbon. He stretched out full in the shade of the cactus, then lit a cigarette, his eyes soft and absent as he watched

Connie and the naked sky in turns.

After Bob went to the brig she got drunk, surprised at the extent of her relief. She scarcely remembered that evening with the Swedish woman and the guy from Iowa, but formed the impression that they'd got it together while she was out of her head. Two days later they bailed out of the city, headed up the coast to Santa Barbara.

'Know what, Irishwoman?'

'What, Injun?'

'I think you should stay up here.'

'I can't. I've got to get back to the baby.'

'It's not yours.'

'That's not the point. I have a *job*.'

'So you have work. Holy-holy-holy!' he laughed, 'There's work up here. Plenty of work.'

'Doing what?'

Blue fell silent. Then he laughed again. 'You could,' he kept laughing, 'you could always give *Irish* lessons.' He laughed till he bent double. Eventually, Connie laughed too, although she didn't find the remark all that funny.

'Yeah, maybe we can trade native talents. I teach Irish, your lot give me a load of native craft for export to Europe. Native American dream catchers, feathers, amulets, headbands,' she snickered.

'Stop right there, Constance.' Blue held a warning hand in the air.

The comparison had had the desired effect.

'It must have been hard, living up here,' she remarked peaceably.

'Originally. It was not something chosen.'

'But doesn't it kill you? Being reduced to this? A reservation, for God's sake! The worst land on the fucking continent!'

'Yes. No. Deep down it's yes. Day to day, less so. Like folks everywhere, we get on with our lives. And think of your own folks. Back when your Constance was fightin' along with them revolutionaries. Y'all lived on a kind of reservation too, right?'

It was true. Theories went out the window, projections about whether and how a people might realise themselves. The Irish had once been the wogs of Europe, Paddys, Shamrock-heads breeding and inbreeding on the other side of the Irish Sea. She thought of home again. Gavin, a banker with Lloyds, lived in Singapore. But something still worked below the surface of their adult lives, something which created a hunger, in all the heat of memory and pre-birth, for acknowledgement. Sometimes she pitied her parents. They did not value the things she knew, not a glimmer of willingness to lean towards the truth of her unfolding life touched them. That blindness she could scarcely forgive. Despite what they imagined it to be, hers was a life of learning.

As the day cooled, Blue and Connie took photographs of one another. The camera lens became a veil with which each could conceal rising shyness, an anticipation. That evening, she said that she might come back to Twentynine Palms.

'Constance,' he said when, eventually, they lay on the bunk in the hut. She gripped his black hair, pulling him down to her face, staring into the brown wells of his eyes. The skin on his cheekbones was moon coloured, smooth and supple. He was like a tree, strong, leaf-trembling as he spread himself around her. His lovemaking was by turns slow, concentrated, then swifter, balancing fire, air as it hit them in waves. It struck up through her, like lightning dancing in sheets around an isolated object, every so often splitting to the core what had attracted it.

'What you going back up to that dustbowl for? San Diego a good place!' Maria's voice rose an octave higher when Connie got back to the apartment.

'I am returning to Twentynine Palms,' Connie spoke firmly, 'because up there it feels like home to me. And Blue's up there.'

'You crazy bitch,' she swung up to high C again. 'Like I suppose you need a home! Ireland your home. Now you have a home away from all that rain and all those people who say the Irish only good for drinking, laughing and making babies. You no need desert home.' Maria poured coffee into a percolator.

'Know something, Maria? You're coming on. You've got a hang of the subliminals.'

'*Madre de Dio*, sub-leem-in-els? What d'hell you mean?'

'I mean the stuff you've picked up about me without thinking about it. The pictures you've put together in your subconscious mind.'

When the coffee had brewed, the women sat back to watch the night. The windows were wide open to the avenue. There was no wind. Cicadas croaked and rustled. Connie and Maria sweated gently, sipped from mugs painted with black and gold Native American symbols, crunched at ginger biscuits. Connie held a flyswatter and waved it idly at nothing in particular. As she did so, a small lizard flicked its tail, then glided over the window ledge, out of sight. Maria kicked off her flip-flops and rubbed oil on her legs.

In the distance, cars cut steadily along the freeway. Connie relaxed, smelled the ocean, the warm earth, Maria's oil. She could just make out the writing on the side of a passing truck. *Kinko's. The Copy Center.*

'S'nice here, huh?' Maria whispered.

Connie nodded. Her mind travelled back the width of a continent, then the width of an ocean, down the vertical tunnels of the past, to summer at Ballyhealy beach. She pictured her father and mother, bent over the Volcano, packing a full *Sunday Times*, sports pages and all, into the cylinder before setting it alight in the sand. She remembered the tea, not the American kind – thin, iced tea with no comfort in it – but good strong Irish tea, the kind where you couldn't see the bottom of the cup.

Come to Me, Maitresse

Since Gwen's arthritis had worsened, every afternoon now began much the same. After lunch, she and Al took a nap. Gwen used the bedroom and her husband lay on the couch in the living area. This was because Al liked the shutters closed but Gwen preferred them slightly ajar. She enjoyed drifting to sleep or slowly waking at around half past four being vaguely aware of a sliver of hot light as it edged through the day's predictable arc.

It was the light that had made them love Carla Bayle from the moment they arrived as passing tourists, fifteen years before; the way it caressed the hot magenta and umber of the houses on the street, their slatted green and white shutters closed to the heat. The dream had always been to have what Gwen called 'a place in the sun'. It would be a reward for the thin years of country living as she and Al came and went to teaching jobs at the local comprehensive, when nobody really expected her to make the break into full-time writing. But she did, though not spectacularly.

The house they bought the following spring stood at the south end of the village, near the bronze memorial with its long scroll of the dead of two world wars. Across the road from the back of the house, off the patio, ancient fortified walls were the last obstacle between Carla Bayle and the plains. The land fell away to crops of sunflowers, barley and maize. Viewed from the ramparts, country roads meandered for miles until they joined with the *route nationale*. Finally, at that point in the distance where the eye relaxes, lay the Pyrenees, mauve-tinged at dusk, crevassed and fissured, the high peaks white and pink.

Today was a break in routine. Calista Stoney was in the region with her niece, Joanna, a rising young poet by Calista's account. Joanna would love to meet Gwen, Calista had texted, it would be marvellous if they could detour on their way to Auch. Gwen had texted back that of course they must come for lunch, giving them a date and a time. Calista had sent a return postcard in her big, looped, forward-slanting hand: *Dying to have a chat. Let me know if there's anything you want brought out from Europe's hottest capital! Love, Calista XXX*

Al's hair was nearly as white as her own, Gwen observed as he leaned over the Cos lettuce at the kitchen sink, separating the leaves for a Caesar salad. She took a selection of local cheeses from the fridge, loosened the greaseproof paper slightly and left them to soften on the little wooden worktop. Sometimes she and Al drove to the far side of Toulouse to the market at Montauban. They always bought things they hadn't set out to purchase – rabbits, fowl, the local *foie gras*, which was different from the one they favoured at Carla Bayle, and, in season, *des truffles*.

'Oh darling, there's a tear in the parasol,' Gwen remarked, almost as an afterthought. 'Maybe you could stick a pin in it or something?'

'For God's sake, Gwen, it needs to be stitched.' Al turned towards her, annoyed. 'D'you think we have a strong needle and some thread?'

Gwen turned her attention to the cheeses again, this time completely removing the greaseproof paper.

'Hmm? Needle and thread?' She poked at one of the cheeses with her finger. Condensation and a slight mould clung to her fingertip. She licked it. 'These cheeses look really good, Al.'

Al gave a quiet snort and went to the food cupboard. 'It's here somewhere, I know it is,' he said, his hands trembling as he felt his way in the cupboard's twilit space.

'Don't worry about it,' she said, relenting. 'It doesn't matter. Really it doesn't. Come here. Kissey-kissey-munchkins?'

He gave that stiff half-turn which had become so characteristic of him in his late sixties. 'Kissey-kissey,' he murmured, smiling. 'We'll sort out that parasol, you'll see.'

Soft-spoken, given to thought rather than swift pronouncement, her husband was regarded by Gwen as infinitely wiser than she, and infinitely wiser than many of the writers of her acquaintance, who sometimes believed themselves to have a monopoly on wisdom. Giving up his teaching career at the school had been a major consideration. Unlike her, he had not had other aspirations.

'Have you done the croutons, dear?' Al called from the rough stone patio. He balanced on a white sun-chair, needle and thread to hand, squinting as he forced the needle in and out through the red and yellow canvas umbrella.

'Hell, no. Forgot.'

'Not to worry. Lots of time.'

Quickly, Gwen cut the bread into small cubes and tossed it into a pan of hot seasoned oil.

'Mmm,' Al sniffed as the aroma of oil, garlic and herbs wafted from the kitchen. He came in behind her then and nuzzled her neck, nipping at her earlobe.

'Now, now, baby, you know Cook doesn't like to be interfered with.' She turned and kissed the tip of his nose. 'At least not in the kitchen. Hell. Visitors.'

'What about 'em?'

'They mean work!' Gwen complained, wiping her brow with the front of her forearm.

'They'll be gone soon. Oh shit!' He gulped his drink. 'I think I hear a car, do you? They're here, aren't they?'

'Shit. Yes. Nice to see Calista though.' Gwen glanced down at her apron, then removed it hastily.

'You look fine. Anyway, they're here,' he breathed out ceremoniously, 'Calista and her young charge.' Al brushed at his loose shirt, then glanced quickly in the oval mirror in the little hallway.

They stood at the open door, beaming a welcome. They extended their arms towards Calista as she ran towards them, smiling shyly.

'God, you two haven't changed a *bit*!' she squealed.

'Oh, go on now!' Al laughed, pleased.

A plump young woman of about thirty stood waiting to be introduced.

'And this lovely creature must be Joanna! Ah, youth, youth!' Al took her hand and embraced her. 'Welcome, my dear,' he murmured gently, his eyes curious.

'Don't smother her, you old fool,' Gwen joked, then rolled her eyes conspiratorially at Joanna.

Joanna, dressed in a sleeveless serge blouse and a matching skirt which swirled around her ankles, met their attempts at welcoming humour with a little smile, nodding at Gwen. With her short, uncoloured brown hair, unmade-up skin and the blue outfit, she reminded Gwen of a newly laicised nun. When she shook hands with Gwen, her clasp, Gwen noted, was firm and cool.

'Welcome,' Gwen said, meeting the girl's eyes, which were also cool. Calista cornered Gwen immediately, enthusing about the house. She admired the wooden furnishings, running her hands over the surfaces of chairs, vases and wall panels.

'What intense light! And the curtains!' she cried, examining the drapes that separated the main living area from the galley kitchen. Joanna, ushered to the swing-seat by Al, sat out on the patio.

'Well yes, I suppose it does look rather grand from the perspective of the school staffroom on a wet November morning,' Gwen said gaily, 'but you must remember that we get the most *awful* rainstorms here too. And winter is hard. It doesn't help my arthritis one bit!'

'Even here!' Calista exclaimed. 'Well anyway, you're well out of the stress palace. The school has gone from bad to worse.'

'So I gathered,' said Gwen, cracking an egg over the Caesar salad. Expertly, she tossed the salad leaves with her fingers until the egg was evenly distributed.

'I think we're ready to go,' she said in a sing-song voice, 'almost there. Calista, be a dear and carry out the bread. Two little baskets.'

They settled themselves in the shade of the parasol, close to a lemon tree.

Calista and Joanna made appreciative sounds when Gwen served the salad.

'*Magnifique*!' Calista kissed the tips of her fingers in her enthusiasm. 'Can't beat it, can you?' She looked to Joanna for a response.

'What? Oh – no, this is wonderful. Really regal,' Joanna spoke quietly.

'*Du vin pour les belles dames*?'

Al was really moving now, Gwen thought, playing the good host. He poured white wine for the three women, then, as an afterthought, offered them water.

'Please,' Joanna nodded, pushing her water glass forward.

'So where do you live, Joanna?' Gwen asked, forking through her salad.

'Bray.'

'What's that like nowadays?'

'Oh, you know. Lively. Hurdy-gurdys. Sugarloaf Mountain. Local radio. That kind of thing.'

Gwen wondered if there might be more to Bray, but didn't say so. 'Have you always lived there?'

'More or less.'

Calista cut some cheese and pushed it towards Joanna, who shook her head and passed it across to Al.

'Now for the good news from home,' Calista spoke coyly, smiling at Joanna. 'Will I tell them?'

The girl shrugged, suppressed a smile. 'As you wish.'

'Jo-jo's first collection of poems has been nominated for a McLachlan Award!'

'Oh wow! Wow!' Al cried, clapping his hands together.

'It's wonderful, dear, just wonderful,' Gwen said. 'If you win, it will be a great opportunity, and even if you don't actually win it will still have been an honour.'

'You'll soon be able to keep a man in style, that's for sure,' Al chuckled, breaking his bread into small pieces.

Gwen could tell by Joanna's face that it was the wrong thing to say.

'Jo-jo's steering clear of men for some time to come,

right Jo-jo?' Calista intervened lightly with a slight frown.

'Well, at least the world of arts and letters is in secure hands,' Gwen said gently. 'I trust you brought a copy of Joanna's book?' Gwen looked across at Calista.

'Of *course* I did. I said to Jo-jo that you'd be really interested in reading her work.'

'Good. I am.'

'Do you review in Ireland?' Al asked Joanna.

'Well,' Joanna was diffident, 'it's a tricky area. But yes, I like to review.'

'Tricky is right,' Gwen chipped in, 'like a rabbit in a tank of barracudas.'

For an instant, Joanna almost smiled.

'I'd imagine it's especially difficult for poets,' Calista said then.

'So?' Gwen's eyebrows shot up.

'They all know one another,' Calista said.

'The dunghill syndrome, you mean?'

'I beg your pardon?' Joanna was staring straight at Gwen, her face very serious.

'Oh, you know. Poets are like dung beetles. All that scrambling around in a mound of S-H-one-T, if you see what I mean.'

Joanna gave an irritated little laugh. 'It's a bit more complicated than that,' she said with sudden vigour. 'Poetry is ...' she hesitated, 'the highest art form there can possibly be.'

Al and Gwen exchanged glances and smiled.

'And there was I, as a mere fiction writer,' Gwen joked, 'imagining it was one of *many* high art forms!'

'No. Poetry is the highest art form there is.' Joanna went on to list her hierarchy of significant poets, the ones who counteracted that free verse patter which the washed-up hippies and feminists wrote during the eighties. 'It's sad!' Joanna shook her head.

'Hmm.' Gwen was thoughtful. 'Now I can't be certain of this Joanna – not being a poet any more. I was one twenty years ago, but then I turned to fiction and found it altogether much more satisfying. An easier habitat, if you like.' She pushed her wine glass towards Al. 'Fill me up, dear.'

'Oh, come on,' Joanna countered.

'In my experience. For what it's worth,' Gwen said lightly.

'Yeah, but there are some really good poets coming along now,' Joanna went on.

'Well, if they're good, they'll be heard, won't they?' Al said softly.

'You're right,' Joanna nodded, 'and the consoling thing is that in each generation of writers, only the best rise to the top.'

'Oh, nonsense!' Gwen's patience snapped. 'In each generation some of the best are certainly there, but side by side with *some* of the mediocre!'

Joanna put her elbows on the table and folded her little hands beneath her chin, regarding Gwen with polite amusement.

'Don't you understand, Joanna, the mediocre is *needed.* It broadens the cultural habitat. That's if you must think in those terms,' she finished with a smile.

They fell silent for a time and sipped their wine. Al looked down at his glass. Calista gazed enquiringly from Joanna to Gwen and back again.

Joanna decided to hold herself at a remove, to at least signal disinterest in Gwen and everything Gwen stood for. As the three older people sipped their coffee, she wandered through the small garden, examining everything with a fierce botanic attention, the deep green shiny leaves of the lemon tree, the olive bushes, a row of ripening vines which Gwen and Al had optimistically planted after they bought the house. She also absorbed the conversation that drifted in scraps from beneath the parasol. All the time, new phrases ran through her head and displaced the words she overheard, snatches of poems she had yet to compose, colours of emotion freshly born from her encounter with these quaint expatriates. There was so much to do, to write, and, she thought savagely, they did not know the half of it.

At the table, conversation flagged. Calista and Gwen fell silent. Al sat rattling the previous day's edition of *Le Figaro*. Joanna moved around with a small camera in hand, then hung over the fence in order to focus on something Gwen could not see.

'Got it!' she cried jubilantly.

'Oh yes, our friends the lizards. All over the place.' Al gave a broad wave of his hand.

Eventually, it was time to go. As they stood up, Gwen felt the familiar twinges in her ankles as the skin of her feet pressed up in little cushions of flesh between the straps of her flat sandals.

'We want to make Auch by nightfall,' Calista said.

Al chased Calista around the garden when she refused to give him a kiss. 'Come, come, Calista,' he laughed, 'for auld time's sake. Gwen understands these ancient staff alliances, don't you, *maitresse*?'

'Indeed I do, *mon capitaine*.' She blew him a kiss, aware that Joanna was observing them. *Damn*, she thought as her ankles throbbed again. She had been sitting too long.

As Calista and Joanna drove away, Gwen and Al waved, calling out long goodbyes. Joanna stuck her arm out the window and waved briefly, but without turning back to look at them. It was strange, Gwen thought, to feel as she did now, of so little interest to this young person that the most they merited was a disdainful backwards toss of the hand.

They cleared up, moving back and forth between patio and kitchen. Gwen lifted the tablecloth and shook it. The movement churned the air, raising aromas of warm lavender and oregano, stirring butterflies on flickering trajectories.

'Here. Let me.' Al took the cloth. 'Come to me,' he said, holding her, pushing her back into the shade of the lemon tree. He stroked her back.

'I'm a fool,' Gwen whispered, leaning on him. 'My knees hurt too.'

'I know your knees hurt, I know. But you're not a fool. Why should you be a fool?'

'Washed up. We are, you know.'

'Did she bother you that much? But she's an innocent! She knows nothing.' Al caressed Gwen's neck with his thumbs, then kissed her on the lips.

'Older people say that kind of thing. It's not always true,' Gwen whispered, her voice shaky.

'In this case, you know it is. In this case.'

'And we're not – we're getting—' Her lips trembled.

They made their way across the garden again, through the kitchen, across the living room and into the bedroom. She dropped heavily onto the bed.

'That girl needs slapping down,' she muttered.

'I daresay,' Al said, removing her sandals. He stroked her feet, cradling her heels, one by one, in the palm of one hand.

'It's all right, *mon capitaine*, they're too tender. Leave them be.'

'*Maitresse*.' He watched, his head to one side as he awaited her response. '*Maitresse*? Let it go. Some things have always been the same. This is one of them.'

'Yes, but …' Gwen thought of the anticipation she had savoured earlier in the day.

'Don't struggle. Not this time, *maitresse*,' he whispered, kissing her forehead. He leaned closer and kissed her again, on the nose, on each cheek, finally on the mouth. As they undressed, she grew less aware of the pain in her feet and the pain that until moments ago had seemed to skewer her right knee.

Twenty minutes later, gasping and perspiring, they curled around one another, their lust still unsatisfied. But her courage had returned. She tilted her head back and kissed him yet again, to signal an end to hopeless frustration; she tried to tease and coax him back to good humour.

'It really doesn't matter,' she murmured, 'not the way you think.'

He sighed, his hand caressing the mound of her pubis.

After he dressed, she listened for a while to the clearing-up sounds that came from the kitchen. Outside, a light wind stirred. The long *cratch-cratch-cratch* of the crickets dipped, then rose again as the wind current rolled, ghostly, along the village walls. Somewhere, a rooster crowed. A car drove across the place, braked noisily, the engine left running. Gwen listened as two men talked and laughed. Eventually, she dozed. The light lengthened to a tawny oblong in the bedroom.

Strong Pagans

The church was in the old graveyard outside the town. It rested in a hollow, close to our family plot and also to the ornate obelisk on which multitudes of angels trumpeted over the Capriano plot. Tender tributes to the dead were inscribed beneath sepia-tinted photographs of fish, chip and ice cream-selling family members who had passed on to the great reward. Nearby was a life-sized statue of Christ the King, seated on a throne. We loved to sit on his knee and swing from his stiff neck, imagining beneficence.

'What reward?' Tara whined insistently.

'Oh,' I bluffed, 'our reward in heaven. There'll be lots of goodies, stuff like that.'

'What goodies?' Anton asked, challenging me.

'Well, lots of whatever you want. And you won't have to look at people you hate,' I explained.

'Does that mean Mrs Blundel won't be there?' said Tara. Mrs Blundel was our music teacher, a woman of venomous loquaciousness who nicknamed every eleven-year-old in her care. Anton was called Specky Foureyes,

Tara became Ducky Darling, Anna Capriano was known as Signorina Chips, while I struggled with Buckteeth.

'Mrs Blundel will certainly not be there,' I assured her.

'But we'd all forgive one another anyway, so it wouldn't matter if she was,' said Anton.

'Oh yes it would!' Tara was not consoled.

We broke into the church one day close to Hallowe'en. The afternoon was warm enough to resuscitate any remaining flies, so that the first thing I remember after smashing the stained glass with a stone is the intense buzz of newly awakened insect life from within.

'Come on!' I whispered to Anton and Tara, who hung back cautiously, Tara's expression shifting between horror and curiosity. Hanging onto the single bar that curved in front of the window, I reached down to pull her up.

'Push her, Anton!' I hissed. She started moaning about the state of her shoes and that we'd all be killed when we got home, but we ignored her, pulling and shoving to hoist her up.

'Now you,' I commanded Anton, who sprang with greater agility than either of us and almost toppled us from the high sill. He banged at the glass panes with his elbow, the old lead latticework giving way easily. We were through.

We gaped, silenced by the atrocity we had committed as much as by the antique beauty of the empty church. Below us was the altar, deep and wide, mahogany topped with white, veined marble. The pews had been removed a century ago, when a new cathedral was built to employ the famine-stricken and also when the need to flaunt a turreted, spired neo-gothic fortress on the highest point above the town seemed most urgent. There, too, it could serve the dual purpose of almost touching heaven and annoying Protestants. What remained here was a simple cream-walled space, at the back of which was a deep marble font, surrounded by small statues of the apostles and thronging angels. Above them, suspended by a fine chain, was the Holy Ghost in all his finery, golden rays sprouting from the dove form and directed at the font over which babies' heads used to be doused.

Anton was the first to spring down to the altar.

'Crikey,' he whispered, dropping nimbly to the floor. Tara and I followed but remained on the altar.

'What if we're caught?' she asked before leaping to the floor.

'Don't be silly. We won't be,' I replied, annoyed at any censure. Why did people always have to spoil anything interesting, I wondered. Why did they worry so much about doing the right thing, about being good?

'Nothing's going to happen,' Anton calmed her from the floor of the church, his voice echoing around the arched ceiling. Then he drew a tin whistle from underneath his jumper and tested it by hooting once or twice. The sound was thrilling. Tara and I begged him to play. He raised the instrument to his lips and began to make sounds. It was nothing recognisable. I knew he was just messing, that this was nothing learned at Mrs Blundel's musicianship hour, but it had rhythm and it gathered momentum, and his body swayed in harmony. It was then I began to love my cousin Anton, feelings of extreme fondness and affection flooding through me, because I knew that our blood was the same, our inclinations rooted in something similar. I didn't fall in love with him for another fifteen years, by which stage I had stopped loving him. It took a long time for the two loves to flow as a single current, for us to discover who we are today.

I danced on the altar, my arms stretched high, fingers curved, limbs raised, back arched to the sound that flew to the full height of the roof. Tara looked on and smiled, regarding us as if from a distance – at least that's how I remember the moment when I sensed her incomprehension, if not her disapproval, of our antics. Turning and circling, I caught sight of the fresco depicting the ascent into heaven. It showed Christ in his purple robes. They flowed and shimmered around his feet so that I wondered how they stayed on. Cherubs and angels spun around him as if they too were dancing to Anton's music, happy and delirious with unnamed joy. The Holy Ghost hovered above his head in the way he always hung around people's heads, and high above was Michael the Archangel, brandishing a sword, his brow furrowed as he glared fiercely at a group of cowering pagans on the far side of the image, his hand pointing heavenwards. I began to grow dizzy, but Anton played on after I had collapsed flat out on the altar, my eyes drifting slowly over the ceiling. Only then did I notice the matted cobwebs, and also, more worrying, bats.

Just then, someone banged abruptly at the door. The fluted curve of the handle began to rattle.

'Who's in there?' a serious voice demanded. We stared at one another. Tara's face was white.

'It's all right, don't cry,' I said, pinching her arms. She ignored me.

'Us,' she replied.

'Who's us?' the voice demanded again. This time she remained silent because Anton held his hand tightly across her mouth while I grabbed her legs. She flailed angrily with both arms while we struggled to keep her quiet. Anton's eyes pleaded with me to do something. I shook my head vigorously, indicating silence. We remained like that for perhaps fifteen minutes, only gradually loosening our hold on Tara, by which time the voice, which I had recognised as belonging to my pious Uncle Kevin, had taken itself elsewhere. By then the bats were flitting above us, Tara was sniffling and we knew it was time to leave. We shinned up to the high window again, pulling and shoving at Tara to lift her clear of the altar. It has always seemed to me that Tara was deliberately helpless then and still is, and that her reward has been a relaxed, orderly life.

Needless to say, we were caught and punished. Uncle Kevin, who frequently took a detour through the old graveyard after his evening prayers in the cathedral, had recognised Tara's voice, assumed that her brother and I were also present and reported accordingly to our parents. Anton and Tara are my second cousins, our parents were on very friendly terms, and the four of them awaited us at my house when we breezed in as if nothing had happened. Tara got off the lightest, considered to have been led astray by two extremely bold older children, Anton was whacked around the legs by his father and I was thoroughly shaken and shouted at, my parents useless as ever when it came to doing anything firm or disciplinary. They went through the motions of being very cross just to show Tara and Anton's parents that they were not softies and knew their duty. I have never been convinced that they did know their duty, but I always loved them because they were so ineffective in Irish terms, because they spoiled me and because to my mind I was spoiled usefully in terms of my future.

Anton and I left school the same year and headed into different careers, if you could call mine a career. I spent one year in Trinity College, acquired a new accent, failed everything but met people whom I considered to be interesting and worthwhile company, and joined the drama society. I was a regular in the various pubs up and down Nassau Street and Lincoln Place and got to know Anna Capriano, whose family still lived in our town and had sent her at great expense to do a course in dress design. Through her I got in touch with Anton again, because they were going out together and seemed to have a rather sedate relationship in which Anton conformed to the Italian mode of courtship. Most girls I knew were either passionately in love, trying to be passionately in love or in the middle of a break-up with one of the poets who lectured us, flattered us, told us we had enormous potential, then dropped us as soon as we began to believe it.

By then, I wasn't really interested either in Anna or in her oppressive family; my sights were fixed more firmly on Anton and I was fascinated by the apparent order and discipline of his academic life as an economics student. I'd imagine him doing something else, like music, arts or oriental studies, but never economics. He took a huge and unwarranted interest in Anna's work, which charmed me and fit my perception of him as a fluid, artistic, sensuous animal. He had grown handsome, slimly built but firm, his hair brown and wavy, the structure of his face and jaw Grecian in proportion. He was very much my aesthetic ideal. What of it if he had chosen economics, I would think, watching him help Anna select samples of fabric from the little pattern books she kept in her bag, observing him finger the satins and velvets, brushing the soft yarns with his fingers.

Tara remained at home to work in the local branch of an insurance office. She had never shown any inclination to move away and got married to a production assistant at the creamery some time after I failed the September repeats. They built a pleasant, airy house outside the town, and within two years her first child was born. Now she has five and her husband heads the production team and travels abroad to stroll around dairies and inspect yoghurt-making machinery in Denmark, Germany and the Netherlands. They are a happy couple. He likes to assume control and treats her as if she was his daughter, but Tara has always liked being looked after, so she's lucky to have found someone who likes to do it. We meet at Christmas in one of the local hotels, when practically three generations of people who either left the town for Dublin or emigrated return and attempt, over a drink, to re-establish points of contact. Those hours are full of 'Do you remember?' and 'Will you ever forget the time when … ?', so it's natural that we almost always recall the day we broke into the church and danced on the altar. Of course, as Tara remembers it, she danced on the altar too, but that is not the case, she merely looked on. Even more surprising, she seems to have completely forgotten how Anton gripped and almost smothered her with his hands while I held her legs – perhaps that's as well.

'We had great fun then,' she mused last Christmas, swirling her cocktail thoughtfully.

'Mmm,' I replied, reluctant to remember.

'You were always imagining things,' she said then, looking at me. I refrained from referring to her failure to imagine anything and forced myself to smile.

'Anton was as bad,' I said, nudging him. She didn't like that. Even though we're married, she regards me even today as a bad influence, someone who may have led him astray at a critical point in his development. Our failure to divide and multiply as she has done seems to reinforce her doubts, even though she insists on regaling me with statistics about the various syndromes that can strike families where the blood ties are too close. Second cousins, according to Tara, are more at risk than first cousins.

'He was impressionable,' she replied, as if Anton's fall from grace must be explained. I held my silence, wishing he would speak for himself. Unexpectedly, he did.

'No, just a bit different,' he said.

'You were impressionable,' Tara insisted, her eyes darkening.

'I found what I was looking for all the same.' He linked my arm companionably through his. I glowed, despite some discomfort at witnessing the mild frisson of disagreement between them.

'He found me!' I almost crowed at her, but she looked through me as if she hadn't heard.

That's the way our relationship has always been. It must be asserted, affirmed and reaffirmed through other people, through responding to sometimes tactless comments. Most of them don't know all that much about us, and those who do are wary of Anton and half-afraid of me because I possess what is known as a 'vicious tongue' and make short work of petty prejudices.

Anton's affair with Anna Capriano continued but was from my point of view an outrage. By that time I was head over heels in love with him, admiring the way he sailed through his examinations, the way he looked and the way he was somehow inexplicably different. I worked sporadically with fringe theatre groups, independent troupes who hoped to shatter many of the cherished theatrical orthodoxies with a brave new vision. Critics no longer daunted me, for what could they know about acting unless they had experienced the living moment on stage as we actors did? Besides, there was enormous safety in the jocosity of our numbers. My main preoccupation was to get a decent part in something as we moved from season to season, and generally speaking, I managed. Anton saw me play Salome, the best part I had ever had, and there's no doubt now that it changed everything. I was fitter than ever before, conscious of the effect my dance before King Herod exerted on the audience. I knew what it meant to be in the right place at the right time, to feel the life flowing in my veins. Anton told me afterwards that it woke him from his sleepy relationship with Anna and pulled him out of himself as nothing had done before.

Our wedding was short and unceremonious, our families and close friends filling the front pews of the cathedral in our hometown. Tara read a poem, chosen by Anton. It was Vaughan's 'Peace', which perplexed me with its references to 'a Countrie far beyond the stars' and the 'beauteous files', presumably of the blessed. Yet I was happier than at any time in my life, although I would be sadder again before long.

'Oh Anton, Anton!' Tara cried on his shoulder in the church doorway afterwards. 'Do be careful, whatever you do.' She wept openly and with a sadness which left me perplexed, her mascara running in muddy rivulets on either side of her little nose.

'Look after him now!' she whispered fiercely, catching my wrists, matronly in a blue Jaeger dress and a matching hat which sat like a plate balanced horizontally on the crown of her head.

'Of course I will,' I assured her, noting that that was the third time I'd been asked to look after Anton in the general mêlée, with rice and confetti settling around us in the October air. It was what they called an Indian summer, the days full of translucence, every saw-toothed leaf tawny and fragile. On our way to the country house where the reception was held, we passed the old graveyard. The church was unchanged, but there was a grid across every window that would have made it impossible to force an entry. Anton looked at me. I nodded.

We stayed late that day, remaining with our twenty guests, who seemed in no great hurry to leave, then watched fireworks and the glow of distant bonfires on the horizon. There was nothing for Anton and me to hurry for, at least; the physical side of our relationship had long been established, so the urgency of new passion was slightly muted. Still, by midnight he was pressing my arm, the pupils of his eyes large and shining. We slipped away to our room and left the others to their memories and the maudlin conversations which set in at the closing stages of weddings.

Part of my attraction to Anton has always been governed by a dull recognition that there was something about him which defied revelation. Over the next two years, although we were occupied and in most respects content, I felt something amiss. Looking back now, I believe that some part of me knew, but uneasy about possible implications, had refused to acknowledge the truth. There had been signs, simple things, all along. I worked as irregularly as ever, occasionally striking lucky for a few months, but otherwise just looking on. I was particularly unhappy about not being chosen to play Aggie in *Dancing at Lughnasa*, which was to tour America. Resigned to tricking about with unchallenging roles, I returned home earlier than expected one Saturday morning after reading for a cameo which didn't in the least interest me.

'I'm ho-ome!' I called upstairs. Anton's work is tiring and he often rests late on a Saturday. I heard rustling sounds. Thinking he was teasing me by remaining silent, I took the stairs in twos, turned the landing and was stopped in my tracks.

He emerged from the bathroom. Clearly he hadn't heard me. He wore my silken robe. It fell open to reveal my one and only white Agent Provocateur bra, with matching suspenders and lacy pants, dark glossy stockings covering his legs. His face was fully made up, the eyes enhanced and made huge by eye shadow and mascara.

'Let me explain,' he almost pleaded, as shocked as I was.

I stood, slack-jawed, unable to utter a sound. Attempting to pull myself together, I began to laugh, to treat it as a joke.

'Good one, baby, really good – is this your evening attire?' I bent double, desperately hoping he'd agree, say it was all a joke, even if in bad taste. He stood watching me, then turned and walked into our bedroom, mincing effeminately in patent high heels which I registered as not being mine. I followed blindly. My breathing came in short little gasps as I went up to him and punched him in the chest, full on one of his ridiculous stuffed satin breasts.

'What the hell are you at?'

The words squeezed from my throat. I recognised symptoms of stage fright in myself. He said nothing. I struck him again, this time more forcefully.

'Tell me!' I whispered, my face wet with tears as I observed the man of my dreams who had been the boy of my dreams, whom I had always, always adored as if he were a pagan god because he was so exceptional and so very lovely. People don't often describe men as 'lovely' or 'beautiful', but he was all that and more – elegant, erect, fully male.

'Why didn't you tell me?'

'I tried. Couldn't get it out.'

'Does anybody else know?'

The question was prompted not by fear of what people thought so much as a possessive need to be the first, the first to the experience I found so utterly repulsive.

'Yes.'

I began to feel faint. Someone else knew him better than I.

'Who?' I whispered, then more angrily, 'Who, for Christ's sake?'

I knew the answer without his telling, then felt all the angrier, all the more astounded.

'You can't be serious,' I stuttered, rage rising like a white heat in my chest. He nodded slowly. Tara. Dear, innocent, helpless Tara, who understood nothing and was supposedly shockable, an impression she herself did little to allay. I would have preferred if it had been an affair, could have coped somehow with another woman, could deal with a sexual competitor. But this was beyond me. I hated them both for the collusion, Tara in particular for letting me patronise her, for never asserting that part of her personality which was ingenious, interesting, which I might have liked had she let me. It struck me, not for the first time, that the brightest of women subvert their talent into cunning and silence, as if they possessed no other means of power. That was Tara. Clued in from the start, tolerating, indulging my uninhibited nature, allowing me to think myself more perceptive than she, all along hugging a secret, avenging herself in silence.

'That traitor!' I muttered, slumping onto the bed beside him. 'Your rotten sneak of a sister could at least have told me, the poxy bitch!'

He sat there, absurd, his face plastered inexpertly with

my make-up. I tore around the room then, my limbs frozen yet violent, plundering drawers, wardrobe, turning automatically to his bedside cabinet.

'There's nothing in there,' he said calmly. 'Try the other room.'

He took a packet of cigarettes from the pocket of my robe and lit one. I burst across the landing and into the spare bedroom. Still, I found nothing.

'Try the recess,' he said helpfully.

The recess was where we kept wine, Christmas decorations and boxes of useless items bought in second-hand shops, things like old photograph albums we liked to rescue so that they'd have a home. The bottles broke on the carpet as I tossed them free of the two racks on which they rested, the air tangy with the scent of fermentation. I didn't care. Carpets, furniture, nothing mattered. Then I found it, a medium-sized box. It contained everything: basques, suspender belts, bras, garters, slips, shimmering sets of knickers, silky stockings.

'You louse,' I said simply, rising and turning towards where he stood in his finery, the silk robe still open. 'And for God's sake close that thing and spare me the view!' I snapped, leaving the room to pour myself a whiskey, cheated without fully understanding why. Hours later, I could hear him upstairs, scrubbing the wine stains from the carpet. I pitied him then.

The funny thing was, we didn't sleep apart that night. I thought I'd want to, that he'd want to.

'I suppose I'd better move into the other room,' he said.

It didn't work out like that at all. We were still friends. In the middle of the night, we found ourselves embracing. We made love and found relief of some kind. I could still smell traces of cold cream from where he'd removed his make-up. Afterwards, I stroked his face, half-healed, but not fully. It was a moonlit night. I could see the outline of his brow and cheekbones. Inexplicably, I thought of that day in the church, when we were children, and Anton's comment about forgiveness, even if we were to encounter Mrs Blundel in the next life. We both had plenty to forgive.

'When did it begin?'

'You'll be surprised if I tell you,' he said, turning on his side, leaning in on my stomach.

'Tell me anyway.'

'Around the time we broke into that church. You, prancing up and down on the altar like some kind of demented sprite.' I had looked wonderful, he told me, intriguing, feminine but wild, my skirt lifted in what he now called 'feathery wings'.

'So?'

'You whirled about and I saw your underwear.'

'Jesus Christ,' I groaned.

He listed the garments. A slip, the loose bloomers my mother had made me wear. 'It was the first time I'd noticed women's things, how soft and colourful they were. It's not sexual, you know, not the way you imagine anyway,' he faltered. 'Would it have made a difference if I'd told you?' he asked then.

I turned away from him. Angry with myself as much as anything. Cheated. I needed to think. He went on and on about the freedom women have and about the freedom they've taken for themselves.

'I don't know,' I answered sulkily.

Today the underwear is still a big consideration. We buy together and we budget for the best, which he approves of. Sensuousness can be expensive. The only thing I refuse is to accompany him down Grafton Street on a Saturday morning, when he's rigged out fully in a Max Mara dress and French Connection boots. I can't bear the possibility of running into someone who knows us, of observing them peer with curiosity at his jaw-line. The street is thronged with the young and fashionable, with pickpockets and photographers, with fortune-tellers, flower-sellers, people linked to our most private dreams. Who knows what could happen. The best I can offer is an opinion on which skirt or dress is more suitable, which shoes are definitely out, which stockings enhance his legs. Once a week the house reeks of depilatory cream. He refuses to avail of the clean swipe of a razor, as I do, on the grounds that it makes the hair coarse. He dislikes the pain of waxing.

Once a year, we holiday abroad. On certain days we stroll as girlfriends through the streets of ancient ports along the Mediterranean. On others we drift as lovers. Either way, there are churches to be visited as a matter of course, where we sit and thrill to the sound of organ music, from *bel canto* to cantatas or a cor anglais vaulting into the baroque spaces above our heads. There is *fresco secco* showing scenes of unadulterated joy in which everyone is either robed flowingly or naked. Then the splendid altars, exotic gargoyles, chorales of angels designed centuries ago by extravagant Italian sculptors. Finally an ancient dance remembered, part of us stirring, strong pagans that we are.

Canticles

I saw Ottiline yesterday, for the first time in twenty years. The president had been ushered into the new Irish Conservatory of Music to unveil the plaque, flanked by the director and professors, the year's Performing Artist in Residence, the John Field Scholar, the Albinoni Scholar and the sponsorship organiser, when Ottiline glided past. She has risen to become senior lecturer and specialist in twelfth-century composition. I too am a specialist in twelfth-century composition. She inspired me to compose and play when all around me were damaging their tympani – blessed membranes of inner ecstasy! – to the sound of the Sex Pistols, Sid Vicious, The Boomtown Rats. She teaches medieval harp, fiddle and the organistrum. It is my privilege to mostly play these instruments. My diary is full for the next two years.

But before I became a music student, I discovered the *symphoniae harmoniae celestium revelationum*. Well, Mother did. One day, as she sat down to practice, she casually tossed a soiled wad of music sheets at me.

'You might have some use for those,' she muttered as

she opened *59 Best Loved Piano Pieces* and grimly flexed her fingers. She had discovered them inside the lid of her piano stool, a treasure for which she had trawled Francis Street, up the hill from where we lived. Having lobbed the yellowing manuscript into my hands, she began to attack Rachmaninoff's Prelude, Opus 3, No. 2, as it should never be attacked. I said nothing and brought the pages – fine as young skin! – into the kitchen. My bag lay on the table, bulging with Leaving Cert books. We were having boiled bacon and cabbage for dinner. I remember the clatter of saucepan lids that foamed and sizzled like lava while mother ran at Rachmaninoff. But old Rach would not be hers that day, despite her lusty *molto agitato*. I turned the knobs on the electric cooker to three, then, at the window, propped open by mother's hazel wand from the water divining days, I examined the manuscript, holding it to the light, separating the sheets. As I scrutinised each one and certain phrases sprang to life, something awakened in me – an excitement, a sense of being a link in a chain of events that I might have the capacity to complete.

Outside, leaves lay in crisp stacks against the walls of the opposite terrace. Crows cackled above chimneys. In the dining room off the kitchen, Mother reached the climax of her prelude. The dark lower notes growled their *fortissimo* and I knew that our neighbours would be hammering the walls again.

Father would sleep until half past four, despite the racket. He was working that night, as he had done every night since Les Trois Canards had taken him on.

'Holiyers next summer, girls!' he would say, rubbing his hands together. We ignored Father's predictions. For one thing, anxiety made him exaggerate, and for another, in the middle of an oil crisis, he refused to sling hash. He only worked in classy joints, with a foreign menu in ornate writing and an interesting wine list. So while Father slept and Mother played the piano, I trembled as I read the phrases, *O vis aeternitatis, O virga mediatrix, O viridissima virga.*

Six months on, my parents were able to tell their acquaintances that I was studying for a 'Bee Muzz'. Within a week in college, Ottiline became my tutor, Ottiline of the fleecy, shimmering hair, that undulant walk across any room, the trail of cigarillo smoke despite her asthma! She encouraged me. She hectored me. I thought of Richard Bonning working Joan Sutherland, or Van Karajan bullying his finest soloists. This was *it*, I thought, how it had to be.

One day as I practised the harp, she interrupted mid-phrase and broke my A string.

'You did that on purpose!' I gasped.

'And you're out of tune!' she screeched. 'For God's sake, keep your instrument tuned! If you can't hear properly, then you've no business here in this college.'

I resented that. I knew I could hear. Later, she apologised.

'It's just that I'm working on something – a version of an Oswald von Wolkenstein. It's' – her voice dropped, she chewed her lips – 'difficult.'

'Von Wolkenstein?' I felt giddy. 'I have something too – a find, a real find!'

She didn't ask what it was.

That night, I removed the manuscript from a box inscribed *Taken from Old Waterloo Bridge, London* – one of Mother's antique treasures, which Father, in an effort to brighten it up, had painted blue, inside and out. Ottiline would be able to tell me about the manuscript. She would help. I thought of her sensitive face, imagined her humming the Antiphons and Responsoriums, the Alleluias and *Lieder*, in the way she had, tilting her lovely head as she tried to hear the music. I had handwritten some of the words, which my old Latin teacher had translated into passable English.

The Spirit, life that gives life,
And moves all things
And is the root of every creature
Wiping away pain
And anointing wounds:
This is the radiant and admirable life,
Awakening and reawakening all things
To their most natural ecstasy!

Whoever wrote those words, that music, was an artist, a visionary. Certain phrases were worked and reworked, as if to induce an ecstatic trance in the listener. She – I always felt it was a woman – addressed the Virgin as a *virga*, or 'branch', or even a *viridissima virga*, 'a most verdant branch'. Ottiline had to see this.

Eventually, I brought her home. As we pushed open the narrow front door and negotiated the tiny hallway, I sniffed the air. To my relief, Mother wasn't cooking. Instead, she was waiting by the piano – poised, in fact – one elbow resting on the cracked inlaid mahogany, dressed to kill in mauve and turquoise satin. She swept towards us, arms outstretched.

'Oh, you're here! You're here at *last*!' she cried.

'We're here,' I replied casually. For a while that afternoon, her need for art and culture made her lose her sense of judgment. Because Ottiline was in the house, Mother was charming and funny. The effect would last for weeks, before the little black balloons that often trailed above her head descended again. Ottiline was pleasant enough, but she coiled herself back in the sofa as if she did not have to make any effort in our home. Her eyes swept over the piano, over Mother, around the little room. As Mother struggled in the kitchen with the fresh Java coffee, bought for the occasion in Bewleys, she looked faintly amused.

'What's funny?' I asked.

'Oh.' She wheezed a little, sliding fine hands into the pockets of her jeans. 'All this, I suppose. Not quite what I expected.'

'What did you expect?' I smiled, feigning calmness.

Before she could answer, Mother staggered in with an overladen tray, piled with cream slices, Danish pastries and our silver coffeepot.

'Oh, Mammy,' I whispered, 'that's heavy! Anyway, Ottie and I were going to make dinner soon.'

Inexplicably, Ottiline fixed me with a long, approving stare.

But she took what she felt to be her due, waiting as her coffee was poured as Mother spooned in the sugar, added a drop of milk. We sipped our coffee, made small talk. Outside on the street, buses tore past in a whirl of dust. Occasionally, one of the sellers would come down from Thomas Street market, her cartload of toilet paper or chocolate or flowers rumbling below our front window.

At eight o'clock the bells of Christchurch rang across the darkening city, the bolognaise was simmering and Ottiline had opened a bottle of Blue Nun. Mother nudged me.

'Show her, Anna, show her – you know!' she urged, excited as a child. I wanted to. I really did. Yet if Mother hadn't been there, I would have wriggled out of it. She sat happily, as if that manuscript marked my natural admission to a world that had been denied her. I laid the manuscript on the kitchen table.

'You know what I think this is?' I was bursting to tell her. The silver eye shadow she often wore made her lids ripple as she glanced quickly over the top page. Something in that glance made me wary, but then her amused look slipped back in place and she shrugged.

'So what is it?' she said lightly.

'It's sort of – it's connected to Hildegard,' I stammered proudly. She put the page down, lit a cigarillo and reached for the whole manuscript as if it was some old magazine. Nervous of that cigarillo, I gently removed it from her hand.

'Somebody's keen!' she whispered. Again she stared at the top page, eyelids glistening. Mother perched on the edge of the sofa. But something in Ottiline had sealed itself off from us. I watched as her face became an unlovely mask, bland with cunning.

She sighed and then spoke. 'That's not from the Sibyl of the Rhine, or any of her sibylettes either.' She actually chuckled. Her eyes fell again on the manuscript, 'It could be anything. It could be some menopausal Victorian having fun with vellum!'

I heard Mother's gasp. She began to pat her hair into place, her face suddenly flushed.

The words came slowly from my mouth. 'I don't – think – so.'

'Have you tried to date it?' Ottiline asked then.

'No.'

'Well then.' She looked relieved. 'And what have I told my Anna-Banana about the value of a little research, hmmm?' She smiled warmly as she tapped the back of my hand with her index finger.

'You're probably right,' Mother cut in.

'I have a friend,' Ottiline drew breath, 'who knows about such things. If I could,' she chose her words carefully, '*borrow* it?'

Mother was frowning. Then I stood up. 'I don't think so,' I said a second time.

'I *could* try—' she went on.

'No.' Mother was firm but gracious. 'Thank you.'

Ottiline turned to me then. 'Anna?'

'Oh,' I fumbled with the manuscript, avoiding her gaze. 'There's no rush, really. It's probably nothing much. Menopausal rubbish, as you say.'

Slowly, I gathered the manuscript and replaced it in the blue box. Ottiline understood. Minutes later, an unfamiliar coolness possessed me as she moved calmly, rapidly down the street. Her cigarillo glowed red as she slid into darkness.

She was right about the value of research. Mine eventually confirmed that the influence of Hildegard von Bingen had, by the late twelfth century, reached the shores of Ireland, where a woman in the forests of Laois put ink on vellum and as a means of raising herself to ecstasy composed her own theology.

When I saw Ottiline yesterday, I thought of Mother's efforts to exalt the bizarre turmoils of *her* life. She now plays in grand style at her own grand piano. As most of the neighbours have gone, she makes plenty of noise. Developers have planned two apartment blocks on the street, with electronically operated gates. Our house, the only one left standing, will be buttressed tastefully between them. Father still waits on tables, in an Italian restaurant that employs the mature type of maître d'.

But time transforms us. A single disappointment finds a lifetime's compensation. One is able to observe from a distance the average humanity of a former god or goddess, whose feet of clay allowed us to go on. Yesterday, Ottiline and I ignored one another. We clapped, one of us with joy, the other with an asthmatic hiss, as the director read from the new plaque: 'This is the radiant and admirable life, awakening and reawakening all things to their most natural ecstasy!'

Passover

Practically every night since the first exhausted ones when the blood leaked out onto her damask nightgown, Rosanna dreamed of still, pale seas. Like a child, she would run breathlessly along the cliff paths, seeking a way to the water's edge. It was a sunny dream, with scattered tribes of summer visitors below on the sand. Children's voices were whirled high on the light wind, a brown and white terrier ran after a ball and Rosanna's body was bent on immersion in that sea. Sometimes Henry was with her, part of the dream. She accepted his presence without question.

One Saturday afternoon when the baby was eight weeks old, she drove over to Henry's place. It was her first visit in the six months since they'd met. Her mother had taken the baby for the day. She'd spent the morning drifting through the warm crowds on Grafton Street and she was still free, free, free. Accelerating across the canal bridge, she overtook a slow-moving scooter, then admired the exultant light that cascaded through the trees onto the windscreens of oncoming traffic. Not once did she relax her excited clench on the wheel. She adjusted her Ray Bans, sniffed at the tang of a new leather jacket draped over the passenger seat, then looked quickly in the mirror. Her hair flew in loose blonde wings around her shoulders, her cheeks drawn and hollow as if with a dark energy. Her eyes were shining and grey. As she scrutinised herself and the car wavered across the white line, an oncoming driver sheared past, horn blaring, then disappeared down Heytesbury Street, a snort of gleaming red, his face maddened. She swerved, barely missing a cyclist. The sound of the red car, followed by the sight of the cyclist's raised middle finger, jarred at her high excitement. Her whole body stiffened in the car seat, then slumped closer to the steering wheel.

'Jesus Christ,' she whispered to herself, 'when will it end?'

The only place she could get a bit of peace and quiet at the hospital was in the baths, especially the demi-tubs. That was her hideout, three or four times a day after the birth, a gushing, echoing haven which contained two such tubs and a standard long one. Conversation between the women, on the occasion that all three alcoves were occupied, was random and sporadic. The walking wounded, she remembered, would sink their bruised lower parts into a warm swirl, sigh and grow still behind plastic curtains.

She had never had a Turkish bath, but back in Washington, Marlene once told her of the exquisite release of handing one's careless flesh over to the hands of women who slough away every trace of time's recent deposits.

Marlene rarely exclaimed about anything. She had travelled from Timbucktoo to Termonfeckin, had boated down the Yangtze as well as the Corrib, never forgot her portable computer, her razor, her vibrator and an anti-spasmodic pill called Imodium. During labour, Rosanna thought fleetingly about Marlene's accurate yet unhelpful advice that every contraction meant you were one stage closer to the finishing line.

As she sat in the demi-tub, she would listen to the other women on the far side of the partition as they bathed. They were like escaped animals, stunned but functioning. When the water cooled, Rosanna would open the taps and blast more anodyne around her thighs.

Sitting there, she sometimes thought about Henry, about the way his forehead had puckered with disbelief, fascination and less nameable emotions the moment he'd laid eyes on the baby.

At the hospital, the ward orderly who emptied bins and mopped residues with sodden towels from the delivery ward floor told her he had once been a pork butcher. The nurses behaved towards him as if his maleness alone accounted for the condition of all the women in the hospital.

'Testosterone overload, if you ask me,' one of them said in an offended voice. 'Brings me out in a rash, he does.'

Rosanna did not dislike him. He understood some of the pangs of mind and body. She knew by the way he had flirted so casually the night before her induction, acknowledging what everyone else seemed to have long forgotten. He was perky. She imagined him down at his local, boasting about the things he knew about women.

The married women in the ward awaiting sections and inductions were surrounded by husbands, mothers and sometimes children. She rested for the last few hours of her pregnancy, blood pressure soaring, fingers tight and puffy, and sparred with the orderly. She did not feel alone. Henry had brought chocolate-covered brazil nuts and a damask nightgown, then left for a night shift at the pathology department up in James's.

Later, the blinds and curtains on the flats opposite were drawn, late spring blizzards ripped across the roofs of Dolphin's Barn, then cleared to reveal a mother-of-pearl moon fixed to a frozen sky. Rosanna could not sleep, anticipating the next day's certain events.

One morning nine months before, she'd invited the child's father back into bed. What she remembered now was a pink aura in the bedroom as sunlight washed through the slats of the blinds, rather than an act of any particular pleasure. She had hooked him around the waist with her arm, without knowing why, without thinking of possible consequences. The reasons for the gesture, she concluded, sprang from some prehistoric place of keen animal perception which never slept, alert to every pharmaceutical ruse designed to outwit the rhythms of the twentieth-century female body.

After the birth, they'd left her in the delivery room for a while, wrapped in cotton blankets, a dimmed light behind her head. The orderly chatted about his last job. Rosanna relaxed and flexed her feet gently beneath the blanket, propped her head with her left arm.

'So it's yerself,' he nodded, recognising her.

'How's the pork butcher?' she whispered by way of a reply.

'Ex-pork butcher,' he corrected, squeezing a mop.

'Pigs bleed like hell,' she said quietly.

'Yeah, bleedin' like a stuck pig, as they say.'

She watched as he mopped and squeezed, mopped and squeezed, pictured him slicing a dead, bled pig down the middle with a glistening cleaver, splitting the sternum, separating a symmetry of ribs and pelvis until the animal lay in halves, like an enlarged, Technicolor Rohrschach image.

'Have you ever looked into a pig's eyes?' she asked drowsily.

He paused, his gaze earnest. One of the nurses poked her head around the door. 'Are you nearly finished in here yet?'

He raised his eyebrows and made a clicking sound with his tongue as the door swung closed. 'Nice girl, that. Don't know what's wrong with her. Now where was I? Oh, yes. Pigs. They're as intelligent as dogs,' he went on. 'Me missus has this bitch and I swear there's no difference between her and some of the pigs.'

'The dog?'

'Jayz,' he snorted.

'Did you mind doing it?'

'What?'

'Killing them.'

'They hardly know they're gone.'

She could see why he was at home in the maternity hospital. Women coming and labouring and going, one of life's greatest emergencies crafted to a medical art.

The first time she met Henry, he was poring over a newspaper in a cramped restaurant off Fownes Street, hungrily cramming a small chocolate Swiss roll into his mouth. Rosanna was five months pregnant. Something about the ripples on the chocolate as it disappeared into his mouth reminded her of the day she and Marlene visited the Hirshhorn Museum and Sculpture Garden at the Smithsonian.

She'd bought a Georgia O'Keeffe print called *Black Hills with Cedar*, which the artist painted while living in New Mexico.

Back home, it aroused mild consternation, even embarrassment. Her choice of souvenir unsettled and amused some of her friends. In time, it became a source of bawdy conversation at parties which had reached the point of no return. Initially, Rosanna had only seen hills fringed by a slightly ominous clump, unaware of O'Keeffe's alleged tendency to turn flowers and mountains into florid genital representations.

On The Day of the Chocolate Swiss Roll, she recalled the Hirshhorn's fabulous bronze anti-war sculptures. One in particular showed the heads and bodies of hundreds of soldiers mounted on a huge phallus.

While in America, she wasn't aware of pregnant women, unlike at home, where they were very much in evidence. Marlene wrote soon after the birth, in response to Rosanna's hastily scribbled SOS.

> *Rosanna dear, your letter arrived and the exhaustion you report is, alas, normal. Particularly when one is over 18 and without a man. I remember thinking I wouldn't survive it, but I did, and you will also. And life goes on. Despite everything (and maybe because of it), life goes on.*

The living and the dying, the about to live and about to die, held the world to ransom. Coming into life was like visiting a season. Perhaps when God created the world, he had imagined a season and called it Eden.

Eden first announced itself to Rosanna while she sat in the demi-tub at the hospital. Now she dreamed about

Eden every night between the baby's feeds. It had all the flora and fauna of springtime in the northern hemisphere. Blackthorn hedges prowled, crows cawed, poplar trees shivered, sturdy seaweeds trailed the piers of ancient estuaries and a vernal light danced on every surface, seeking apertures, crevices, dusty corners.

It was as if she had been reborn. She brimmed with something imponderable. Whatever it was, it felt dangerous. Yet she still pushed Henry away, gently but firmly. He'd call by on his way from the laboratory, freshly scrubbed after a day dissecting cadavers, removing organs bequeathed in advance of death. His attention, on top of everything else, was almost too much. When her visitors had left, after swamping her with good wishes, flowers and teddy bears, Eden would overwhelm her again. Sitting in the tub, she knew she'd been cut away from the past, had survived a primitive journey across a river of casual slaughter.

Rosanna slid beneath the surface of the water, felt it lap up along her neck, over her ears, finally over the top of her head. Beneath the surface, the sensation of warmth throughout her coiled body was so pleasurable that she realised she would have to postpone drowning in lieu of pleasure. She surfaced, took a deep breath and again submerged herself. It obliterated everything, the thundering sound of water pouring into cisterns somewhere above, random echoes from the corridor, the laughter of visitors come to scrutinise the newborn.

Seven months pregnant, she'd cycled to the shop late one evening, skidded and fell on a patch of ice. Monstrous ice-laden mists rolled up the river. For a split second, her head reeled as she lay on the road.

'Are you all right?'

It was Henry. For a while she said nothing, afraid to move until the child turned inside her again. He pulled her in as the traffic thundered across a nearby intersection.

'I'm fine,' she eventually replied, as near to tears as she had ever come in those months. 'You keep – turning up,' she added.

'This is my beat. Pathology's just up the road,' he said, helping her to her feet.

He insisted on walking the remaining stretch to the shop with her, wheeling the bicycle with his left hand, guiding her elbow with his right. Up the hill at Christchurch, bells pealed through the freezing fog. Traffic was at a standstill, each driver locked in an elongated metal capsule, breathing dampness and sulphur, bent on the homeward trail, thoughts focused on fires, television viewing, the prospect of rest.

She bought three Walnut Whips and two bars of orange chocolate. There were pink blotches on Henry's cheekbones and she caught a whiff of spirits from his breath. He paused once and turned to her, placed his hand gently on her stomach. To her surprise, she felt blessed by the touch of this near-stranger. Then, embarrassed, she asked him about his job.

'Nobody,' he said, turning puce, 'has ever before asked me why I do what I do.'

'I wonder why?'

'Bodies. People are afraid of dead bodies.'

She laughed. 'So they think you've a vested interest in death?'

'Something like that.'

He continued to guide her from the shop, until they

stopped outside a café. The smell of fish, chips and vinegar raged warmly from within Burdocks along the queue that wound around the street corner. Her stomach rumbled.

'Come on. You do need something to steady yourself.'

In Kennelly's Tea Rooms, she smelled soda bread and clovey apple tart. For the first time since she'd become pregnant, the aroma of strong tea did not make her stomach heave. She rested her chin in her hands and smiled at Henry.

She and Marlene visited the famous site at Appomattox. Marlene had rambled on about her ex-husband, whose new wife had the IQ of a piece of wallboard, was very sweet and perfect for him.

'Why do we do it, Rosanna, why the heck do we bother with 'em?'

'Because they are different. Because they are other,' Rosanna had speculated.

The pork butcher-turned-orderly would be more impressed with the site at Appomattox than some of the people who came to view it before whizzing off to Monticello, President Jefferson's specially designed home. It was he who had worked ambivalently for the abolition of slavery while retaining his own retinue of black workers.

'How come you're no longer a butcher?' she'd asked in the delivery room, after the midwife took the baby to warm up in an incubator.

'Business went bust.'

'So what brought you here?'

'It's a job.' He shrugged, then cocked his head and looked at her quizzically. 'If you wanted to cook marrowfat peas, how would you cook them?'

‘*What?*’

‘Would you steep them overnight with the white tablet, or what?’ He propped his chin on the mop handle.

‘Ah, fuck off.’

‘Go on. Serio, like.’

‘What kind of a stupid question is that?’ she asked as the blood spurted beneath her onto the brown wadding the nurses had slipped beneath her exploded, new-stitched perineum. She regarded her hands, fingernails ridged with dried blood, her left hand and arm streaked with it. The smell was sweet as a balm.

‘Just to see if you’d make a good wife,’ he muttered and resumed his labours.

Unhesitatingly, she told him that she’d go right out and buy a tin of marrowfats, pre-cooked. He rolled his eyes, smiled sadly, then shook his head.

The ward orderly’s experience would be welcomed between the covers of a hardback novel or a slim volume of angry poetry, particularly if he dared to articulate it himself. Yet the difference between his written life and his lived one was like the difference in distance between the Milky Way and Andromeda.

Her most physical and violent work over, she watched him idly, imagined a future for her child, her daughter. Yet the future, she knew even then, could be terminally shocking. She took a deep breath. More blood spurted from her.

Take it day by day, lady, she hushed herself. *Enter Eden. Remember Eve.*

In the weeks after the birth, she struggled to contain the panic of her love. She was wet with it, sweating with it, hot with it. Even her nipples pranced with it. Was it for the child alone? There seemed so much feeling that the only way she could cope was by lavishing her excesses on

Henry. If only he'd stayed away instead of pursuing her, she might have felt calmer. Yet she kept phoning him, at any hour of the day or night, whether he was in the laboratory or in his bed. One night when the baby almost choked because the teat on the bottle let the milk run too freely, she rang him in a panic, her body trembling uncontrollably. The child had gone purple in her arms. Rosanna had held her in the air like a doll, tried desperately to remember what to do. Was it the Heimlich method or did she hold the little creature upside down and rub her back vigorously? In the end, the baby coughed and spluttered, then cried, and everything was all right. Henry came over anyway and slept on the sofa. Every time he smiled, she feared she might collapse against him or beg him to hold her and mind her forever. She wanted to be held. Yet she could not ask him, not yet. She remembered Eve in Eden, what her first spring must have been like after the birth of those awful brothers.

Rosanna and Marlene saw the servants' quarters behind houses dating from the Civil War – pristine, whitewashed little shelters which would have been stifling in summer and freezing in winter. They didn't look so bad until she heard how many black servants they housed at one time. Meanwhile, up in Monticello, Jefferson worked on his inventions. He had a bed built into the thick wall which separated the bedroom from the study. In that way, whenever an interesting possibility struck, he could leap straight from bed to study.

Before, Rosanna used to regularly hop from bed in her night-clothes for preliminary work on some plan, a fan heater blowing across her bare feet as she sat at the computer. Now the central heating was on day and night for the baby. And she had to sleep.

In Washington, she'd sat in McDonald's with Marlene after a visit to the Torpedo Factory. The Smithsonian was high culture and Torpedo Factory was hands-on but definitely lower culture. Marlene had talked about her plans to have a second family some day, she wasn't sure when exactly, but some day, if her biological clock hadn't stopped ticking.

'Who'll be the father?' Rosanna asked.

'More like who'll want to be father,' Marlene grumbled. 'The choice isn't limitless, I guess.'

Outside, it began to drizzle. The last stifling fall days had ended. Temperatures plummeted overnight and Rosanna had bought a cardigan in a shop off Independence Avenue. In a matter of hours, the cicadas went silent, signalling an end to thirsty days and the beginning of freezing nights. The two women paused for a moment, their eyes drawn to the street outside. The silence continued longer than it should have. They watched, transfixed, as a wizened Vietnamese man tottered past the window, feet rag-bound and filthy, his body emaciated.

'In some parts of the world, people work magic in order to ease suffering,' she told Henry. 'Remember that bit in *The Right Stuff*?'

'A cinematic trick,' he scoffed.

It was the film's climax, the critical moment when the astronauts are locked within their capsule, far from Earth. Images of bushmen chanting around a bonfire intersperse the high-tech action. At the point of maximum danger, one of the astronauts witnesses an inexplicable drift of sparks around the spaceship, brilliant as fireflies. The men are saved because (the viewer is expected to deduce) the Aborigines had intervened.

Rosanna had speculated about the Aborigines, the Carmelites and unorthodox priests banished to outposts of either Ireland or the Third World, psychics and healers within every community. Why, she wondered, could a blazing Aboriginal bonfire, a pointed bone or a possessed dancer leaping over hot coals not relieve the hunger and pain of an ancient Vietnamese man thousands of miles from his home? During her delivery, when she had felt like a cornered animal, the thought of the Aborigines flashed through her mind, but most of all the sense of having been conned.

Now, she pulled up on the broad footpath outside a renovated building above the brewery, braked hard and switched off the car engine. She sat for a moment, wondering if she should go home again. Her gaze rested on a small holly hedge that scratched and tapped at the building's low windowsills. She had no right to be away from the child, out gallivanting with Henry. The blaring car horn, the accusing face of its driver, the cyclist she'd almost hit as a result, were still vivid. It took so little to make her feel small, to sense her energy in retreat to God knows where.

The drone of traffic rose from below on the quays. It was too late to turn back. Henry stood in the doorway, making funny welcoming gestures.

'Where's baby?' he called out.

She stepped stiffly from the car. 'With my mother,' she replied, 'I didn't think …'

'Never assume anything, Rosanna. Never assume.' He smiled, wagging his forefinger. 'I wanted to see the little witchette, you know.'

She shrugged and made an apologetic face. It was too late now. Once inside, she removed her jacket, tossed her hair back from her shoulders and looked around.

She eyed the bottle of Bordeaux, two glasses and the

cheese laid on a low table. Henry fiddled with the CD player, then turned as a thought struck him.

'Do we need music?'

'I don't know. Do we?'

'Hmm,' he deliberated. 'Perhaps not.'

She sighed, relieved. Atmospheric music might break her. The room had absorbed the odours of all the meals Henry ate while watching satellite television late at night. Despite herself, she sniffed. Chips and spag bol, curry, eggs and toast and garlic. A musty odour that she could not quite define underpinned everything.

'Mice.'

'Mice?'

'I saw you sniffing,' he explained. 'Mice. An interest of mine. No doubt you hate them.'

'Actually, no. Never assume.'

They laughed.

A scrap of bacon rind curled from beneath the table and a succession of yellow notelets stuck to the cracked glass panels of a bookcase. In Eden it was the apple that did it, not the serpent, she thought. Eve didn't need a bloody reptile to draw the attention of historians and scholars to the phenomenon of an exploring feminine conscience.

Rosanna's body was tired. Leather boots kicked and marched once more within her breast. Henry passed her a glass.

'Hell, I shouldn't. It makes me want to sleep.'

'You can do that here. Nod off,' he said quietly, pouring, not looking at her.

She flopped back against a cushion. She had pushed a child to life, yet there had been a death. Despite that death, she would explore Eden, she must ascend to meet it. It was like choosing to love or not to love the child, to live or to die. There was no choice.

'So what'll we do?' she smiled at him, stirring herself.

'Nothing.'

'Nothing?'

'You're too exhausted.'

Suddenly, the new leather jacket, the Ray Bans, even her long hair, made her feel silly. Her skin was as slack as his but for different reasons. She wanted to be held and she wanted to weep like a child battered for no reason, beaten black and blue with no court of appeal, ripped to pieces by the birth of a baby.

Her baby. Child. Daughter.

They sat and gossiped for an hour. He made no attempt to touch her. Gradually, she felt better.

Later, she drove away, hair dishevelled, cheeks livid from wine and the unexpected exertion of hunting for an escaped mouse. Henry had blathered on about dominant and recessive genes.

She chugged into the sunset, snared in the traffic near the estuary bridge. Unlike Jack Kerouac, she wasn't on the road anywhere but to her mother's to pick up the baby.

That night, for the first time in eight weeks, the baby slept right through. Rosanna slept and sweated. Sometimes her shoulders twitched, her eyelids rolled and darted as she dreamed about the hot bush country, watched shoals of sparks drift into a southern midday. Already, the future beckoned. Eden had come and the world was ablaze; the pylons and satellites, the pulses and connections were alive and singing above and below field and savannah, jungle and mountain. Night passed effortlessly into dawn. The angel of despair had passed her door without stopping, daubed as it was with the blood of new life. The baby snuffled and turned. Rosanna stirred.

'Let me hold you. I just want to hold you,' she whispered in the frail light.

She swung the baby from its creaking basket beside the bed, leaned into the warmth of its drowsy body, her lips brushing the down on its head. She inhaled the scent of her waking child.

Charlie, St Joseph, Big-Hands & God

A single plank bridged the pool of rain water outside the house every winter. It reminded her of the plank she'd once thrown across a rock pool in Antigua, on the brink of finding her first ever *Tectus nilaticus*, the hat-shaped shell with bands the colour of dried blood. Now the plank dipped and creaked beneath Charlie's weight as he raced down the steps with Eva in his arms. Rosaleen followed, almost slipped, then steadied herself. Between them, they forced Eva's body along the back seat of the car.

On the main road, Charlie accelerated. Rosaleen bent over the convulsing child. The blue eyes stared blankly, pupils huge, the throat worked, released uncontrolled gushes of sound.

They'd have to give the toys away – if others would accept the playthings of a dead child. She thought of the house, silenced by Eva's absence. She imagined the bedroom air sucked clean of infant smells – powders and creams, the sticky odour of spilled Calpol from times when her sleep-drugged hand would pour shaky spoonfuls in the middle of the night.

Blood trickled from Eva's nostrils: Rosaleen willed herself silent. It felt like a punishment for the times she'd looked forward to turning undistracted to her work again.

'Woman, there's more to life than shells and stones,' Charlie would mutter.

But life had a way of fulfilling almost every wish, if not quite in the manner one wanted. People everywhere neglected what they most loved. Hadn't they forgotten the glad moment of Eva's arrival, a thing as rare as it was common, as triumphant as it was overshadowed by the planet's important doings?

Rosaleen grasped the child's stiff fingers as the car lurched along. She felt for a pulse. It was pebbly and rapid beneath narrow, stiff wrists.

The doctor smelled of work and fatigue. He took the child and made soothing sounds, then swiftly cracked open a syringe and answered Charlie.

'No, she's not going to die.'

Diazepam, inserted rapidly. The small body relaxed. Rosaleen wiped the child's cheeks with her knuckles, watched the dazed, rolling eyes.

'Is she blind?' she asked.

'She's disoriented,' the doctor said lightly. 'Her brain is flooded with heat. Best take her to the hospital.'

'Smile for Daddy,' Charlie waved across the room. The skin on his face quivered at the child's titanic struggle. Her eyes rolled, words without edges tumbled from her mouth and tongue, primitive *oooh-aaah-werrgh-ghaaaa* sounds as the storm blew off her brain and up into the stratosphere.

In casualty, parents, bawling juveniles, smells.

'It could be a couple of hours,' the young nurse smiled.

Rosaleen headed for the canteen, left Charlie and Eva on a leatherette couch. The walls were hand-painted with familiar heroes. Mickey Mouse. The Seven Dwarfs.

In the corridor, she raked her memory when a familiar-looking woman in a hound's-tooth mini-suit passed from the opposite direction.

Then the muggy canteen air hit her full in the face. She recalled a time when she'd been determined to sail and shell hunt, to comb humid tropical shores – whatever it took – to find her treasures. Shells were a mixture of the divine and fleshly. Descriptive words like *posterior canal* and *spire* put them in context, betrayed the nature of objects which could digest and transcend at the same time. Now she ignored shell and cornucopia-shaped pastries filled with jam and cream, bought a mug of coffee, a chocolate bar and an orange. Her lip wobbled as she sat to peel the fruit. A blood orange. Eva loved them. *Tectus nilaticus*, she repeated sternly. *Think Tectus nilaticus. Tectus nilaticus, nilaticus, nilaticus.* She gulped the coffee and the contraction in her throat subsided.

She split the orange in quarters, kept a couple of red-banded crescents. She considered Eva's pleasures. Ice cream, chocolate, chips, oranges. Yoghurt in the absence of ice cream. Oranges in the absence of chocolate. *Crescent, first quarter, gibbous and full.* Her own mother had demonstrated the phases of the moon by using an orange.

A figure at the far side of the canteen distracted her, someone more remote than the unidentified woman in the corridor. Yet recognition was easy. Davnet O'Reilly, unchanged in twenty years, the little self-conscious tilt of a head as she chatted with colleagues.

Davnet came straight over. Aware of looking haggard, Rosaleen wished she had a bit of make-up to hand. Then she heard her own voice boom, 'I thought it was you, but I was afraid it mightn't be!'

Davnet laughed. 'And there was I over at the table saying to someone, I *know* that girl from *somewhere*!'

This was Davnet's court, the palace of food, oils, sauces and beverages. From student hostel days, Rosaleen remembered the catering school vocabulary. Things to do with costing, food values, onion sauce and how to skin a chicken. They'd enjoyed Gilbert and Sullivan operettas when everyone else liked Thin Lizzy.

'Well, how are you? Every time I think of you I think of The Gondoliers!'

'Lord, that old stuff?' Davnet scoffed. 'Don't mind me, I'm barely back from maternity leave.'

'Married long?'

'Five years. Yourself?'

'Ten. Kids?'

'Five. Steps of stairs, twins included. Yourself?'

'One. That's why we're here.'

'Kids. Desperate, aren't they?'

Rosaleen nodded, then detested herself. 'Sometimes,' she compromised.

'Well, we're having no more. Lord, all I have to do is look at himself and I'm pregnant!' Davnet said.

'Time for the old snip-snip, what?' Rosaleen began to relax.

Davnet looked surprised. 'Oh Lord, I don't know if we'd go *that* far.'

The conversation died as rapidly as it had begun. Rosaleen grinned and got up to leave. Davnet, she guessed, had done her sums, and they totted up to a life.

'Orange,' she said lamely to Davnet, who stared at Rosaleen's left hand, 'for Eva.'

She watched as Davnet trotted off through the far door of the canteen. Their paths would never cross again. It struck her as odd that someone like that should have acquired such self-assurance.

Rosaleen thought of her own life at the faculty, the books and shell displays, computer discs filled with post-doctoral research. Her samples were arranged within slim, wooden-fronted drawers, annotated by hand in hard-backed science copybooks. Hardly anyone outside the faculty burned to know anything about shells and minerals. Now, she felt apologetic about her passion. She saw her colleagues' over-certainties as if for the first time, observed the smooth insincerity which was indispensable to many knowledgeable people.

On the way back to casualty, she almost collided with the mini-suited woman, who burst this time through the double doors carrying an X-ray.

Then she remembered, recognised her obstetrician's secretary in the unfamiliar territory of the children's hospital.

'Hello, Laura,' Rosaleen called. The woman responded in the way of someone more recognised than recognising, her face polite.

Just when she'd almost forgotten the obstetrician, his large hands. She didn't find it as hilarious as she felt she ought. She remembered a single, scalding emotion: adoration. The child, she thought, could have been osmotically conceived thanks to obstetric spores wafting secretly in the air, seeking her, finding her. Charlie was surplus to requirements. Charlie's paternity was a mere front to pacify an unforgiving world. A bit like the way God pulled a fast one on St Joseph when he wanted to impregnate Our Lady.

She passed a statue of a saint with an electric blue halo over its head. St Francis, she supposed. Or did he deal with animals? Still, children and animals, what was the difference?

Charlie deserved a rainbow of halos over his head for putting up with her and her epiphanies. Eva's birth, and a moment later the onset of *devotion*. Not to Charlie, but to old Big-Hands, the divinity who'd seen her through the pillaging of her posterior canals, which strongly resembled the pillaging of *Tectus nilaticus*'s canals by sea parasites.

Two weeks later she was tearing around the city in the car, leaving Charlie to handle the four-hourly feeds. Her left hand pumped in time to rock hymns from the 70s. The smile on her face was beatific. Instinctively, she knew that she must not speak of this madness to anybody.

Once, she pursued the obstetrician's olive-green car along the Stillorgan by-pass, but the sports model accelerated and finally broke the lights at Shankhill junction.

Since the business with Big-Hands, she understood how fanatics felt. She'd even told Charlie. One evening three weeks after Eva's birth, she slid weakly against the kitchen wall, groaned about being in love, watched his back as he poked at the frying pan. At first he'd said nothing. He listened, then turned and held her as she blubbed against his trembling body.

'I want to go away!' she sobbed.

'But where to, love? Where would you go in mid-winter?' he reasoned, then released one arm to poke the stir-fry again.

'I'm tired. Tired. Tired. *Tired*! I'm in love!'

'What about Eva?'

'I want to *die*!'

'What about Eva?' He juggled the vegetables around the pan again. It had infuriated her.

'Go to hell!'

'What about Eva, and,' he dropped his voice, 'and *me*?'

What about Eva and Charlie? They weren't the only ones to claim her. Not by a long shot.

She paused before turning again into casualty. At least her face didn't flash her psychological history in neon lights for everyone to ridicule. The presence of an erotomaniac had passed unremarked in the children's hospital. She had kept her nerve as nurses slipped by on quiet shoes, doctors with stethoscopes. Nobody but Charlie had known that she was temporarily bonkers. From her left, she heard the bawling, wailing and puking of the casualty department. She turned and watched as a father struggled to lift his son from a wheelchair. The boy howled, throwing his head from side to side, his mouth lax. She stopped then, felt a rushing perspective, a gravity that pulled her towards Charlie and Eva.

The doctor had been. Rosaleen expected X-rays and an overnight stay.

'It's very normal. She can come home,' said Charlie.

'So is a heart attack. So is cancer,' she grumbled.

On the way home, Charlie switched on the car radio. The evening anchorman badgered the Minister for Justice about the criminal underworld. Rosaleen dug deep in her pockets for some jellies, a soother, anything to please the child.

They slipped onto the motorway, listened as the Minister fought her corner. The traffic thinned as they passed Lucan and Leixlip. Then came familiar landmarks, an old barn and an obelisk; finally, the country road again. Eva slept. She glimpsed a farmer in a field, a newborn glistening lamb slung between his fingers.

The wheels of the car crunched on potholed tarmac as they approached the house. Rosaleen observed the broken slats of wood along the fence, the lopsided nameplate on the gate, how brittle the garden was in twilight. Weeds sprouted from guttering on the roof. In the front window, a Pacific conch rested between two ailing spider plants.

She made her way up the plank, over the puddle, waited while Charlie unlocked the front door. The child dozed against his shoulder. Rosaleen looked down. She could have wallowed in a vast puddle like that after Eva was born, preferably with the obstetrician, the pair of them floundering like two lovesick elephants. Anything to soothe the stinging passions of parenthood and something not quite lust, the need to lean in close to Big-Hands, to rest until a hurricane subsided.

The moment they got into the hall, Eva stirred in Charlie's arms.

'Down! Down!' she demanded.

They watched as the child waddled towards the kitchen, still in the nappy, vest and boots which was all she had on when the convulsion happened. Rosaleen pressed the button on the answering machine and listened to a message from her opposite number at Sheffield University, an invitation to join a field trip to Madagascar in November. She replayed the message, watched as Eva staggered back down the hall, small eyebrows dipped in a frown.

'Chips!' she yelled, opening her mouth, pointing to its pink, empty space.

'Chips,' Rosaleen smiled. Her hands trembled with relief, and not just for the child. For herself, that she had passed through her own sickness without being committed to an asylum. Back then, it was she who would have needed nursing, not the baby.

Well, it subsided. Above, birds on the telegraph poles. The vernal outpouring from throats and bills no longer upset her. She picked Eva up, wrapped her in an old jacket, then opened the front door again. Outside, a crescent moon tilted westwards. What was it people said? Something about making a wish and looking away. Because a waxing moon held in its belly the wet sac of the world's grief. And too much grief and longing gave rise to unlit swamps and puddles which light could never reach.

Border Crossing

I spend my life trying not to be a goody-two-shoes. It is 1974 and I am hurtling across the switchback hills of County Cavan in a fast car driven by a young man who is everything I ever dreamed of, even when I did not know what I was dreaming about. His name is Peter – a reliable name for a very unreliable young man. The car is metallic brown, with a long, gleaming snout, reclining seats and a good radio. At night, when we pull into some laneway or field, it plays Radio Luxembourg. Right now we're both humming along with Abba and 'Waterloo'.

Thanks to Radio Luxembourg, I have discovered one important thing about men. They can stop, when they really want to. They don't have to go *all* the way, or even part of the way. They are well able to pause in the middle of all that hectic touching and cuddling, even when the Danger Zone is involved, if something more interesting or important comes on the news. Current affairs, it appears, is my main competition.

On one particular evening, the news headlines are all about Intervention. Peter is knowledgeable about Intervention and cattle. Just when I am on the brink of passing out with the pleasure of his kisses, he stops suddenly.

'Hang on a wee minute,' says he, cool as you like, turning the volume up.

On another evening, we pass the house in which Senator Billy Fox has been murdered. I do not understand exactly why he was shot, but I know that it was brutal. The house stands darkened, so innocent and ordinary despite what has occurred. On many nights we drive along that stretch, tar and asphalt burning away beneath us as Peter accelerates – fast – to wherever we're going. I feel as if I'm at the centre of whatever is worthwhile in life. He has made me a woman, not by doing *it*, which we haven't so far, but through his kisses, the first of which removed the remnants of my childhood once and for all. The fact that he also wears no underpants beneath his trousers adds to his mystique. Seven years older than me, he is experienced. He has known many girls, but none like me, with what he calls 'education'. I have outlined my ambitions to him, and even if I am repeating the Leaving, I am determined to be a vet with my own practice.

'Yur not a womon, not yet,' he remarks with gentle authority one evening, 'yur still a gurl. Gotta lotta learnin' to do yet.' He goes on to compare me with a real woman who was older than him, but who would not commit herself one way or another. He says he loves her, that she is the only one. Because I am certain I will die if Peter dumps me, I barely comment.

Even though I am from the border area, there are things I have never noticed until now. I do not understand the kind of politics that occurs at the end of dances, when some fellows make people stand for the national anthem with their hands clasped behind their backs. The local girls take to the fellows from the North, to the wild-weed streak to them. They arrive in Cavan for discos or for Chicken in the Rough, in cars that play the first notes of 'Hitler Had Only One Big Ball' and 'Yankee-Doodle-Dandy'. The girls that come south are different too. They wear more make-up, and their platforms are higher than ours. The sleeves of their blouses are even more flounced at the wrists, their coloured denim jeans tighter and more flared. They remind me of returned adventurers, their way of speaking somehow smarter, their laughter out-laughing ours in knowingness and sophistication.

Out on the roads again, the Guards are about, checking who you are, where you're going and what your business is in the South. Peter knows most of them by now. He drives regularly across the border from his town to Cavan. There are discos on Sunday, Wednesdays and Fridays, which is where he met me.

'Well, Payther,' says one of them in a strong Munster accent, leaning in and looking quizzically at me.

'Och, yur all right, Jack,' Peter laughs, 'No bowms here. Only a blonde bowmshell, ha ha ha!'

'Off with ye so,' says the Guard.

We roar off into the night, along the shore road between the lake and the woods. I have drunk too much vodka. I roll my head along the headrest and close my eyes for a moment. I'm good for him, he sometimes says after a couple of Pimms No. Ones. Some part of me knows that this will be the night. We're crossing the border on our way to his house. By dawn, I'll be his and he'll be mine. Forever. I know he will love me if I give myself to him. It's as simple as that. I imagine us at some future point, farmer and vet respectively, cutting a dash at the Hunt Ball, the New Year's Eve Ball, the Horse Show Ball in the Shelbourne Hotel.

Peter's mother is Italian. She will not be at home because

she is visiting her sisters in Italy. I have never met her, although Peter has met my parents, neither of whom approves, but who manage to humour me in the hope that Peter will pass out of my life like a temporary, upsetting virus. At the end of our second date, my mother leaves out slices of chocolate Swiss roll and cups and saucers on a tray for us, even though Peter's father was a half-tinker who, years ago, pulled the wool over a visiting Italian girl's eyes, even though Peter himself is a wheeler-dealer farmer, and on no account to be trusted.

Peter is in awe of his mother. She has an octopus-like grip on him and his feelings. When he speaks about her, it sounds as if he is referring to royalty, or to someone who lives on a very high pedestal indeed. I am not good at paying homage to invisible women of influence who get in my way, neither the former girlfriend – the *real* woman – nor his mother. But I am curious. He is the first man I have ever met who fears and needs women in equal measure.

There's a ten-minute delay as we go through the checkpoint. I sit dead still until we go clear. Some people say the soldiers can hear every word that's spoken in a car. Frequently, when I go north with my mother, we deliberately speak to one another in crumbling Irish while crossing the checkpoint. I observe the khaki faces and bodies, the huge rifles, bullet-proof vests, aware that to my left two more soldiers are crouching down behind a bush. As I can clearly see both of them, that surely defeats the purpose of their hunkering down like that.

'Noime please, suh,' says another, squinting at Peter's licence. 'Wot's y'business, suh?'

'Dealer. A'm on m'way home.'

'And the young loidy?' He bends and takes a good long look, then winks at Peter.

'Gurlfriend. From Cavan. She's a nice wee gurl, don't worry, Corporal,' says Peter. The pair of them laugh, like boys who have just peeped up my skirt and are about to run away.

Finally, we get the all clear. The car zooms down the last stretch of road and Peter turns sharply into the gateway of his house, up the short, stony drive. It reminds me of pictures of houses in former British colonies, an old stone bungalow with gable windows and a south-west-facing veranda painted dark green, except that it's not half as smart. Little effort has been made to preserve outside appearances and ragwort sprouts all over the drive and the front lawn.

First, he shows me his horses, a chestnut hunter and a Palomino. Then he lets three liver and white pointer bitches out of another shed and talks to them as if they were women: 'Oh my loves,' he croons, 'oh, my great wee darlin' gurls.' Finally, he walks me around the house a couple of times because I'm still feeling woozy from the double vodkas I didn't ask for but which he bought anyway.

'Inside, sweetie.' He guides me into the hallway.

The house smells damp and uncared for, yet the peeling and bubbled classic wallpaper in the long hall suggests former glory. But this is where he lives, so it is important.

I wait in the sitting room while Peter goes out to the kitchen. He has switched on a transistor radio and my all-time favourite song comes on, The Hollies singing 'The Air that I Breathe'. Immediately I want to dance, to hold Peter close. But I wait, assuming he is making tea, getting the biscuits out, maybe even laying a tray with a couple of mugs. To pass the time, I examine some photographs on the mantelpiece. One shows Peter when he was a little fellow, dressed up in a sailor suit. A wave of pure love sweeps over me as I pore over this image of him. *Adorable*! is all I can murmur, *Adorable*! It reminds me of a photograph in my school history book of Alexis, the haemophiliac son of the last tsar of Russia. I pick up another picture, this time of his mother and dead father. The frame is tarnished. Peter strongly resembles his father, a medium-sized man with sallow skin. Even though the photograph is in black and white, I guess by the tone that Peter's father's eyes were also an intense blue.

The mother is terrifying. Now that I see her, I do not ever want to meet her. Tall and thin, beautiful in a tight-skinned way, very unsmiling and poised. I remember Peter having said that she was sixty-three. I do a few quick calculations now and decide that, by the look of her, it will be another twenty years before she relaxes the clench of that jaw and goes to her heavenly reward.

Instead of tea and biscuits, he arrives back with a striped bath towel.

'Who was a good little sailor boy then?' I tease.

'Och now,' he smirks and rolls his eyes. 'Mother wouldn't have it any other way.'

I'm sure she wouldn't, I stop myself from saying, further evidence to me that I am almost a real woman, capable of mustering some savage sarcasm when necessary.

He stands by my side, smiling, swinging the towel like a lasso.

'Ming Dynasty?' I enquire as casually as possible, stroking a large blue and white Chinese-looking vase. I have read a short story which involved a precious Ming vase only recently.

'Eh,' he hesitates, as if unsure what to say. 'Eh, yeah. Ming. Ming she is.' He pauses again. A lustful smile steals over his lips and he approaches me, his blue eyes soft with need. I feel myself begin to melt.

'Sit down thur, thur's no hurry, sweetie, no hurry at all,' he whispers, then kisses my lips. I melt some more.

'Now, sweetie.' He catches both my ankles firmly in one of his hands. '*This* is what happens' – the effort of binding my ankles in the towel makes him grunt – 'to naughty gurls who enjoy too much kissing.'

I laugh as he sweeps me off the sofa, ankles bound, and carries me through the sitting room door, down the long hall and across a broad wooden threshold into a bedroom. Triumphantly, he deposits me on the side of the bed and undoes the towel.

'My wee slave-gurl!' he murmurs fondly.

An image of his mother flashes through my mind. I sit up.

'Whose room is this?'

'Mother's'.

'You're joking.'

'So what? She's gone till the weekend. Relax, baby, enjoy yourself. You need to let your hair down! Please?'

Naturally, I am well able to block out illumination of any kind, using the word LOVE as a mental shutter to prevent the slightest ray getting through. As it turns out, I have far more bedroom theory at my disposal than he does, thanks to *Cosmopolitan* magazine, but he has the practical mileage up and that's what counts.

'My wee slave-gurl!'

'Sailor-boy!'

'Slave-gurl!' he growls back.

'Sailor-boy,' I whisper, 'but don't go *in*!' I warn.

'Don't worry, sweetie' he sighs, his ardour increasing by the second as we lurch around the bed and I think of his Italian mother and what she would think and say if she should see the pair of us, him working me over, guzzling my flesh, twisting my long hair in his fists, telling me not to be shocked or surprised. It strikes me that he will probably not even bother to change the bed sheets afterwards. Then he rolls to one side, his expression satisfied, his mouth curling upwards in a smile. It is over.

He dozes for about five minutes while I stare at the ceiling.

'We'd better move, sweetie,' he sighs then, hoisting himself out of the bed again in a busy way I do not like. He is not in the least bit interested in looking at my bare body or in watching me reassemble my garments. Already, he has disappeared into the kitchen.

When dressed, I gather my bag, my jewellery, my scarf and follow him. In the kitchen, I perch on a low stool in order to fasten the sandals which, earlier, he so enjoyed removing. He has opened a pound tin of Italian plums with the word Mangiamo on the label. Leaning over the big Belfast sink, he forks them quickly and greedily into his mouth. They are deep, sunset-red-tinged-with-purple plums. The juice dribbles down his chin. I would just love one of them because I am parched from vodka and courting. But he does not offer any. He stands slurping plum after plum, his mouth crammed full the whole time until they are all gone. Then he drinks the juice straight from the tin.

Everything becomes clear. My mental shutter flies open and a new, icy illumination blows through me. His mother probably suspects this kind of carry-on. She lets her twenty-six-year-old son have his fun, so long as she doesn't know too much about it, so long as he doesn't ever leave her. I tell him I've forgotten something, then cross the hall again to the bedroom. Quickly, I unclasp one pearl earring and fling it far down beneath the sheets. Then, just as he calls my name with a new and unfamiliar impatience, I take the pillows and rub them thoroughly along my neck and chest, then sniff. *Good.* Then I take my mother's bottle of Nina Ricci Eau de Toilette from my bag and sprinkle it randomly on the sheets, the bedside rug, the mattress. *Even better.* The delicious odour wafts around me gently. Now Peter's mother need never more suspect what her son gets up to in her absence. She'll know for certain.

'I've made the bed,' I tell him.

As we set off back across the border, the southern sky is full of stars. Cars coming north whiz by the lake to our right, windows rolled down, headlights flashing, horns tooting.

'Must've bin a good night in Belturbet,' Peter remarks.

'Yeah,' I say, watching a white hook of moon on the water.

Jethro

Now that the trees were cut and sold, Jethro imagined the following summer. From his bedroom he saw how patches of light would waver in small clearings between the remaining spruces.

He could sit and anticipate his new life, its smooth, sure prospects. So unlike anything he had yet known. He'd be well away from domestic sounds like his father's confident baritone as he read the new lines added to the tenth rewrite of a rejected play. Or he could distance himself from the music that vibrated the book-crammed walls of his mother's study while she scribbled every morning.

He eyed the islands of exposed ground, trying to decide which would be best for sitting in. Since Christmas, when Mum and Dad's old London friends had descended with guitars and pan-pipes, hash and wine, the matter of space and privacy had acquired even greater urgency.

Why couldn't his be like most other parents? Why couldn't they get on with life without drawing attention to themselves by setting up a solstice commune? Of course, he clicked his tongue in annoyance, they revelled in exhibitions like that, reared as they were on a diet of permanent controversy. Nowadays it was different. His generation didn't go in for rebellion and individualism.

He left his room and went down to the kitchen, then groaned gently. Soon, he'd have to break the news. He was going to tell them. There was his mother, a brown wool jumper beneath her dungarees, sharpening a carving knife in time to the overture to *The Marriage of Figaro*. If he squeezed his eyes hard, she might dissolve. Perhaps it was all a figment, a hallucination transmitted genetically from one of her forgotten acid trips. Perhaps in some other waking life, he had ordinary, plodding parents without artistic ambitions for themselves and their son.

'Tea, Mum?' he asked, filling the kettle. Her eyes registered annoyance at the intrusion as the overture built to a flamboyant finish.

'Oh,' she sighed, 'that piece really sends me. I know who I am when I hear it.'

He smiled and got himself a teacup. It would be churlish to be anything less than agreeable where his parents were concerned. Not for him the holidays which his friends boasted about, where food was recognisable and days fell away in a blue haze of swimming pools, with bougainvillea and garlic wafting on the air. Oh, no. *They* had to get half a dozen injections before setting off by mule to discover inhospitable tracts of the East African hill country. It was too much for the mules, he threw up every second day and his father kept proffering advice about drinking enough, to be sure to rehydrate himself: 'Only another hundred miles to go, son.'

After that, he swore that when he was truly free, he'd never, ever inflict the savagery of an African holiday on any of his friends or family – if he ever got married. And it would be marriage or nothing, none of this living together nonsense or the half-hearted commitment of a registry office.

'Well, son, it's important to find the right person, not to be tied down if things don't work out,' his father had drawled in one of his man-to-man pep talks.

'They'll work out for me,' Jethro had insisted between his teeth.

'But if they don't, you're not to blame, you know that, don't you?'

Typical of his father in middle age, to display no sense of responsibility whatsoever. Typical of him to refuse to join the golf club because of something to do with women's rights, typical of him to flaunt pink shirts and big, floral waistcoats because he opposed the sexism of colour categorisation.

Jethro sat down with his tea and awaited his father. He'd tell them now. It had to be now or never. He would tell them on this crisp winter morning, in the lull of January, and the cruelty of the blow might kill them.

'I'm a lumberjack and I'm okay, I sleep all night and I work all day,' he hummed uneasily.

'Whassat, Jethro? Have I heard that piece before?' his mother enquired, her hair spilling from its single, greying plait.

'It was on TV at Christmas. *Monty Python*.'

She shrieked with delight. Of course, *Monty Python*, why, herself and his father had been mad about *Monty Python* years ago, wasn't it anarchic, wasn't it so clever?

'Generally speaking, Mum, it was vulgar and pathetic,' Jethro replied. His tone was not harsh. His mother smiled and shook her head.

'All the same,' she mused, 'you remembered that song. It must've caught your imagination!'

'No, Mum. The tree-cutting caught my imagination. Before Christmas. And that's why I'm singing the lumberjack song.'

It had been one of the most wonderful experiences of his life. His father and mother, wanting to keep the planet green and at the same time generate a little future income, had planted six hundred Norway Spruce some years previously. They'd all watched, summer by summer, as sparrows and swallows flew over the plantation, or dived to scoop flies and spiders from the moist new buds. Last summer, before his final school year began, Jethro reminded his father to make enquiries at the gardening centres in the area.

'They'll all have trees organised if we don't act now,' he urged.

'Time enough, son,' his father replied easily. 'Sure, Christmas is four months away.'

Jethro's instinct had proven correct. Most of the larger centres had already ordered their trees from the huge plantations up in the mountains, which left smaller centres, shops and supermarkets.

For two glorious days after the school holidays began, they cut and sawed and carried the young trees to the trailer, their gloves stiffening with resin and sweat and frost, pine needles sticking to their clothes. Then the slow journey to the shops on icy roads, past country homes with coloured lights and decorations in windows, Jethro watching the side mirror to see that none of the trees toppled out.

The larger ones still remained in the plot, and between them, those open spaces which he would hog to himself in the summer, before he went away.

His father came in, a play script bulging under his elbow, a necklet of amber beads, his wife's Christmas gift, visible beneath an open-necked shirt.

'Brigid, I think I've got it!' he whispered. She grinned.

'Oh, major moment! Wow! Next stop, Broadway!' she joked, kissing him. Like two huge, purring cats, they gazed into one another's faces.

'Dad. Mum. Can we talk?'

'Of course, Jethro, of course, but isn't it amazing? It's working out, son!'

'Great, Dad. Just great.' He could never bring himself to tell his father that he was wasting his time. 'Mum. Dad. Just listen, will yis?' he entreated.

His parents sat down at the kitchen table and held hands – when would they realise that people their age looked *stupid* doing crap like that? Their eyes were trained on him with their usual searching earnestness.

'If you're about to tell us you're gay, that's all right, Jethro,' his mother interrupted. 'It's – it was always on the cards anyway. And we love you.'

'No, that's not it!' Jethro hissed. 'Look. It's like this. You know – what you were hoping? University and all that next year?'

'Oh. Well, what is it? Have you decided you'd prefer to study Japanese instead of the Chinese languages?' his father smiled casually, his eyebrows raised.

'No. Yes. No. I've changed my mind. But …'

They sat forward, beaming and expectant.

At first it came out in a whisper, caught in his throat and slithered forth on a gasp of air. His father leaned forward in his chair.

'What's that, son? What's that? Manx? *Celtic* languages, is it?'

Jethro inhaled and this time the words had a shrill power.

'The *bank*, Dad. I want to go into the bank.'

They stared at him, ashen faced. His mother hunched

her back as if she were suddenly cold. His father's lip trembled. For one awful moment, Jethro thought a primal scream was in the offing.

'The *bank*? Is that what you're telling us?' he said quietly. They sat in silence for some minutes. Jethro's mother hyperventilated. He watched as she joined the thumb and third finger of each hand in an attempt to calm herself. Then she screamed at him.

'You're serious, Jethro? I mean, is this what we marched on Washington for in '72? Is this why we marched against Regan in the Eighties? Did you know that we signed a petition to the World Bank on behalf of Third World countries?'

Encouraged, his father joined in. 'And is this why we literally *starved* ourselves outside the Dáil for a week? So that you'd end up in a *bank*? A shagging *bank*?'

He'd never seen them so angry before.

'I'm sorry.' He stood up, left them to their outrage. He looked back from the kitchen door. His parents faced one another from opposite sides of the table. As they glared with disappointment at one another, their hands no longer touched.

'Christ!' his mother whimpered accusingly.

'Well don't look at me!' his father replied in a trembling voice.

'What have we done? Jesus Christ Almighty, what have we done to him?' his mother shouted at the air above the table.

They would not harangue him for long. He knew that. In the end, they wouldn't grant him the enjoyable conflict of rebellion. It had to be his choice, they'd reason, his choice.

Outside, his boots crunched through frozen grass. He entered the plantation. He'd need this sanctuary, would camp out if necessary, paying tribute to flickering sunshine and phosphorescent stars.

Before his career began, he might write a few poems, a *lyric* or two – wasn't that what Mum called them?

Aphrodite Pauses, Mid-life

It is an August afternoon. Carol scans the street, her judging eye roving along gaudy shop fronts, over the preening, gilt-titled books and Celtic CDs in each window. As she walks on, one eyebrow flickers, her attention caught by a display of purple pottery, Hessian lampshades and other emblems of authentic Irish family living.

Upstairs in the big tweed and pottery store, a man from somewhere east of the Danube and west of the Volga makes sandwiches to order. His expression is polite. Because he does not turn a full, carnal, vagabond smile on his customers, Carol instinctively admires him. She orders a tuna sandwich, then observes as he flips two slices of fresh white bread between his plastic-gloved hands. He stops and turns to her. 'Butter?' he inquires in a heavily accented voice. She nods and he spreads the butter, then tops it with tuna fish and mayonnaise, pressing one slice lightly over the other. He transfers sandwich to plate, then cuts the whole piece diagonally and pops it to her waiting tray.

She is one of the youngest customers in the store. The age profile must be, what – from fifty till death us do part?

People move quietly, softly shod, mostly trousered. Hands have age spots. The Americans no longer wear plaid. Touring agencies direct them to this part of the city, where traces of culture are sold. It reminds her of the Turkish men who offer dusty replicas of the goddess Aphrodite to dehydrated tourists outside the ruins of Ephesus, from which people derive inspiration in times of need.

Need drives us all, Carol thinks, questing for solace, for one final clue which would make sense of the hodge podge of a life. She considers her womanly options, the open avenues as she waits for Godot, the unlikely possibility of one last rejuvenating fling, the definite matter of death. Her children are grown, her husband happy. Is that the word? Happy? *Sometimes* he is happy. Sometimes, she too is happy. She even sings around the house, a spontaneous response pours out and her notes, a scratchy warbling, are in the air before she knows it. He likes it when she sings. It releases him. He need no longer feel responsible. Occasionally, she has sung deliberately; she too feels a responsibility to make his life tolerable, even pleasurable, outside of the bedroom, where, she readily acknowledges, standards have never slipped.

She leaves the store, briefcase in hand, and heads down Nassau Street again, towards the university. The students await her, twelve twenty-year-old Americans who have come to Ireland to write literature. She, being a writer, is present to assist in the implantation of literary embryos if not at the actual long-term delivery of fully fledged entities, grotesque beauties of rampant imagination.

She stops to rummage in her case and finds a packet of spearmint gum. As she unwraps it at a stand outside a snack bar, her eye falls on an evening newspaper, drawn by the picture of a beautiful young woman. *That French model*, she deduces quickly and with a pang, before bending to confirm that it is indeed Marianne, the woman on whom the French national ideal of womanhood has just been remodelled. Her picture will appear on stamps, her statue will dominate drowsing country squares from Normandy to the Languedoc. Momentarily, Carol is awestruck. The girl is in her prime, with wings of thick hair in flight behind her shoulders and a noble and feminine profile. Some things are not relative, she concludes. Things like this creature's beauty, or evil and cessation. They simply are.

She steps absently onto the road to cross to the horse chestnut tree that shadows the university's side entrance, then jumps with a start as a car cuts in front of her, its horn trumpeting, the woman behind the wheel throwing her a cutting, laser-lipped look. Carol smiles through the tremor which grips her body, recognising incipient signs. One day she will have become a brazen woman who creeps into rush-hour traffic, indifferent to the psychology of the city automobile, which means so much more than getting from point A to point B. On the pavement, she stares after the elegant machine that almost ran her down, double exhaust snorting. *Silver*, she tuts: a safe colour for safe new money, new discretion, showing a repulsion for strong pigment and any kind of singularity. She fancies owning a hot yellow number, the kind that goes from nought to sixty miles in seven seconds, which looks frivolous and fast.

The young man who stands most days beneath the tree outside the university offers her a magazine, which she accepts. Again, she dips through the mesh of visitors exploring The Dublin Experience that the university offers each summer. A familiar sense of panic rises in her, like a chill wind of foreboding.

In the basement cafeteria, an elderly Japanese man sits at the corner table, exactly where she has observed him for five weeks now, a heap of manuscripts spread before him. Although it is twenty-one degrees outside and the sun is shining, he wears a black woollen hat and a padded anorak. Suddenly, he gives a start and lets out a shout at no one in particular before resuming the study of his papers. Tourette's syndrome, she diagnoses automatically, before passing through the double doors and ascending to the fourth floor.

As she climbs, she considers how well she feels, then emits a little puff of dismay as she recalls that the past six months have gone unmarked, uncalendared with red, anticipatory rings. Her body is quieter, in a new and startling way. Perhaps she should listen to that. There is no pain, heat or discomfort, nothing but a new, unfamiliar stillness. She hesitates within its portals, not quite ready. It seems far too soon and she is too absurdly young!

Not for the first time, she discovers that the classroom door is locked. Students sprawl across the seating cubes at the centre of the hallway, their folders thrown down. One of them – a half-Indian, half-American boy – heads towards Carol, his face lit with diligence. He thrusts a late assignment into her hand, mumbling something about a migraine. He hopes she'll accept it now.

Carol watches, hearing in the breathless voice the sounds of Boston. She is sceptical. A migraine. Party-induced, she suspects.

Just so long as you get it done! She uses her warning tone, but then breaks off to laugh, wanting to encourage, regardless.

He gazes soberly at her. He is concerned about his final grade. Carol sighs, then encourages again, telling him that from her perspective, it's the story that counts. His voice drops with relief. He thanks her. She looks at his eyes, at how the skin close to the eyelashes is naturally darker, as if lined by mascara; she sees his shapely, plum-coloured lips and just then, it is a wonder to her that anybody should be so preoccupied with something so insipid as a *grade*.

She tells the students to wait while she goes to get a security guard to open up the classroom. *Monday, Wednesday and Thursday*, she tells the guard. She speaks as lightly as possible to conceal her irritation. Again, she trudges up the stairway to the fourth floor with the man, who asks what she teaches. *Writing*, she says, *creative writing*.

He wonders what exactly that is and she cringes at her own explanation. As they chat about the number of people now interested in being writers, he mentions discipline. Is it all discipline, he wants to know. It takes discipline to *live*, she almost says, but doesn't. Instead she gives the usual reply. *Ah well, God loves a tryer*, he remarks pleasantly before selecting a long silvery key from the bundle attached to his belt.

In the classroom, the students wait. Three are to read from work in progress. Today, they are all giddy. She senses it, like an invisible laughing gas in the air. At the end of week five, mixed moods – mainly discovery and lust – hang in the air. Trips to the Wicklow Mountains, a journey to Newgrange, even a momentous week in Belfast in the wake of the 12th of July have cemented friendships, spawned love and tenderness.

Two hours pass. One student emerges, gratified by her peers' opinion of her work, the two others less so, but ready to go back and rewrite. *We are all*, Carol consoles them, *apprentices to writers who have gone before us. We absorb their traditions, then freely break them to the point of reformation. Reform, reform without fear*, she urges.

Later, she pushes down the stairs through a group of excited historians and, on the ground floor, around the registration queue for a psychotherapy conference. Out of curiosity, she peeks over the cement wall of the mezzanine, down to the cafeteria. The Japanese man is asleep, a trail of brown, like chocolate, encrusted between his lips and chin. Around her, the clamour of foreign visitors seems symphonic. Apart from the Japanese gentleman, who may or may not have Tourette's syndrome, the people engrossed in The Dublin Experience are busy and directed, putting best feet forward. She wonders what they are like at home, when they hang up their fiddles.

Suddenly, a new misery swells within her, because her own public face is at times so reluctant. But what, she speculates, is the alternative to a public face? War? Enmity? Madness? People are incredibly brave, she thinks, when who-knows-what things are defining their private lives outside of the cool and welcoming university.

Again, she considers her tide-less, about-to-be-permanently-silent body. She moves out onto the street, wondering whether she should go home. In her briefcase, the students' final assignment, which she must evaluate for signs of craft, courage, ingenuity and talent, as assiduously as a jeweller sifting through a heap of unpolished gemstones. Like a jeweller, she will have to grade the work. Sometimes, she realises, you sell your soul, even if you've managed to delude yourself that all you did was buy in.

The thoughts of selling her soul make her decide to stay. Outside, the light on the street flickers like amber on the windscreens of passing cars. The sense of urgent business at the corner of Dawson and Nassau Street no longer bothers her. A cup of coffee would be the thing, maybe a slice of well-sugared apple tart, both with cream.

The thing that had defined her since the age of thirteen, that stormed suddenly into her when The Beatles were on the brink of splitting up and her mother was wearing long dresses with psychedelic Indian patterns, which defined parts of every month for thirty-three years, was being withdrawn as suddenly as it had arrived.

As Carol stands poised at the traffic lights, it works within the province of her body, like a spy returning gathered intelligence to another, more native place. A man looks her quickly up and down and in that moment, she knows herself transfigured. She considers her pale, still body as that stranger would never see it, encrypted by a watching source which could not think as humans did, which had never thought; she considers her strong hair, once too thick to manage, now thinner; and, transfigured, she passes through the portals of stillness, aware of the tide in retreat, driven out along the estuaries of her body by this knowing counter-intelligence, in its wake a new secret, naked and white as death itself.

Yugoslavia of My Dreams

Within an hour of their arrival at the hotel, Katherine meets Mikael, the Yugoslavian waiter who serves in one of the Bundesbahn restaurants. She is stunned by so much that is new, timid in the city's vastness and bustle, although it is Sunday and therefore quieter than usual.

At the hotel, Katherine and Laura introduce themselves to Frau Schlang. Swiftly, the housekeeper's eyes take both girls in from top to toe. She looks relieved, as if they have confirmed a prior impression that Irish students are polite and not surly or resentful. The other girls they will meet, she informs them, are mostly dirty, lazy and unreliable. They come from big, dirty families in hot, dirty countries where the politics are most *unzuverlässig*, unreliable. They are not used to our standards, *ja*?

'*Aber Ihr seid müde! Jetzt müßt ihr essen*!' she purrs at them.

Katherine and Laura are ravenous. They are only too happy to hear the word *essen*. Frau Schlang directs them to the hotel basement, where the staff canteen is situated. They wander, lost despite her crisp directions, through the bowels of the building. Inches of fatty liquid slosh across the concrete floor of one corridor. Coarse-featured men and women push enormous trolleys of dirty laundry. The word *Scheißarbeit!* resounds at every turn. Eventually, they find the canteen.

Katherine stares. The hotel underlings, to which group they now officially belong, sit hunched over white platters of odd-looking food, pork knuckles and pasta, dull green sauerkraut. They pull and gnaw as if half-starved.

'How are we going to stick it?' Katherine gasps. She thinks of Sunday roasts at home, gleaming tableware, the aromas of moist lamb, mint sauce and thick gravy, the radio switched to BBC Radio 2 and comforting overseas requests from BFPOs in Germany and Palestine and Hong Kong.

'Christ above.' Laura wipes her brow with the back of her hand.

'*Bitte beeilen Sie sich!*' one of the serving women snaps at Katherine.

'*Bitte?* Oh yeah, *zum Essen bitte!*' She points to her mouth in a struggle to supplement her unreliable German.

Immediately, both their platters are piled with pig's knuckle, gravy which contains large globules of fat, a mountain of stringy sauerkraut and what they later come to know as *Knudeln.* They want to sit together, but almost every space at the long trestle table is occupied. Fortunately, one smiling young man urges his companions to make room for them.

'*Bitte, bitte, hier ist frei!*' He pats the space and they join him, grateful for shelter from the disinterested, gawping and even hostile stares that have followed their every move since they entered the canteen.

Very quickly he finds out that Katherine and Laura come from Ireland, students, yes, twenty and nineteen years old, respectively. Me, he says, I am Mikael, I come from Yugoslavia, you know it?

'*Ja, natürlich kennen wir Jugoslawien*!' Katherine replies as she attempts to separate a morsel of pig meat from its gristle.

He offers to show them around the city whenever they wish, he knows it very well. 'You like to dance?' he asks. 'Then I show you the nicest places. You like film? I bring you there.'

Eventually, they give up the struggle with the pork knuckles and wonder if they should go to a restaurant.

'*Was würden Sie empfehlen*?' Laura asks Mikael casually.

His eyes widen. You can afford to eat in restaurants every day, you Irish students, *gel*? Well, maybe just this evening, Katherine answers carefully, not wanting anyone to think that they might be rich. He puts his hand to his chin, considering. He hems and haws, then tells them to try Restaurant Attaturk just off the Marienplatz. He'll show them the way if they wish. But they decline. They are both too tired to communicate any longer in another language. Politely, they excuse themselves. Out on the street again, after buying four slabs of Milka chocolate, they immediately lose all sense of direction and wander into the U-Bahn but on the wrong platform, so that they end up miles from their accommodation. The girls squabble, blaming one another for the mistake.

By the time they reach the room which the hotel rents for its *Gastarbeiter*, they are still in the sulks. It is beyond Teresienhöhe, on the sixth floor, directly beneath the roof. There is no elevator. That night, they sweat in their beds, kept awake by the sound of music and loud laughter from the Yugoslavian restaurant on the other side of the street. By the time the restaurant closes, they are on speaking terms again. It is almost time to get up. The hotel provides no catering facilities, which means they have to turn up for breakfast in the hotel by six fifteen, or else clean twenty bedrooms and bathrooms on an empty stomach.

On the tram, Katherine feasts her eyes on the more fashionable women, some with massive bio-waves, others wearing embroidered Afghan waistcoats even in the heat and high-heeled tight leather boots. She longs to be free and independent, shopping, not working. Posters and hoardings advertise soaps and deodorants called X mal 4 and Fa. Another, for *echt kölnisches Wasser*, shows a blond, tanned, sporty man patting his smooth jaw-line. His teeth are fluorescent white. Already, in August, preparations are underway for the Münchener Oktoberfest. Long tents have been erected and posters of frothing tankards and fleshy Bavarian faces advertise the revels to come. As they leave the tram, two Turkish men make clicking sounds, the strains of Pink Floyd wavering from the transistor radio one of them holds to his ear.

'Funky!' Laura sighs.

'Yeah,' Katherine agrees with another sigh.

'Ah well, just one more year in college.'

'World, here we come, right?'

'Right.'

After bolting two white bread rolls with butter and jam and coffee, they meet the chambermaids who will train them in. Katherine's co-worker is called Teresia. Heavy boned, her face is tired and her legs bulge with veins. Laura will work with Lucia, flaming haired, skinny, with very mobile lips, also, like Teresia, from Yugoslavia, but from a small place called Porec. Within two hours,

Katherine knows all about Teresia's family in Zagreb. Having had four Caesarean sections, she is proud to hoist her pink and white chambermaid's uniform to waist level so that Katherine can see the thickened weals of birth butchery. While Teresia stands displaying her stomach, Katherine looks on with bemused sympathy. Such things – birth and all that – are vague possibilities in the far future. There is no room for them in her head.

By the end of their first shift, the girls' backs and feet throb, but after a meal of *Wiener Schnitzel mit Pommes frites* and a couple of beers, they are ready for real action. That first afternoon, it is in short supply. They keep getting lost. The local accent defies them and Turkish men tail them and chat them up so that they feel hunted and a bit annoyed.

Gradually, they learn to elbow their way sharply past unwanted men. Gradually, too, they grow accustomed to the pace of work at the hotel, harder and heavier than they ever imagined it would be.

'*Keine Tropfen, meine Damen*!' Frau Schlang constantly warns on her early afternoon tours of inspection, smirking at both of them whenever they meet. Teresia and Lucia roll their eyes heavenwards and perform exaggerated muscle-man actions with their arms and shoulders by way of imitation.

'*Damen, nur Damen für Frau Schlang*!' Lucia tells them with a laugh.

Every tap must gleam dry and drop-free, every plughole surround must reflect the ceiling above, the white enamelled baths must be absolutely dry. However, Frau Schlang has a soft spot for the *irische Damen*, rarely criticises their work but constantly warns them against their companions from Yugoslavia and Turkey.

'*Schmutzige Leute! Sehr schmutzige Leute*!' she shakes her head in distaste.

Teresia is an expert bed-maker. She shows Katherine how to put the cover on a duvet without ending up in it herself. She demonstrates how to make the corners of the covered duvet point sharply to the four points of the globe.

'*Siehst du? Nord, Süd, Ost und West*!' she announces mock-seriously.

She shows how the pillows are arranged at the top of the bed, just so, with *genau zehn Zentimeter* to spare on either side of the mattress. She shows Katherine the small tape measure which she carries in her apron. It's a long way, thinks Katherine, from the sixteenth-century Middle High German consonantal shift, but at least there's the money to look forward to.

After work, they wander the streets, searching, searching. They want X-rated films, strip joints, bars and clubs. They also want romance, excitement, to be swept off their feet. They examine window displays of green, red and blue vibrators as well as the usual skin-coloured ones. Their eyes widen at the selection of chain wear and leather, at blinkers, gags, bits, rings and stirrups. They discuss the possible function of what looks like a double vibrator and wonder who would use such a thing and how. Is it for men and women, or for men only, or is it for women only, they ponder aloud. Katherine turns away from that window, from such hugeness. To her puzzlement, she feels queasy.

They almost go to a porn show. Just as they are about to pay, a departing English tourist draws back the red velvet curtain which separates that secret world from life on the street. Katherine catches a glimpse of what could be beefsteak, of flesh impossibly close to camera. Then she hears the phoney intense moans and groans. Instinctively, she draws back. There are also, she quickly notes, only men inside.

'C'mon,' she tells Laura.

'But—'

'Not this,' she insists.

'You're so fuckin' bossy, d'ya know that?'

They take the U-Bahn to Schwabing, *ein Studentenort*, according to Lucia, who has never been there.

'This is more like it!' Laura clicks her tongue and does a hip swagger.

'Musk or patchouli?' Katherine offers Laura two small bottles of oil.

'Ta,' says Laura, taking the patchouli and rubbing it on her pulse spots.

They listen to the *croo-croo* sound of pigeons roosting above on the nooks and ledges. They wander streets lit by small lanterns and coloured lights, where very fashionable shops stay open late, the windows full of the most extreme of everything – boots, leather gear, jewellery. The sound of Led Zeppelin fills the air. From a couple of streets away comes the chiming of bells, and more distantly, the clamour of the bells of the Marienkirche. It is nine o'clock.

'Great stuff!' breathes Katherine.

In the end, they pay into a night club, die Nacht Eule, and settle themselves down at a table. A red, encrusted candle flickers gently before them. Unlike at home, there is no stampede between dances. The dance floor is a small rectangle in the middle of the club. In less than a minute, they are approached and politely asked out to dance. Laura moves off on the arm of a fair-haired German, into the smoky, gently strobed, dark heart of the club. But it is Mikael who asks Katherine to dance.

'*Ach, Du*!' she gasps.

Mikael could not be more charming. While dancing, he is polite and respectful, at pains to ensure that her every need is met.

'*Zu laut für dich*?' he enquires during a David Bowie number.

'*Nein, nein.*' She assures him that it is not too loud. When the sound fades, he thanks her for the dance, escorts her back to her table. Laura's man has done the same thing.

'What d'you make of that?' Laura grins, then breaks open a fresh pack of Camel cigarettes.

'No mauling. No pawing. Don't look now – there's another pair heading this way.'

The music starts again. An hour passes. Just when they have grown a little tired telling every man who tries to guess their nationality that they are neither Swedish, Dutch, American nor indeed from Iceland, Mikael returns. Laura sits this one out, smoking moodily, sipping a glass of Pils.

Katherine likes Mikael, without feeling much more. He does not attract her in the way she has imagined herself being attracted to someone. She has expected more of this summer, and although Mikael is kind and attentive, he fawns too much. She suspects he cannot help his cravenness. But perhaps she is not used to such large helpings of flattery either. She wonders if this is the norm among Continental men, then reminds herself that places like Yugoslavia, Turkey and Greece are not exactly 'Continental', no more than Ireland is, even if Ireland is in the EU and they are not. Yugoslavia, at least, is exotic in comparison to home.

Weeks roll away. The weather is warm, sometimes thundery. They decide to buy nightdresses for their mothers back in Ireland, spend ages in a small lingerie boutique on the Leopoldstrasse. Finally, they purchase slippery, shell pink lace and silken garments. Laura is less certain about the wisdom of her choice.

'The old lady will flip when she sees this,' she grumbles.

'Yeah, maybe. I bet your old man will like it though,' Katherine replies, adding that her folks have sent a telegram to the hotel wondering why she didn't phone home the previous weekend as arranged.

'Christ. They never leave off, do they?' Laura shakes her head.

'Never. Worry worry worry, that's my old folks.' Katherine shakes her head in turn, puzzled, feeling a wave of panic in her stomach which she cannot quite explain, which she hasn't had since coming out to Munich – well, apart from the day outside that sex shop.

'Pathetic,' says Laura.

Mikael continues to court Katherine. He is ardent but not pushy. He calls her *Katarina*, which she enjoys. He holds her hand as if it is made of porcelain. He stands back and opens doors for her. He will not sit until she is seated. She doesn't know how to tell him that she has had enough. It seems unkind.

The night he brings her to a film called *Mandingo* at one of the multiplex cinemas off the Marienplatz, she plans on finishing with him before he smothers her. Mandingo, a huge black slave in the American South, is practically raped by his white boss's frustrated wife. When the husband finds out, he blasts Mandingo with a shotgun straight into an enormous cauldron of boiling water. The image of the screeching, screaming black man being boiled alive is more than Katherine can bear. Mikael runs after her as she flees the cinema, on the brink of throwing up. She controls herself. The feeling subsides. This has happened before in Ireland, she explains. Sometimes in crowds, or during very intense moments, she needs to escape. Even good emotions overwhelm her. It even happened, she reassures Mikael, the year before in Rome during the papal audience, when all the different nationalities began to behave like raving groupies as Pope Paul VI was hoisted on his throne and all the cardinals lined up on the stage of the auditorium like a long chorus line of men in red dresses. Instead of standing and cheering with her old folks, she ran out. Mikael, who is Muslim, has only a vague idea of the significance of this. It's nothing, she tells him apologetically, at the same time fascinated by the efforts she makes to assuage other people's alarm at her physical distress. It should be the other way around, she knows that; why does nobody ever see that?

As he walks her back to her room, Mikael talks about Yugoslavia.

'*Es ist sehr schön, ein sehr schönes Land*,' he whispers dreamily, then adds that Germany is *ein Scheißland.*

'With mountains?' Katherine asks.

'*Ja, Jugoslawien hat Gebirge, grüne Bäume, sehr nette Leute.*'

'You are lonely?' she probes.

'*Manchmal*,' he says, turning to face her. Yes, sometimes he is lonely, sometimes he dreams of Yugoslavia, of the dark forests, the clear sea, the fountain in the square of his home village. He speaks the word for his home country tenderly, as if it is sacred, then leans and kisses Katherine's cheek. '*Aber jetzt nicht so sehr*,' he beams – not so much since he has met her.

Three nights later, she breaks it off. He has brought her to a smart restaurant. The candles flicker, his hand reaches across the table to clasp hers and all of a sudden she can no longer bear it. She stammers something at him, the words *Schluß machen* tumble forth. He gets the message all right, he is raging mad. He tells her that she has insulted him. She does not reply, then murmurs that she is sorry.

'*Aber was soll denn das*?' he fumes across the table, a vein pulsing down the centre of his smooth brown forehead. Why did she keep going out with him if she felt like that, he demands, why has she insulted him? Then he storms out of the restaurant. Feeling small, mean but also a little relieved, she makes her way back to the stuffy room on the sixth floor which has become their safe place, hers and Laura's. Mikael was too much, like a thick, warm, stultifying blanket.

The girls gradually learn how not to work so hard. They uncover haunts in which to hide for fifteen minutes or so, certain toilets on certain floors which seem permanently empty, where they can sit and smoke and gossip and rub one another's sore feet. Or they offer to water the plants throughout the whole hotel. Anything to avoid the bedrooms and, more especially, the bathrooms.

No drops of water, no marks – Frau Schlang, at pains to signify what she means by marks, jabs her long forefinger at the toilet bowls.

'*Alles muß sauber sein*!'

'*Ja, ja, Frau Schlang*,' the girls chorus automatically.

Some guests leave good tips. Others leave nothing. Some guests have clean habits. Others have been very badly reared indeed, Katherine thinks. Occasionally some geezer has a few too many and pisses the bed. One morning, Lucia and Laura find a sodden mattress. Lucia throws her hands up in horror.

'*Er muß bezahlen*!' she shrieks, then races like a blue-arsed fly down three floors to reception to report the calamity.

But the man has already checked out.

Up on the fourth floor, Katherine does her best to restore a bathroom to order for its returning guests. The words *sauber und schmutzig*, clean and dirty, circle her brain like a mantra. She casts about for a lavatory brush, to no avail. Nearing desperation, her hands grow clammy as she stares at the lavatory bowl. In an inspired moment, her eye falls on two toothbrushes in a glass over the washbasin. They are pink and blue. After a moment's quick speculation, she selects the blue one on the grounds that men seem generally less prone to physical upsets of a minor nature than women. Quickly, she scrapes the offending marks off the lavatory bowl, flushes, then disinfects beneath the rim with a generous green squish of Schwarzwald Frisch. Calm again, she rinses the toothbrush at the sink, then replaces it beside its pink companion and a pack of dental floss. She takes a final glance around the bathroom and leaves, satisfied.

Outside, the city awaits. They enjoy the very first *Emmanuelle* film, about a young woman's sexual awakening. Then they go to an explicit Dutch film with German subtitles, *Türkische Früchte*. The film has artistic merit, they both decide. This mad young couple fall in love. When the female lead gets a brain tumour and her artist lover, on a hospital visit, watches her stuff her face to choking point with Turkish Delight, Katherine feels a little like she did at *Mandingo*, except for the fact that she is with Laura, and so she can just be herself.

She grows to love their strolls and night-time adventures, the foreign cigarette smells, different perfumes, spicy aftershaves wafting on the air. She enjoys emerging from the U-Bahn to the lovely floral-decked space of Marienplatz, the grey and gargoyled Rathaus, with its lush window-boxes, and on the door of one restaurant, an ornate brass representation of Germany's legendary jester, Til Eulenspiegel. The bustle and buzz of the warm nights, the clacking of heels in the cobbled Altstadt, the fever, frivolity and sheer ecstasy of the frescoed façades strike her as declarations of a love of existence itself.

She meets another young man, a light-haired German from near Augsburg, called Karl. He plays soccer (he is limping from a knee injury when she meets him) and lives on a farm with his parents. Still grieving after the death of his brother in a car accident, he talks freely to Katherine about his loss. She listens, and even if she cannot always exactly follow his strong Bavarian accent, she understands enough, she feels enough. At that point in her life, sad things find a route through her quite easily, at least as much as happy things.

Karl collects her outside the apartment block a couple of evenings each week. Laura has met a Turk from Istanbul who sells silver and turquoise jewellery on the streets and tells her that he has never, no never, met a girl with such lovely hands and feet before.

'I'm in love!' she crows excitedly.

'Well, at least he's different from the others.' Katherine's voice betrays the doubt she feels towards most of the Turkish men they have met so far.

'At least he's into hands and feet, not tits and ass,' Laura retorts.

'Karl isn't like that.'

'No?'

'No.'

To be Irish for Karl means also to be unsullied by the smut and filth of the world in general. Katherine has done little to dissuade him of this romantic vision. Yet, towards the end, she half-hopes they might sleep together and wonders vaguely about contraception and how to use it.

She tells him one night that her heart will be *gebrochen* when she leaves. He bursts out laughing and explains that this verb is usually applied to a piece of crockery and not to one's heart. *Du fehlst mir*, he tells her, and, repeating the words, she means them.

At the hotel, Katherine and Laura become even more cavalier about their work. Frau Schlang is anxious that they should not run off back to Ireland with the keys to the room at Teresienhöhe. She nags so much that it annoys them.

'*Schlüssel nicht vergessen, meine Damen*!' she warns constantly, wagging her finger whenever she meets them, her eyes still slightly flirtatious.

On the last day, they say goodbye to the girls they have worked with. They take photographs of one another in various stances along the hurtling length of the hotel corridor. They promise to send copies to Lucia and Teresia. The Yugoslavians are sorry to see them go, but, Katherine realises, will quickly forget the two students who flitted in and out of their lives briefly and inconsequentially. Their work supports relatives in Yugoslavia, just like the money Mikael earns as a waiter.

She takes the elevator down to the Bahnhof restaurant where he works. She feels that she should say goodbye. She stands for a moment in the doorway, watching. In the process of explaining something on the menu to an American backpacker whose voice carries and who keeps throwing his hands in the air as if to say *what can you expect*, Mikael's expression does not grow annoyed or even vaguely impatient as the man, who is about his own age, grumbles and grouses. Eventually, he takes the order and weaves his way efficiently across the restaurant. Then he sees Katherine. She smiles and waves. For a split second, he hesitates, a smile almost breaking across his face. His mouth – she just knows it – is about to form the word *Katarina*. But no. She is mistaken, he has changed his mind. Just as smoothly, the face becomes a mask that neither she nor any other student foreigner has the right to remove.

In the bus on the way to the airport, they remember the keys. Too late.

'Ah, fuck it,' says Katherine.

'Yeah,' Laura drawls.

They cross and uncross their legs, compare their new flares and the new high-heeled leather boots bought in Salamander, what Katherine calls sluts' boots. Laura has dyed her hair auburn. They have both got springy bio-waves. Their curls bounce and shine, big and soft and doll-like. Suddenly, Katherine remembers their first sensation-seeking days in the city, dawdling outside the sex shops, how some part of her backed away, reviled, afraid. Yet it stays in her head, the image of those things, pushing at her, pushing into her until it seems she is nothing but orifices, and such is the anger that builds, inexplicably, that she has to giggle until she giggles away her sickness, the feeling that she may well be going mad.

The girls swirl the keys on the ends of their fingers, then laugh some more, excited at the thoughts of seeing the old folks, lined up and waiting for them at Dublin Airport, the beaming faces and relieved expressions that will greet their return to the fold before college starts again.

Little Africa

Fifteen years ago, when her son was born in a village ten days' walk from the city, Angela decided to name him after the strange, beaded flower she had seen in a magazine. He had been born sweet and slippery, scented with birth. At that time she called him Hyacinth. But as soon as they arrived in Ireland, his mother renamed him Mosi, meaning first child.

Since then, five others had come, but they had died in a local war at the same time as their father. Angela and Hyacinth had fled to the forest and cowered there, shivering and still for a long time. Hyacinth's heart had pounded so hard he thought his whole body was pulsing with movement. He tried to silence his breathing, to keep the air in his terrified lungs silent. During the two nights in the forest when he sometimes dozed beside his mother, he would occasionally awaken to see her dark eyes, staring, moving anxiously from side to side or up and down as she peered into the night. He remembered how thirsty they had been and how his mother continuously smacked her lips together, as if searching for moisture within her cheeks. Hyacinth was afraid of snakes, but his mother told him that snakes were the least of their worries. Then she put her arms around him and held him close. The moment she did that, they could feel one another's hearts, and it calmed them a little.

Two days after the massacre, Angela and Hyacinth had crept back to the scene and run around in circles, sending strangled screams up into the deserted clearing. They sounded like the birds of the night forest, producing high utterances of different rhythms, their weeping full of long and short notes and truncated, unmelodic passages. There was no time for proper graves. They found the bodies and covered them with a thin layer of red earth. But the termites had begun to work. No amount of brushing the broken remains with their bare fingers would keep them away and in the end Hyacinth and Angela had piled twigs and branches over their kin, laying them in a row of six. They did not forget the exact order of the bodies and arranged them according to age. On the left was Chinua, Mosi's father, his grey face still frozen in a rictus of terror, and to his right all the children, beginning with Adanna, the smallest. When Angela saw how the killers had even ripped the gold studs from Adanna's tiny ear-lobes, she howled at the sky. After Adanna came Violet, who was four, then Chima, Kwesi and finally Hyacinth's last brother, Dragon, named after the snapdragons Angela had seen on a gardening programme on foreign television.

Now, in Ireland, he was Mosi. Boys were not usually called after flowers. He must forget Hyacinth, Angela said. They had to make things as easy as possible for themselves.

But after a year in Ireland, Mosi still found it impossible to forget. His mother found it hard too, having to forget and learn so much at once. He would watch her face across the small square breakfast table in their inner city attic flat and observe the determination in her eyes. Son, I need to think, she would often say. Sometimes, Angela's new man Colm stayed over at the flat. Mosi tried not to suspect him. He was white, his features as vague and unformed as most white people's. The only thing that distinguished him was his hairy nose. Mosi would peer with dislike at the small gingery hairs that grew inside his elongated nostrils and wonder if his mother had lost her mind from too much death and thinking.

While his mother was thinking, Mosi went to school in Denmark Street and afterwards walked through the north city. The school had taken him in as one of three boys from Africa and he was happy enough there. Before he had come to Ireland, he never thought about happiness, but in the past year it was a word he heard frequently from adults and on the radio. Everybody in Dublin believed in happiness, but in his previous life it was not discussed. That did not mean happiness did not occur, merely that it was not a subject considered worth discussing.

Mosi grew accustomed to the rushing city. Many years before, he had once been to Kano with his father. There, everybody was black and ordinary. The fact was – and he could not admit this even to Kevo – that in Dublin he sometimes found it difficult to tell one white person from another. He had spent the first three months in school talking to people he only half recognised because they looked just the same as someone he had spoken to only a minute beforehand. Gradually, he developed codes that helped him. He began to observe hair, the shapes of heads, lengths of noses. Not all hair was as straight as he imagined. Some people had hair like wavy rivers and others had short, totally straight pale hair, worn very close to the scalp. He began to see that not all eyes were pale blue, but that there were various shades of blueness, and that there was light brown and dark brown too. Their teeth were small and they had small jaws. That did not help matters. But mostly it was the skin – chicken pale, bloodless looking, which they wore with such casual pride, not seeing anything remotely startling about themselves.

At school, they did not ask about Africa. It was understood that he might not want to talk about some things. But sometimes he spoke up. Sometimes, in class, there was an opportunity to describe how something had been or what a certain place looked like. In Geography, he had spoken about the equatorial climate and about the animals that came to the watering hole at sunset.

Many of the boys in his class were rich, but not all. They wore black blazers with an emblazoned crest, and so did he. His mother had not had to buy the uniform, because the Jesuits had taken him on and were looking after everything. Mosi made an Irish friend. For some reason, although he often spoke with the two other African boys in his year, he had no desire to play with them or to know about their previous lives. He was certain that they too had experienced awful things but he had no more room in his head for such sad furniture.

The preparations for the school Christmas concert were in full swing. Mosi knew instinctively that he would be drawn in, whether he liked it or not, because he could sing. That was what everybody expected of an African boy, but he had to admit that he enjoyed singing, and that in Ireland many people were afraid of song unless they were drunk.

Before long, Mrs Fitzgerald had swept into the classroom during French class to liberate the boys she wanted for that day's rehearsal. Like a thrown blade, her eye hit on Mosi and she smiled greedily.

'You, Mosi! Kevo! Dylan! I think the Three Wise Men and choir need a little practice, eh?'

The boys waited.

Mrs Fitzgerald turned to the young French teacher, who had been in the process of teaching the class how to tell the time. She smiled unctuously at Ms Elliot.

'Ms Elliot, may I borrow a few of your boys for this period?'

Ms Elliot did not return the smile. 'Yes, Mrs Fitzgerald, you may borrow them for today,' she replied.

'Eh, eh,' Mrs Fitzgerald hesitated and wrinkled her nose in annoyance, 'it's for the Christmas play, as you know, Ms Elliot, and the music department is putting the finishing touches to its Wise Men and angels … and shepherds, of course.'

Mrs Fitzgerald went *heh-heh* before her voice petered out. Ms Elliot stood waiting for her to leave. Eventually, Mosi, Kevo and ten others stood up and looked at Ms Elliot. Finally, she nodded at them. Mrs Fitzgerald shuffled out hurriedly.

Occasionally, Father Headmaster, who was fond of musical entertainment, stuck his head into the concert hall or wandered in, hands behind his back, his sharp eyes darting as he observed proceedings. Mosi suspected that Father Headmaster kept appearing so as to watch Mrs Fitzgerald and the other music teacher, Mr Colley. The two disliked one another. If Mr Colley did the piano accompaniment, Mrs Fitzgerald would suddenly bring the whole choir to a halt and start rolling her eyes and sighing impatiently.

'Eh, eh, I think we need that D chord to come in a little more quickly, Mr Colley, if you don't *mind*?'

Then, when Mr, Colley came in with his D chord, he came in too soon. Mrs Fitzgerald put up her arms and began waving them criss-cross style, like the man on the tarmac at Dublin Airport the day Mosi and his mother had arrived in Ireland and the plane was taxiing into its parking bay.

'Now what is it?' Mr Colley said archly, looking up under his glasses at Mrs Fitzgerald.

'Timing, timing, Mr Colley. But not to worry!' she went on brightly in an artificial voice, '*Poco a poco* as the Italians say, eh, eh?'

Eventually everything went the way it should, and 'Ding-Dong Merrily on High' was sung and played at the right tempo and with festive verve. It was at this point that Mr Colley suddenly stood up from the piano and pointed towards Mosi.

'Listen to him! Listen to that boy!' he gesticulated excitedly. 'Mrs Fitzgerald, when have we heard a low baritone F like that? Tell me that, when, when?'

Mrs Fitzgerald, rattled by Mr Colley's enthusiasm for Mosi's harmonising very low F, took a moment to reply.

'Indeed, Mr Colley,' she murmured, not wanting to appear as if she herself had not already observed Mosi's talent.

A number of things were settled that day. Mosi, as well as holding the strong baritone line together for the other low-voicers in the choir, would now take the part of Balthazar. Kevo, inexplicably, would be Melchior, and Caspar would be taken by a broad-shouldered boy from third year. He was a boy who would be given no lines, unlike Mosi and Kevo, for whom Mrs Fitzgerald had now amended and expanded Father Headmaster's Nativity script. The third boy was chosen despite the fact that he couldn't sing, couldn't remember lines and couldn't follow any instruction, but because he was unnaturally large for his age and would look convincing as a grown man.

After school, Mosi and Kevo wandered along Parnell Square. Kevo was in no rush to go home. His mother would be in the shops along Henry Street, doing the shopping, he grinned at Mosi, then nudged him.

'It's a good time of year for shoppin',' he added for good measure.

The last time Kevo's mother went shopping, a security man had intervened and she ended up at the Garda station.

'Does your ma ever go shoppin'?' Kevo asked, shoving his hands deep in his jeans pockets.

'No,' Mosi replied darkly. 'Not like that.'

'But she has a boyfriend,' Kevo went on, as if that confirmed something.

Mosi said nothing at first. Then he decided he might as well tell Kevo everything.

'My mother is pregnant now,' he said quietly, feeling ashamed.

'So's mine,' Kevo countered. 'When's she due?'

'I'm not sure. Soon,' Mosi frowned a little.

'Funny, that.'

'What is funny?'

'If they both ended up in the hospital together,' Kevo laughed.

'Then we would both have new brothers,' Mosi took up.

'Or sisters.'

'From different fathers,' Mosi sighed.

'Wise up, wouldya?' Kevo pushed him with his shoulder. 'That's how it is.'

They turned into the shopping centre in Parnell Street and strolled down the mall. The sound of carols echoed down the long shopping halls. Sometimes they were intercepted by competing sounds, like an announcement from one of the big stores of a sudden pre-Christmas half-price sale. Turkeys hung by their feet from metal hooks in the butchers, thin threads of blood dangling from their beaks. They were fat birds, unlike the wild black-feathered turkeys Mosi's family used to occasionally catch and eat.

As the boys had only a few coins between them, they gawked into shop windows, chatting about electronic equipment and wide-screen televisions. Both wanted a picture phone. Ten different models were on display in one window, with golden tinsel and little glittering baubles attached.

Show someone how much you love them was written beside the latest picture phone. Mosi eyed the colour screen on the phone, which showed a smiling blonde girl with a Santa hat.

'Me ma's new fella says he'll get me a video phone for Christmas,' Kevo remarked.

Mosi would have liked to say the same of his mother's Irish boyfriend, but could not. So far, he and Colm had gazed across the breakfast table each morning in a state of mutual caution, not meeting one another's eyes. Yet he had begun to be able to read Colm's face. Now that Angela was growing bigger with the baby, he stayed over at the flat quite often. He had done some useful things. He fixed a leaking tap and re-plastered the wall where a damp patch was showing, then painted it to match the rest of the room. He often arrived with boxes of food, with a whole roast chicken from the supermarket – which he knew Mosi particularly liked – and bread or eggs and vegetables. At other times he brought beer, and Colm and Angela would sit and watch television, drinking beer from a shared can. Mosi did not like to see his mother drinking beer in this way and told her so.

She reacted instantly, angrily. 'Son, don't you start to order me about the place!' She loomed up out of her chair and faced him.

'It's not good for you,' he insisted in a sulky voice.

'Hey, Mosi-my-Hyacinth!' she whispered more softly then, stroking his cheek with her thumb. 'I know you're growing a beard now, but you're still my Hyacinth and you always will be. If Colm brings beer, don't worry. It is a gift, that's all. I only drink a little. To tell you the truth, son,' she giggled, 'I only take it because he offers it. I could never drink a full can of beer!'

But Angela hadn't drunk beer before she met Colm, Mosi thought anxiously. He hadn't made up his mind about this new man who shared a bed with his mother and was trying to make himself a father. On the other hand, he thought as Kevo led him into a long hall with slot machines, Colm didn't pretend to be his friend. He didn't try to be too nice.

Mosi and Kevo turned their heads quickly, alerted by a racket outside in the mall. People were shouting. They ran out, eager to see what all the excitement was about.

All the auld ones were ranged around, necks craning like curious birds to see what they could see. A child had been lifted. She was a girl of his dead sister Marigold's age, perhaps eight years old. The security men handled her roughly and she screamed at the top of her voice, terrified. Mosi's stomach began to flutter. People were yelling and name-calling. *They're everywhere, her kind. Should be locked up. Should be bloody exterminated.*

'Look!' Kevo's eyes surveyed the scene eagerly.

But Mosi turned away. He smelled the little girl's fear, could hear the tears in her voice as one of the men shook her. Out of the corner of his eye, he saw the kicking of her legs as they dragged her along the mall.

'What will happen to her?' he asked Kevo, his eyes wide.

'Nuttin,' Kevo said confidently. 'They're makin' an example of her.'

'An example?' Mosi was confused.

'Showin' us they'll have no mercy and all that. Straight to the children's court.'

'They will not kill her?'

'Of course they won't bleedin' kill her!' Kevo laughed, then stopped suddenly, as if remembering something.

On impulse, he jagged his elbow at Mosi and grinned. 'Chocolate-head! She'll be all right. Her ma or her da will get her out.'

'Snowflake!' Mosi replied easily, shoving his hands deep in his trouser pockets.

They walked on. Mosi wondered if Colm would bring a roast chicken that evening or if Angela was making one of her thick broths, the kind he liked, made from yams bought on Moore Street, mixed with onion and lentils. Gradually, they made their way along, turned left, then crossed at the traffic lights. Traffic thundered past, an angry animal dragging its huge tail as it hurried, hurried. People walked briskly, some chatting into mobile phones, trying to overtake slower pedestrians with buggies and children. At the bottom of Mosi's street, they stopped. Kevo would turn back in the opposite direction, towards Dominic Street, but Mosi would walk up the hill of the old Georgian street to what the locals called Little Africa and climb four flights to the attic flat.

'Shaggin' homework!' Kevo grumbled.

'Shaggin homework,' Mosi agreed.

They slammed their fists into one another's shoulders for a few seconds. Then Mosi caught Kevo in a headlock and Kevo managed to jab his knee in behind Mosi's knee so that he almost fell. Finally they disengaged and went their separate ways.

The Christmas concert took place a week before holidays. As usual towards close of term, the school crime rate escalated and boys filed through Father Headmaster's office on a daily basis. Stern warnings were given, parents called in for urgent meetings with senior staff. Two boys were suspended until January for getting drunk on the way back from a rugby match, another was expelled for selling cannabis to the fourth years, and ten third years had to take over the domestic work of washing and scrubbing the corridors of the cramped building.

On the day of the concert, Mosi sat at breakfast with his mother and Colm. Colm had lit a bit purple candle every morning for a month. It flickered gently as they ate their cereals and drank tea. By now Angela was sitting propped with cushions at her back, the soft light of the candle making the skin of her face more luminous than usual. Her belly was enormous. The evening before, he had caught Colm reclining with his ear close to that great belly, listening hard. He felt as if he had stumbled on something so private it hurt. Tears sprang to his eyes. He remembered his father, whose body no longer existed because vultures would have easily penetrated the thin graves he and his mother had made.

'So this is the big day, what?' Colm said in a genial voice.

'Are you coming too?' Mosi asked.

Colm looked at him. Then he looked at Angela, as if trying to read the correct answer to Mosi's question in her face. 'I won't come if you'd prefer I stay away,' he then said quietly. 'But I was just thinking your mother might need somebody with her. The footpaths are slippery these evenings.'

Angela turned to Mosi. 'What do you want, son? Tell me. Do you want Colm to come or not?'

He knew then that his mother and her man were a team. They would do whatever was necessary.

'Come,' Mosi stated, resigned.

'I'll look forward to that,' Colm replied, not meeting Mosi's eyes.

At lunch hour, Mosi left the school and wandered down to Moore Street. He had two euro in his pocket. That street reminded him of his old home except that here they sold fish instead of dried dust dogs. All the vegetables in the stalls were like those he had seen in his other life. The air throbbed with voices and footsteps, with patient women calling out prices. People stopped and haggled over apples from South Africa, yams from Zimbabwe, over livid oranges and hairy kiwis. Finally, he saw what he was looking for. A ripe pineapple, deep yellow, notched with little brown patches from which leaked small droplets of syrupy sweetness. He stopped and examined it more closely. It was perfect. Of late, Angela had wanted as many sweet and dripping fruits as possible, but especially pineapple and mango.

The woman behind the stall reached over and held it out to him like a golden lamp.

'It's yours, love. Sixty cent,' she said in a smoky voice.

'Forty,' Mosi responded automatically.

‘Fifty-five,’ she eyed him knowingly, replacing the pineapple in its straw-lined box.

‘Forty-five!’

‘Fifty and not a cent less!’

She stood back and folded her arms as if daring him to answer back.

He nodded, then passed a euro coin into her hands. She handed him the pineapple and his change. He smiled, pleased at this compromise, then pushed the fruit into his rucksack.

A fog was descending as he made his way back to Denmark Street. The sun was gradually being soaked up, like yellow ink in the blotting-paper sky. Only a thin light touched the broad footpaths where people jostled and avoided collision, hunching shoulders, pulling scarves around their throats.

At the school, Mrs Fitzgerald swept down, a huge, red-faced bat.

‘Where were you?’ she hissed, pushing him through the front hall where an arrangement of pink hyacinths were set beneath a long purple candle. The sweet aroma filled his nostrils, making him vague and distracted.

‘Out, out,’ he stammered.

‘Come on, Mosi, it’s time to get ready. The parents are due at four.’

He was taken to one side by two young teachers and shoved into the adjacent classroom, which was now the cast changing room. Immediately they began to tug at his blazer, to unknot his tie. Instinctively, he put up his hand, shielding himself from invasion.

‘No!’ he spoke abruptly. ‘I dress myself!’

One of the teachers, a plump blonde girl with creamy white skin and silvery braces on her upper teeth, told him to get a move on, that they hadn't all day and he had to be made up.

His costume was hung, ready, from the top of a picture frame. It was magnificent. There were black suede boots with suede straps which criss-crossed up along his shins. An inky purple satin shirt, gathered softly at the wrists, and matching trousers also awaited him. Quickly, he undressed and pulled on his finery. Then he drew down the cloak. Someone had stitched in large wads of shoulder padding so that as the garment dropped over his body, he realised he now had a splendidly broad form. He stood before a cracked mirror and lowered his headgear, Balthazar's silky, tightly bound turban, onto his crown.

'Aren't you the handsome young king!' the blonde teacher exclaimed, adjusting the cloak and fixing the neck-band more securely. 'Look at him, Mr Kane, isn't he the real McCoy?'

Skinny Mr Kane grabbed Mosi by the arm and began to drag him away.

'Time to get you made up, young man!' he said in a drawling voice. 'We'll make you even more …' he hesitated, as if daring himself to say it, 'even more handsome than you already are!'

In the next classroom he was immediately set upon again by two volunteer mothers, bright-eyed and pecking, who fixed his cloak again, adjusted his headgear. They had just finished making up Kevo, who stood gazing at himself in the mirror, pretending to be disgusted.

Mosi began to feel strange. It was strange, he thought as one of the women leaned over him and studied his eyes.

He held his breath and tried not to notice the scent of her body, which was an arresting mixture of her natural body odour, a sweet perfume and garlic.

Before he could get too distracted, Father Headmaster walked in and regarded him.

'Aha, I see our Wise Men are preparing to set forth!' he intoned in a mock-serious voice.

Mosi smiled and said nothing. The young teacher was in the process of putting some orange colour onto his cheekbones, on either side of his temples and just beneath the line of his turban.

Suddenly the school orchestra had tuned up and six violins were scratching through a series of carols. As the last notes of 'The Coventry Carol' faded, the audience settled itself expectantly in the large theatre.

Angela was about ten rows back, sitting with Colm. The strange feeling which had swept over him while he was being made up returned. Although the Three Wise Men didn't have to do anything just yet, they were nonetheless on stage, keeping very still, mostly so as not to upset the donkey. The audience went *aaaah* in sympathy, then burst into spontaneous applause. All around was movement, activity, the flight into Bethlehem, a real donkey led by Joseph, a hugely pregnant Mary sitting side saddle as the animal was made to circle the stage. All of a sudden, Mosi wanted to laugh. Kevo nudged him and murmured something. The communication made him giddy, even though he didn't hear what Kevo had said. Father Headmaster had been dubious about the donkey. What if it decided to relieve itself on stage, he had enquired only a few hours before. They'd cope, Mrs Fitzgerald, beyond the point of negotiating with anybody, replied briskly.

Things went according to plan. Lights dimmed as darkness fell on Bethlehem. The sound of gunshot and bombs could be heard in the background. The Virgin Mary was a Sacred Heart girl borrowed from across the river. She stood with a belt of bullets across her swollen midriff beside a glowering, dark-browed Joseph who knocked again and again at each unwelcoming inn. Finally, there was nothing for it but the stable, and the refugees settled themselves rebelliously into a raised area of straw, Joseph propping his rifle carefully to one side.

As his moment approached, Balthazar felt himself tighten like a coil. He straightened his back, feeling kingly and good, the words of wisdom penned by the politically minded Mrs Fitzgerald stacked in his throat, awaiting release. The Wise Men moved forward bearing gifts, scrolls on which were written the words *Liberty! Equality! Fraternity*! Balthazar bowed low before the newborn infant, then opened his mouth to speak.

A low moan rose from within the audience. A gasp of surprise, perhaps. Pleasure at the beauty of the Three Kings, Mosi guessed, and released the words which had burrowed so deeply into his imagination that he believed them. He had travelled many months to pass on the news of human freedom, he said. Five moons had passed and they had been guided by the comet to proclaim this gift to all men and women.

Again, a moan was heard, then the scuffle of feet, of chairs being pushed back. Mosi carried on regardless, blinded by the footlights. He had learned his script. He had become that king. He had made the long journey to a new place and would speak the truth.

Later, the audience applauded loudly. One couple in the second row rose to their feet and everybody else followed. Mosi scanned the crowd. He wanted to see his mother's smile, her eager, competitive stare which would gobble him up with pride and love. Then he remembered the moaning sound. He looked again at the row where she had sat, perched beside Colm. A movement to his left attracted him. Father Headmaster, beckoning.

'Mosi, Mosi, your mother has gone into labour. Now, you mustn't panic. She's not in any danger, I believe. But she's gone to the hospital ...'

Father Headmaster followed Mosi back to the classroom, where his clothes lay.

'Can I go?' Mosi replied, ripping off the turban, flinging his majestic cloak to the ground. Automatically, he grabbed his rucksack.

'Hurry, hurry, Mosi!'

It took five minutes to run around the square to the maternity hospital. He hammered along through the thick fog, still wearing his purple shirt and pants, darting rapidly around cars caught in the usual evening snarl. The swirling, cold fog peppered his skin with icy darts, penetrating the thin material, but he hardly noticed. His heart had been pounding even before he began to run. By the time he raced in the entrance of the hospital, he felt as if a fist was squeezing his chest, that he would faint for lack of air. He gulped and gasped, holding his stomach, aware of people looking at him strangely, with his carmine-red eyelids, his deep brown, glossed lips, his purple garments. He stammered his mother's name at a number of people who looked as if they could help. Finally, a nurse came and walked him to a bench and told him to wait. Minutes later, Colm arrived down in the lift, barely recognisable in a green theatre gown. Even his head was covered with a green cap.

'It's a sterile area, apparently,' Colm said ruefully, tossing his head self-consciously.

'Is she okay?' Mosi demanded, squaring up to Colm, arms slightly akimbo, as if at any moment prepared to strike out.

Colm pressed the knuckles of his right hand against his mouth, as if afraid of what would tumble out. 'She's doing fine. They think it won't be so long.'

Mosi kept staring at Colm. Who was this man? What had he done to his mother? As if they hadn't been through enough already. His whole body tensed up as he regarded Colm, staring hard into his face, breathing heavily.

'I'd better get back in there,' Colm said quietly. 'I'm … needed. Is that okay, Mosi? Can you wait? I'll come out and let you know how—'

But Mosi struck him full on the side of the jaw, as hard as he could manage it. He hurt his own hand, so it must have hurt Colm too. The interloper in their lives fell back, then rolled to the ground. Immediately a security man descended on them and began to intervene.

'It's okay,' Colm was breathing heavily, staring up at Mosi. 'It was a misunderstanding. Don't remove him, he didn't mean it … a family thing,' he insisted, dragging himself to his feet.

The security man watched Mosi and Colm as they faced one another. Mosi's head was in uproar, bits of spittle had gathered at the corners of his lips, his breath came in gasps as he stared despairingly into Colm's white, white face, one side of which has begun to swell.

'I … I …' he stammered.

'You'd better put ice on that,' the security man advised.

Colm ignored him. He took a step towards Mosi. 'Mosi! Mosi! You – I—' He shuddered and shook his head, unsure of his ground before the angry boy.

'I want to see my mother!' Mosi shouted. 'I want to see my mother!'

Colm took Mosi by the elbow and turned him towards the lift.

'Mosi!' Angela called out as she squatted on the bed in the delivery room, half-smiling, half-snarling through drawn-back lips. 'Stay here, Mosi!'

Mosi waited and willed his mother on. He had heard her in labour before, many years ago, and was not frightened. There was a cord between them, an invisible cord that tied the many aspects of their lives together. Colm could never know what they had known together. But Colm realised that. Mosi observed, calmer now, as his mother's lover held her head, cradling it gently, urging her on as she did what she would do with or without him.

As the child slid out, Angela's eyes closed to two puffy slits. She gritted her teeth and gave a final shudder.

The baby, a girl, was not so pale, Mosi noted. He regarded his half-sister with amazement, this little slowly blinking, waxy-skinned girl who was causing so much fuss and excitement that he was now weeping, with relief, with happiness, and secretly for his first father, of whom no trace remained except perhaps in the earth of Africa.

Later, he went down to the foyer. The security man had held onto his rucksack. Mosi opened it and removed the pineapple. This time he didn't bother to take the lift up to the third floor. He took the stairs in twos and threes, bearing the pineapple eagerly in both hands. The baby, Angela had already announced, was to be called Daisy. Propped up against her pillows, his mother surveyed the world. Colm trembled as he observed his daughter, already at the breast. When Angela saw Mosi's pineapple, she cried out with delight.

'Oh, great!' she squealed. 'I'm parched! Oh, you good, clever boy to think of me so much! My throat is so dry!'

Mosi cut the skin off the pineapple, removed the inner plug of fibre, and began to slice the succulent fruit. It filled the room with its sweet perfume. He watched as his mother gorged a yellow slice, the juice trickling from her lips. Then he passed a slice to Colm. Mosi and Colm ate with more restraint, glancing at one another every so often. Colm's jaw was swollen.

'Have more.' Mosi pushed the plate towards Colm and allowed himself to smile.